THE CLIFF DWELLERS

THE CLIFF DWELLERS

A NOVEL

WILL LA PAGE

SUNSTONE
PRESS

SANTA FE

‡

Sunstone books may be purchased for educational, business, or sales promotional use. For information please write: Special Markets Department, Sunstone Press, P.O. Box 2321, Santa Fe, New Mexico 87504-2321.

Book and Cover design » Vicki Ahl
Body typeface » Book Antiqua
Printed on acid free paper

Library of Congress Cataloging-in-Publication Data

La Page, Will, 1935-
  The cliff dwellers : a novel / by Will La Page.
    p. cm.
  ISBN 978-0-86534-836-3 (softcover : alk. paper)
  1. Park rangers--Fiction. 2. Homeless veterans--Fiction. 3. Ozark Mountains--Fiction.
4. Pueblo Indians--New Mexico--Antiquities--Fiction. 5. Archaeological thefts--Fiction.
6. Wilderness areas--Fiction. I. Title.
  PS3612.A589C55 2011
  813'.6--dc22

                                          2011040977

WWW.SUNSTONEPRESS.COM
SUNSTONE PRESS / POST OFFICE BOX 2321 / SANTA FE, NM 87504-2321 /USA
(505) 988-4418 / ORDERS ONLY (800) 243-5644 / FAX (505) 988-1025

To Susan, for the inspiration and encouragement.

We are all cliff dwellers staring into the abyss.

I
THE BUFFALO KNOWS

1

ON THE TRAIL

The two young hikers had other things on their minds as they approached the artists' bluff overlook along the Buffalo River Trail that glorious June afternoon. So, it didn't strike them as particularly odd to find an easel and a partly finished water color, along with the artist's satchel spilling its paints and brushes onto the rocks nearby. Having lagged well behind the rest of their group for most of the day, they'd left the trail, ostensibly to explore an abandoned cabin, and lost track of nearly an hour as they stripped off their clothes for a cool skinny dip in a crystal pool hidden by a lush stand of cane.

The girl had been sending signals all day. She kept falling farther back from the others, insisting that he stay with her. She was the one who suggested checking out the abandoned cabin, sixty yards off the trail, while the rest of their group took off up the ridgeline on an easy but unmarked shortcut to the bluff top and the quickest way back to Steele Creek.

The boy knew that an old settler's cabin wasn't on either of their minds as they sat by the river waiting for the others to disappear into the woods. He was, nonetheless in a state of disbelief at the speed with which she was suddenly out of her skimpy hiking shorts and halter top and standing naked in the pool taunting him.

Eager as he was, he knew he was even clumsier than usual, struggling with his clothing, not knowing which way to look, and then the almost paralyzing shock of the icy cold water! How could she just stand there laughing? He was glad that she took charge. It was his first time. And she knew it! Later, hiking out, he kept wondering what she, with her beautifully proportioned suntanned body, saw in him — the end result of four generations of Ozark farmers! He'd been embarrassed at how white his body was compared to hers. But then, he was red-haired, a fact which seemed to particularly intrigue her. For the first time in his seventeen years, he was forced to reevaluate the possible assets of his heretofore embarrassing red hair, freckles, and skin so light that he was still searching, at eighteen, for signs of the genetic disorder that had graced him with the unwanted nickname of "Albi" ever since fifth grade.

They'd left the pool and its special pleasures only reluctantly and had been hurrying to catch up with their classmates when they came upon the abandoned overlook. "Must be answering the call of nature," casually remarked the boy taking a quick look at the canvas. The girl said, "Yeh, this is pretty cool, let's take it," and she started to twist the turnbuckles and remove the board from the easel. "Hey, are you crazy, we're probably being watched right now." The ensuing struggle ended with the easel being knocked over the bluff, and the damaged, unfinished, painting precariously balanced as though about to take flight.

"Come on, I'm getting out of here," said the boy as he started jogging down the trail in the direction of the Steele Creek trailhead. The girl stayed behind just long enough to pick up the picture, look at it with obvious disdain for the brand new scratches, and send it sailing, Frisbee fashion, in the direction of a low-circling hawk.

Perhaps, if she'd taken a moment to look over the edge of the bluff, she'd have noticed a pink silk neckerchief caught on a weathered old cedar stub protruding from the face of the bluff. She might have even heard a faint moan or a call for help. But, then, she had other things on her mind. There was a picnic waiting at Steele Creek Meadow, and she was pretty sure that she'd seen the boys hiding some six packs in the stream before they all left on their hike. And now she was late, and the beer would probably be all gone.

Cassie easily caught up with her red-faced hiking companion less than two-hundred feet down the trail, where he'd stepped behind a tree to relieve himself. She ran on by, laughing at him, yelling, "Come on, Albi, you're pissing the day away!"

2

CROSS PURPOSES

Homer Stankey was starting his seventeenth year as a seasonal ranger on the Upper Buffalo District. It was a good job, a job that allowed him to do his own thing for nine months of every year. Few people on the Upper Buffalo knew what Homer did from September through May. Homer, himself, wasn't quite sure what his own thing was, but he did like the sound of it. His guv-mint job allowed him to pay the minimal property taxes on his cabin over the hill in Possum Trot, do a little trappin' a little guidin' in the huntin' seasons, and meet a lotta dumb city slickers who'd pay ridiculous amounts of money for the chance to see a bear, or a deer, or an elk in the wild.

Homer had been hired in the early days of the park, when they wanted to have a few locals on the staff to build support in the county, and to provide a certain amount of local knowledge—a liaison with the natives as it were. Homer's strategy on the job was simple: keep a low profile, keep those paychecks coming, build a nest egg, and above all, avoid controversy. The first thing he'd learned on the job, was that the feds did not like controversy, especially the kind that got reporters to snoopin' around.

Homer didn't know it, but his strategy had just hit a snag. A really big snag! When Lucy Duckworth, the local amateur naturalist and volunteer interpreter, hailed him as he was pulling into Steele Creek campground from his trash collection run of the district, he'd muttered "Oh Christ" under his breath. He was sure she probably had an exciting new bird or butterfly spotting to report. Lucy could bend your ear for hours on the mating habits of the great purple hairstreak, or where to find morels in the spring, or lion's mane mushrooms in the fall.

Lucy was right out of central casting for the little old lady in tennis shoes with her antique open-top Jeep, flamboyant pith helmet hat, and a voice that was somewhere between fingernails on a blackboard and Washboard Willy's rendition of "By a Babbling Brook." As founder and perpetual president of the local garden club, Lucy was the kind of president that the younger members of the club, and most of them were younger, would think twice about before offering a mildly contrary opinion about the species of any of the local flora and fauna, or how to put on a flower show. As many of them said, in private of course, Lucy's school marm glance could be enough to wither the flowers on a poison ivy vine.

Homer had a love-hate relationship with Lucy. He coveted her endless knowledge of all things wild and natural, and he hated her proving him wrong time after time. He would never admit it, but most of what he really knew about nature, as opposed to what he thought he knew, had come from Lucy.

Homer never could get over Lucy's ability to casually pick up a snake, any snake, and set it down well off the trail, or how she knew what every native plant could be used for, even though she'd only lived here since retiring from a teaching job in St. Louis six years ago. As for Lucy, her encyclopedic knowledge of nature did not extend to her social skills. To her, Homer, whose name she could never remember from one time to the next, was the park trash collector, a nobody in uniform, something of less value than a common weed in the campground. But then, she knew Homer wasn't one to put a snake out of harm's way, Homer was the epitome of harm's way for every snake in the district.

True to form, she hailed him as "Horace." Homer didn't bother to correct her, generously putting it down to distraction, for today Lucy was in a hurry, and so was he. She only stopped him because she had something to give Horace for the lost and found closet. It was a satchel she'd found on the trail, full of paints and brushes and stuff.

Homer thanked Lucy. Mostly he was thankful for her being in a hurry. He dropped the satchel on the floor of his pickup, and took off for the campground dumpster. Homer was anxious to empty his truck of the dozens of bulging trash bags and head for the Elkhorn where a nice cool can of Coors, or maybe two, were waiting with his name on them. The satchel could wait.

3

STARTING OVER

Sarah Pingree had taken up painting right after the divorce, two years ago. Her four-year marriage with Theo had roller-coasted into a fairly comfortable life style. She had the Albany condo, the furniture, and a nice monthly income that allowed her to live a life relatively free of money worries. She'd always liked art. In fact, she had minored in art at Boston College, but Theo had always discouraged her. He liked a nice clean apartment. She hoped he had one. He needed a partner that doted on his endless craving for praise and adulation. With his money, or more correctly, his father's money, she knew he'd find one. And she hoped to never meet her.

She'd felt elated at being able to turn the entire condo into a studio within a week of Theo's departure. It had always been his condo. Now it was hers. It was pretty weird, really, she'd thought. Their separation was not just amicable, it was, for both of them, a blessing from the gods, and goddesses. It was more like saying good bye to a classmate at a graduation party, than the painful messy divorces she'd known about. It was so giddy, she almost felt like she'd been cheated out of some ritual rite of passage. There wasn't even the messy business of a name change. Most of their acquaintances had always assumed that Theo Price and Sarah Pingree had never married.

For nearly four years, Sarah had had almost no friends of her own. Theo had no time for anyone who wasn't one of his associates at the law firm, or politicians that he needed to line up in his corner for his hoped-for career move into politics. Except for Corey, her older brother and her one and only life-long friend, Sarah had become a loner. Corey's job as a game warden in the Adirondacks, headquartered in nearby Saratoga

Springs, made it possible for them to see each other fairly frequently. Almost from the day of the wedding, their get-togethers had become therapy sessions for Sarah. Corey rarely came to the condo. He'd never been able to warm up to Sarah's husband, possibly because of Theo's nervous laugh that somehow reduced every conversation they'd ever had to the level of trivia.

Sarah was a good artist, maybe even very good. She had a knack for putting something into her paintings that could make them come alive. She particularly liked to work with images of wildlife. During the year following the separation, Corey had brought dozens of mounted specimens to her new studio, a Great Horned Owl, a coyote killing a rabbit, an eagle, and whole collections of songbirds, field mice, squirrels, even a sleeping fawn. Her imagination placed them in perfect wild settings where they came back to life, like magic. Each painting seemed better than the last. Corey was entranced with her ability and was able to get her a small contract with his agency for illustrating a series of children's pamphlets on Living with Wildlife.

Over Thanksgiving dinner at the condo, Corey showed Sarah an announcement that had circulated among the folks at his office announcing an artist-in-residence program at the Buffalo National River, in Arkansas. "Why don't you apply? With your skill at painting wildlife, and the experience of having done those brochures, you'd be a shoo-in," he insisted.

"Oh, no, I don't think so," Sarah replied. "I'm not interested in Arkansas, and, besides, look here, the deadline is next week. I couldn't possibly pull something together in such a short time."

"Okay, nothing ventured, nothing lost, I guess. But, I think you need to get away from the city for a while and see some real wildlife and some wild country. Did you notice they even have an elk herd?"

Nothing more was said about it as they finished dinner and took a drive out to Olana, the magnificent estate of Frederic Edwin Church, just a half-hour's drive south. During her brief and tedious marriage, Sarah's escape from boredom was often found in the refuge of either Olana's breathtaking setting and Church's private collection of paintings, or at nearby Cedar Grove, and the equally awesome collection of Church's teacher and mentor Thomas Cole. Often, she would spend an entire visit studying a single painting, as though she was rationing herself for the years of tedium that lay ahead. It was during a visit to Olana that she'd made the decision to broach the subject of divorce with Theo. She couldn't look at these great landscapes without feeling a deep inner need to paint. It wasn't just that she wanted to paint, she was beginning to desperately need the freedom to paint, the freedom to be herself. With each visit the feeling had progressed to an almost physical longing. And, she knew Theo couldn't stand the thought of coming home to find her with paint smudges on her hands and face. She was just another trophy in his life, like the framed photos in his study of Theo and the mayor, Theo and Governor Pataki, Theo and Senator Clinton.

To her surprise, Theo had embraced the idea immediately, taking ownership of it in fact, claiming he'd been meaning to suggest it himself for many months but hadn't done so "for fear of hurting her."

For the next several weeks, Sarah would often wince at how their marriage had taken on its first real shared purpose, a glow of planning together that she'd never known before. She began to idly wonder whether Theo had been having an affair all this time. But she quickly dismissed the idea as being totally inconsistent with his obsession for a political career and a record so squeaky clean that the press couldn't find a speck of dirt to scratch and sniff.

It was that same obsession that greased the way for what must have been the friendliest divorce in New York history. Theo insisted that Sarah didn't need a lawyer. He would draw up, and file, the paperwork for both of them. She merely needed to dictate her terms. She'd been mildly uneasy about his retaining ownership of the condo. But, she didn't want to sound grasping by mentioning it. After all, it was hers to use, free, for as long as she wanted it. And, of course, it was his condo, and he was giving her $2,000 a week. Theo called her a few times after the divorce from his apartment in the city, and then she hadn't heard from him for six months.

As they strolled Olana's beautiful gardens, Corey noticed that Sarah was lost in thought. They rounded a bend in the path and came upon a rabbit bounding down the trail ahead of them as though it hadn't a care in the world. The rabbit seemed to pull Sarah out of her reverie. She realized, at that moment, that she had freed herself of one trap only to entrap herself once more in the condo, his condo. She almost shouted in elation her sudden announcement:

"You're right, Corey, I do need to get away for a while, and Arkansas might be just the place I'm going to do it! Well, at least I'm going to apply. Wish me luck!"

"You know I do," Corey said. "But, you know what, even if you don't get it, there are probably dozens of other opportunities just like this that you could apply for."

"I'm sure you're right," Sarah replied "But, I have a feeling about this one. You know, you've always been my good luck charm!"

Before heading back to Saratoga that evening, Corey toasted his sister's newfound freedom at Catskill's Creek Side, just across the Hudson. Two months later, she heard from the Buffalo. Could she come in June for three weeks?

4

STEELE CREEK

Sarah Pingree pulled into the parking lot of Buffalo National River headquarters in Harrison, Arkansas, early on a hot Monday afternoon. She was five days early. Too soon to move into the artist's quarters at Steel Creek campground, but she thought that she'd stop in anyway and see if there might be a chance to get in.

The drive down had taken less time than she'd planned. Once on the road, she'd just kept driving. The exhilaration of freedom seemed like an emotional high that kept drowsiness at bay. Tiredness was always somewhere down the road, somewhere outside the little self-contained world of her gray Honda Civic. She'd planned to arrive early in order to have some time to familiarize herself with the local area, billed as something of an artists' haven, with scores of studios and places with intriguing names like Eureka Springs and Morning Star and Snowball.

Sarah had been disappointed to find the person in charge of the artist program was away until Friday, and no one could tell her if the apartment at Steele Creek was available or not. The bureaucracy was definitely overspecialized she thought as she headed back down the road to a little "Authentic Mexican" restaurant she'd spotted on the way into town. A hot chile relleno and a cold Cuervo was just what she needed. She wasn't disappointed in the food, but it was a dry county. She had a six-pack of Cuervo in the Honda, but it was warm. During her college years, Mexican food had been her mainstay, but Theo had always insisted on nothing but "American food." In fact, he tended to find her vegetarian leanings just a little un-American!

As Sarah lingered over her meal trying to decide her next move, her mind wandered back to Theo and his totally predictable life. She'd called to let him know that she was going to be away for a few weeks, not so much because she felt he should know the condo was going to be empty, but because it was an excuse to let him know that she'd achieved some success on her own as an artist. She knew that having been selected as an artist in residence at a National Park wouldn't really impress him, but still, she had to do it.

Now, she regretted having made the call. It left her feeling like she was trying to prove something to him, which she wasn't, was she?

And, besides, he hadn't been touch with her for months. It was a mistake she vowed not to make again.

Sarah knew she should call Corey and let him know she'd arrived. But, first, she needed a place to stay. She had her camping gear from her college days in the back of Civic, so she decided to check out Steele Creek campground. If she couldn't find a ranger to let her into the apartment, she'd find a vacant campsite. It was still early in the season, and there would likely be plenty to choose from. Something right along the Buffalo she imagined, thinking back to those wonderful weekend trips to the White Mountains when she and a group of friends from Boston College would flee the urban scene in search of a quick getaway and that exhilarating mountain air. Too bad, she thought, that there wasn't an artist residency program on top of Mt. Washington.

Steele Creek was just what the brochure had said: awesome bluffs rising right up from the river. It was a peaceful world, so far from the one she'd left that she felt as though she was coming home—home to the days of her youth. Not just far in miles and in years, but in growing and appreciating real places and real people. All the miles and all the years just didn't seem to add up to one day in a place like this. Sarah knew now that she didn't just want to paint the things she saw in nature; she had to, needed to, like she needed food and freedom. Why had she waited so long to admit it to herself?

There was no ranger on duty, and no cell phone connection. In a way she was glad, it completed the mental picture she had been painting as she drove the thirty miles from Harrison. She picked a campsite along the river, found some firewood for her evening fire, and took the river walk in response to the call of those incredible bluffs.

The next three days were the most deliriously happy interlude that Sarah could remember across the entire span of her thirty-one years. Sleep fulfilled all the functions that sleep was supposed to, and never did in the city. She woke refreshed, restored, vital, and eager for the new day. And, yet she could clearly recall the night sounds, the soothing song of the river, the inquisitive call of the owl, the wind in the trees, the fading glow of her campfire, and the pleasant drumming of a light rain on her small tent.

During the days she hiked for hours along the river, filling her sketch book with ideas to flesh out later. And yet she seldom felt hungry. It was as though she had been starved for years, and was now gorging herself on the sights and sounds and smells of pure air and sparkling water that pulled her around the next bend, and the next. It was a feast of the senses that can only be found in wild places. Sarah had the feeling of being immersed in the wild, of being an inextricable, but nonessential, part of its wildness. She had somehow managed to find her way inside all those landscapes that Cole and Church seemed to be seeing only from the outside. She found herself wondering how you paint something that you're part of? She remembered, from an almost forgotten freshman-level art appreciation course, how Chinese and Japanese landscape artists often placed a tiny, insignificant human figure in their paintings. The lecturer said that it was done not for purposes of scale, but as an expression of humility toward the magnificence of nature. But she thought that she had a better way. Why isn't it just like making music, becoming one with your instrument? She'd brought her flute with her, though she hadn't touched it in years. The singing river seemed to be calling for a little flute music to complete the picture.

By evening, she knew what it felt like to be tired, honestly tired—not the drained feeling that comes from boredom, or having to wear a phony smile and chatter over cocktails in a crowded parlor. Too tired to fix an evening meal, she'd drive into the little town of Jasper for Mexican food or a salad at the Ozark Café, grab a four-pack of bottled cappuccino and some fruit bars for breakfast and drive back over the mountain for another delicious sleep.

Friday came too soon, and Sarah headed back to Harrison to officially check in as the artist in residence and get the key to the apartment, never once having crossed paths with the local ranger. She mildly resented having to take the time, but getting officially ensconced in those quarters up over the old stables meant that she could finally get down to the serious business of painting. And, she needed to talk to Corey. She'd tried reaching him twice from Jasper, but ended up leaving a message both times. It was a rarity to ever get Corey on the first call. As the lead investigator on wildlife crimes, like poaching, he would often be gone for several days at a time. At least he'd know she'd arrived safely, when he checked his messages. Now she needed an hour or so to tell him how much she'd already learned about what she wanted to do with her life, and to thank him for encouraging her to take this wonderful voyage of self-discovery.

5

ARTIST'S BLUFF

Settling in was a ritual for Sarah. Even a stark apartment like the one over the stables, with its fly-specked windows, and cast-off office furniture, could be made homey with just a few small touches; a sprig of wild flowers on the scarred kitchen table, some curious pieces of driftwood and interesting rocks that she'd picked up on her walks in the river bed nicely covered the scratches and gouges on the coffee table. The tired linoleum floor cried out for a couple of scatter rugs. She made a mental note to pick some up, and donate them to the cause on her next trip to either Jasper or Harrison. Her spattered old work easel and a couple of unfinished water colors of a wild iris and a lupine that she'd found down by the river, finished her decorating for now. She stood back, admired the results, and decided to move the easel and a rocking chair onto the porch where she could sit quietly with a glass of iced tea and plan her first week.

She was just settling in with her tea and the loose-leaf collection of "Rules for Residents" when a shiny Park Service pickup pulled into the stable yard below her porch. The driver gave her a friendly wave as he headed for the stairs.

"You've got things prettied up real nice," he offered, looking around the apartment. "I just need you to sign these forms, and I'll be on my way," he added in a very business-like manner.

Sarah was hungry for information. There had been little to none at the check in at Harrison, and it didn't seem as though there'd be much from the ranger unless she initiated it. Ignoring the clipboard on which he was rapidly checking off items on a very official-looking form, she extended her hand, saying, "Hi, I'm, Sarah, Sarah Pingree."

"Yep, that's what it says right here—Sarah Pingree from Albany, New York." He paused, then added, "Name's Quint, my number's on your copy of this inventory form. Need anything, just give me a call."

Sarah signed Quint's form, noting that Quint's last name was Speaks. Great name for a man of few words! He gave her his best attempt at saying "Thanks" without sounding either sincere or encouraging, succeeded admirably, and was gone. Do they really think somebody's going to steal this sorry imitation Naugahyde furniture, she wondered. She was mentally going over the list of questions she'd saved up for this occasion when she heard his steps returning up the dingy stairwell. He stuck his head back in saying, "If you see some folks at the stone house they'd be from the university down at Fayetteville. Would you tell 'em to get in touch with me? I've been trying to catch up with them too."

"Yes I will, Ranger Speaks," Sarah replied thinking, wow, that's more words than he had for me! "And, oh, by the way," she quickly added, "I've been wondering about a taking a float trip down the river. Could you give me some names of people who might rent canoes or offer guided float trips?"

"There's several. Just check the brochures outside the ranger station. We're running short handed this summer, so most days you won't find nobody there. But you can slip a note under the door, if you need anythin'. Either me or my assistant Homer will get back to you. Big weekend coming up, Father's Day. We always fill up." He closed the door and was gone.

Sarah, was so bemused by the whole experience that she couldn't remember, for the life of her, the other questions she had wanted to ask. Not important, she thought. Tonight would be the first night's sleep in her apartment, and tomorrow morning she'd hit the trail for Artists' Bluff. She had read several comments in the artists' log about what a great place it was to get a view of the valley and the bluffs across the river.

Reading always induced sleep, so she read for an hour about how artists had helped create the national park system through their spectacular images of places like Yellowstone and Yosemite, and Grand Canyon, even Acadia, the first national park in the east.

After tossing and turning for an hour, she decided that the apartment just didn't have what the river offered, so she slipped on a loose polo shirt and Levi's and headed down to her old campsite, where she'd left her tent standing that morning. She was surprised to see so many campfires winking in the meadow. And, then she remembered what Quint had said about Father's Day weekend. She seldom thought about her father; it seemed as if he'd been gone forever. In fact, she realized it had been almost half of her life. Life is so unfair she thought; Dad would have loved this place! The moon was so bright she didn't need a flashlight to follow the trail. The river was still chuckling its same soft tune, and she was asleep in minutes.

Artist's Bluff was even better than the rave reviews in the resident's journal. By Saturday afternoon, she had roughed in three small paintings, one of the river winding through the trees, one of the campground in the meadow, and one of the bluffs across the Buffalo. It was the bluffs that really intrigued her. She made a mental note to come back on Sunday with binoculars so she could study them in more detail. Her curiosity was aroused by what looked like a totally inaccessible cave entrance just below the rim. Probably just a shadow, she mused.

Sunday, Father's Day, dawned as another beautiful day in the Ozarks and found Sarah already on the trail. She wanted to have a head start before the sun made the hike something less than the joy it had been yesterday. Even with the lightweight traveling easel, she still had a lot of gear to lug up the mile-long ascent. The pack was heavier today with the addition of her father's old Army 7/50 binoculars. She liked to travel light, but it made a nice touch for Dad's Day she thought.

She preferred not to think about the combined weight of her

equipment, but guessed it had to be nearly one-half of her own one hundred twenty pounds. Thinking about unrelated things always made for a nice diversion when hiking a steep mountain trail. And, it was natural that she thought about Dad. Before dying at the ripe old age of forty-one, from a massive heart attack, he'd constantly encouraged her to eat more, to build up her weight, and strengthen her immune system. So much for that theory! At least Tom Pingree had left his two children well cared for. That had been his sole obsession as a single parent for more than a dozen years. Idly, she thought that whatever might come of this residency she would dedicate it to his memory. It was the least she could do.

Diverting her thoughts from the strain of the steep ascent worked. Almost before she knew it, Sarah had arrived at the overlook. There had been no one on the trail to slow her down with questions like

"Good Morning. What's that thing on your back?"

"An easel."

"What are you going to do with it?"

"Paint."

"Paint what?"

"Scenery."

"So, you're a painter huh?"

"That's right."

"Well, have a nice day."

"Thank You."

She set up the easel in a hurry because the early morning light was creating a masterpiece of the bluff across the river. She quickly took several photos of the scene, knowing that it wouldn't last long.

Putting the camera away in her bag, she saw the binoculars and decided to take a moment to study the opposite bluff in detail. Focusing in on what looked like a cave entrance she noticed movement just above the entrance, back in the woods. The old field glasses might be heavy, but they couldn't be beat for bringing detail up close. There's a man in the woods, she realized. That's odd, because the map shows no trails on that side of the river, it's all designated wilderness. But, of course, it could be a park employee. She scanned back and forth across the top of the bluff and finally found him again. Wearing camouflage? Not likely to be a park employee, she muttered.

She continued scanning farther along the bluff to see if there were others. When she scanned back to where she'd seen the figure, he was now sitting on a log and staring right back at her through his own binoculars and an enormous growth of black hair and beard. She was feeling a little embarrassed at being caught spying and was thinking she ought to, at least, wave a greeting as an apology for intruding. She held the binoculars in one hand and was about to raise the other in a feeble wave, when he shot her a very aggressive gesture. Sarah gulped. Not a park employee, she decided. If he is, his public relations certificate badly needed updating!

Sarah hurriedly put the binoculars back in the tote sack and tried to put the incident out of her mind. She tried to focus on finishing at least one of the water colors, the one of the bluffs. But her heart wasn't in it. She felt as though the day had lost its magic for her. There was always tomorrow. Anyway, with the digital photos, she could work on the paintings at the apartment. And, if necessary, she could hike up again tomorrow and fill in the detail. She wanted to finish these three, because her sketchbook and her head was filled with ideas of ways to paint nature from the inside out. She was too excited to let one little crappy incident spoil her plans.

Another hour of half-hearted stabbing at the canvas and she decided to pack up and head for the less-than-inspiring apartment.

The hike back took a lot longer than the one up. Crossing Steele Creek she became enchanted by the polished stones in the low water of the streambed and began to follow the gentle meander upstream to where it disappeared around a bend to the left. Each new curve in the narrow shady vale pulled her on to the next one. Half a mile upstream, weighted down by a pocket full of smoothly polished white, pale green, gray, and pink stones, she sat to rest against the rotted stump of an ancient tree and dozed.

Awakened in what seemed like a bare half-hour by the complaints of an empty stomach Sarah headed downstream with a warm feeling for a glass of wine, a quick dinner, and a good sleep. Within just a few steps, she realized she'd been asleep for more like two hours, and that she'd had a dream about the bearded man on the bluff. The dream came back in a rush, adding to her warm feeling. The man in the dream was her father, and his seemingly angry gesture was his strong encouragement to let go of the past and move on. Sarah smilingly agreed:

"Screw the past! And Happy Father's Day Dad! Let's go have a drink!"

6

DEATH OF AN ARTIST

Corey Pingree got back to his Saratoga apartment Wednesday afternoon. It was mid-afternoon. He was mentally and physically exhausted from a five-day sting operation with federal and Canadian wildlife officers. It had been the culmination of a year-long investigation of international trafficking in wildlife parts and rare species. It was a carefully planned undercover operation, but something had gone wrong. The suspects had never shown up for the buy. The last day had been spent in an exhaustive review of all that might have gone wrong, ending in the conclusion that there had to be an informer in one of their agencies.

His eye caught the light blinking on the answering machine, but he needed a bath more than he needed to get involved in a dozen messages. Later, he'd curl up on the couch with a cold beer and find that most of the calls had already taken care of themselves. There was bound to be a message from Sarah, and he wanted to relax and enjoy it before calling her back.

Half an hour later, feeling decidedly refreshed, he took his frosted glass and an extra Fat Tire to the couch and pressed the message button: "You have fourteen new messages. Press ONE to hear your first message." Pretty good guess, he thought. Corey had learned that it was better to ignore the tedious instructions and play the last message first. It tended to save a lot of unnecessary note taking when people called several times. Instead of pressing ONE, he skipped to the last message to hear an unfamiliar and very authoritative male voice: "This is a message for Corey Pingree. My name is Seth Greer, I'm the head ranger for the Buffalo National River, in Harrison, Arkansas, and I would appreciate a call back as soon as you get this message. I am

30

calling to see if your sister has been in touch with you during the last forty-eight hours. Sarah appears to be missing, and we have initiated a local search, because her car is still in the parking lot. I don't mean to alarm you, but I would appreciate a call back anytime day or night. You can reach me at either of these two numbers . . . "

But, there were no call-back numbers; Corey's answering machine had run out of tape. Trying not to panic, Corey called his office, and was slightly relieved to hear that there were no emergency messages waiting for him, until he realized that Sarah probably hadn't given the Park Service his office number. He asked his secretary to find a number for a Seth Greer at the Buffalo National River in Harrison, Arkansas, and to let him know as soon as she had it. Meanwhile, he started playing the rest of his messages. He pressed thirteen. Good, he thought, it was Sarah's cheerful voice.

"Hey, Bro, must be one hell of a big case. I've been trying to reach you for days. It's Sunday evening, Father's Day, and I was hoping we might reminisce together. I have a dream I want to share with you. Don't try to call, I have to drive about two miles out of the valley to get any cell phone reception. Talk to you tomorrow. Luv Ya."

His secretary hadn't beeped him yet, so he pressed twelve: "Hey, it's Saturday night, and I didn't really expect to get you, since there's no messages on this end and you're the only one who has this number. I'll try again tomorrow. Just wanted to let you know that I love this place, and I am sooo thankful that you pushed me into doing this. I don't know if I can do it or not, but nature painting is what I want to do for a living when I grow up! Love Ya!"

Just as he was about to press eleven, Corey's secretary broke in with a number for the Buffalo National River. "What's up boss?" She asked. "I don't know, Jen, I'll call you back in a few minutes. But see if you can clear my calendar for a few days, will you?"

Corey dialed the number. "Mr. Pingree, thank you for calling. I am very sorry to have to tell you this, but we found Sarah's body about two hours ago. She apparently fell from the top of a bluff here in the park." Corey dropped the phone. This can't be happening a voice inside him thundered. He stared at the black bug of a phone on the floor, thinking that if he stomped on it everything would go away.

"Mr. Pingree, Mr. Pingree, are you all right?" the little black monster on the floor was saying. Numbly, instead of stomping on it, he reached down and gently picked it up. "Yeah, I'm okay", he muttered "just give me a minute will you please?"

"Of course, take your time, I'll be right here."

Ever so gently, Corey set the phone down on the coffee table. He picked up the still frosted glass and the two bottles of beer and went to the sink. He set them down very carefully in the bottom of the kitchen sink and stared out the window, bracing himself with both hands on the side of the sink, and groaned a sob that came from some unknown place within him. He turned on the faucet full blast to drown the sounds of his anguish. After what must have seemed like an eternity at the other end of the line, Corey managed to pull himself together and go back to the phone.

"Is there anything else you can tell me, anything at all, Mr. Greer?"

"No, I am truly sorry, Mr. Pingree, it's too soon. The recovery is still going on. I will update you just as soon as we know anything more. Would you be able to come to Arkansas in the next day or so?"

"Of course, I'll come right away."

"I can get you on priority if you'd like, Mr. Pingree."

"No, I can do that myself. And, please, under the circumstances, call me Corey."

"Thank you, Corey. Call me Seth. Are you quite sure I can't help with the flight arrangements. You can fly either into Little Rock or Fayetteville. Fayetteville may be a little closer. I can give you directions, or we can have someone meet you, whichever would be easier."

"Let me see what flights I can come up with, and I'll call you back."

Corey sank into the couch, feeling numb and tired and aching all over. He knew that he should be doing something, but what? Just then, the phone rang. It was Jennifer, his secretary.

"Boss, what's going on? Some reporter from Little Rock has been trying to reach you. Something about Sarah being lost in the Buffalo Wilderness? I didn't give him your number. I hope that's okay? And, I've got some flight information for you, if you're ready."

"Thanks, Jen. Yeh, they found Sarah's body a couple of hours ago. If anyone calls, just take a message and tell 'em you don't know where I am, okay?"

"Oh God, Corey, I am so sorry. Is there anything else I can do?"

"No, not right now. Just give me the flight information."

Jen didn't push. Never, in all their years of working together, had she heard Corey sound so completely hopeless. She quickly gave him the information, asked him to stay in touch, and hung up before she started crying herself. He didn't need to hear that right now!

7

BAD NEWS TRAVELS FAST

Seth Greer met Corey's flight at the Northwest Arkansas Airport at 4:00 Thursday afternoon. The last thing either of them wanted was to have some rental agency person drop the word that there was a Corey Pingree in the area. The news of Sarah's death was all over the front pages of the local papers. Further, Seth needed time to have a private chat with Corey before he arrived on the scene and let him know that there would have to be an investigation, even though nothing looked the least bit suspicious. Or, perhaps just because nothing looked suspicious, he needed to know something about the deceased's mental health. And, above all, he had to remember to avoid using that phrase!

After the initial pleasantries and condolences, nothing was said for the first dozen or so miles. Finally, Seth broke the silence:

"I understand you work for New York Fish and Game?"

"Uh huh, been with them for almost twelve years."

"I'd like to talk with you about wildlife management if we get a chance. But, I need to take advantage of our time today to learn all I can about Sarah. I'm sure you understand that we have to conduct an investigation. Sarah was, in a way, very much one of us, though none of us really knew her. She was under contract, as a volunteer, with the Park Service. As you can imagine, the press is watching our every move."

"I understand completely," Corey replied dully, still tired and still numb from the events of the last twenty-four hours.

"Had you had any contact with Sarah since she left New York?"

"She left several messages for me, but I'd been away for nearly a week and just heard them yesterday."

"Did you hear anything, in any of her messages, indicating she was despondent or depressed?"

"Look," Corey snapped, "Sarah was not in the least bit suicidal. Furthermore, she never experienced depression, at any time in her life, even through several years of a less than perfect marriage!"

"I'm sorry, Corey, but it's a question we have to ask. As near as we can tell right now, Sarah slipped and fell. The only other possibility is that of foul play. So, I also have to ask you if anyone other than yourself knew that she was here? You mentioned a less than perfect marriage. Would her former husband have had any reason to follow her here?"

"No," Corey said, trying not to sound impatient with Seth's questions. "The divorce was very amicable. Theo Price is a very high-profile New York lawyer, and I think he was even more pleased than Sarah with his freedom to pursue his own interests. The idea is not just remote, it's as far beyond belief as the idea of suicide."

"Okay, as I said, we have to ask. Now, it gets even tougher. Are you prepared to identify Sarah's body?"

"I guess I have to, don't I?"

"It's a formality, but a necessary one, even though they have fingerprint certainty. I'd like to go by the morgue, before going to my office, if it's alright with you?"

"I'd really prefer to see the spot where it happened first, if you don't mind."

"It's a bit out of the way, and better than a half-hour hike in, so I thought that we'd do that tomorrow afternoon, after we stop by the Steele Creek residence. I haven't been to the bluff yet, myself, and I wanted to do it, if we can, at approximately the time of — uh, that is, at the same time of day we think that Sarah fell."

"Sure, I just want to get Sarah home. You should know that I'm the one who encouraged her to apply for this. So, I'm probably not thinking very clearly just yet. There is one thing that you could explain for me. Your call on Tuesday just said that she was lost.

"Twenty-four hours later you're telling me that they've just found her body and are recovering it. What was that first call all about?"

Seth paused, trying to recall the exact order of events as best as he could. "Well, as best as I've been able to piece it together, one of our volunteer naturalists found Sarah's tote bag on the trail late Monday afternoon and, since there was nobody around, she picked it up and brought it with her to the parking lot intending to leave it at the ranger station. There was no one on duty at the time, so she was going to drop it off at our office in Ponca, but on the way she ran into Homer Stankey, one of our assistants, and gave it to him.

"Homer turned the bag in Tuesday morning, and his boss, Quint Speaks, looked through it and, realizing that it must be Sarah's, he took it to the apartment, the resident's apartment at Steele Creek. It's upstairs over the stables of what was a dude ranch in the old days. What with the value of the stuff in the bag, cell phone, binoculars, a lot of art supplies, he didn't want to just leave it outside her door, so he let himself in and took it upstairs. He also thought it strange that she hadn't reported it missing. When he found the apartment empty, and no sign of anyone having been there recently, he remembered seeing the uneaten lunch in the tote bag, and began to think that things weren't adding up. Sarah's car was parked in the shade in front of the apartment, and it still had the morning dew on it."

Seth paused again, realizing that there were still some blanks he needed to have filled in. "Quint drove over to the campground, hoping to find someone who might have seen Sarah, but he struck out. The campground had been full for Father's Day and had pretty well emptied out by Sunday night. There were a couple of campsites with rigs on them, but no one around. He did find a small Green Mountain tent set up by the river with Sarah's name written in Magic Marker on the door flap. But, nothing in it and no indication that it had been used recently. At that point, Quint called my office to report that he had a possible missing person, and to see if we might know anything of her plans.

"The clerk who checked Sarah in on Friday said that she seemed really eager to get back to Steele Creek and get started painting, so they hadn't talked much. That was when I placed a call to you. Yours was the only emergency contact she'd given at the check-in.

"I instructed Quint to start a search of the immediate area and see if there was anyone on the trails or on the river who might have seen her. By dusk on Tuesday, we had a full search team out. But, we were hampered by not knowing exactly where Lucy, she's the volunteer naturalist, had found the satchel. And, we were unable to locate Lucy until nearly midnight.

"Early Wednesday morning, the search zeroed in on the overlook and a searcher noticed a pink piece of cloth caught on a snag below the bluff. It's a difficult place to get climbers in to, so we weren't sure until after 10:00 that morning that she was even down there. Like many of our bluffs, the overhang conceals a lot. And, it's equally difficult to see much from the base, because of the foliage and the shelving rocks of the bluff."

Corey sat silently, deep in thought. His investigator's mind carefully recording and cataloguing every bit of information Seth provided. His own surprise at how easily he'd switched roles from that of a bereaved brother to criminal investigator kept him from asking any further questions for the moment at least.

"When you called yesterday afternoon, we were in the process of trying to trace you down, but I gathered, from your secretary that the press found you faster than we did!"

8

MUDDIED WATERS

It had been an abnormally hot July and August in Saratoga Springs. Corey Pingree sat in his air-conditioned office, trying to decide if it was worth venturing out in the blistering heat for a quick lunch or whether to just skip it. The decision was made for him when Jen buzzed him to say that Seth Greer was on the phone.

It was the call Corey had been dreading. He knew that he needed some kind of closure, but he also knew that Seth couldn't provide it. All Seth would have to offer would be more sad memories and unanswered questions. The box containing Sarah's personal effects had arrived last week. He hadn't had the heart to open it yet, but he knew that it signaled the end of any formal investigation, and a final report would be coming soon.

The lightly attended memorial service for Sarah had been held on Independence Day. Corey thought it would be appropriate should Sarah's free spirit decide to attend.

To his surprise, Seth had shown up for the service, representing the Park Service, as had Theo, Sarah's ex, both leaving immediately after, in answer to the call of busy schedules. He couldn't blame them; the luncheon at Creekside was going to be painful for everyone. It would be especially so for anyone who hadn't really known Sarah for the gentle soul she was. A bud just beginning to open. Corey had spread her ashes, without permission, among the flowers at Olana. That also seemed fitting. It was where she had been happiest. And, it was a place where he could visit her and know that she'd found at least a few answers. Something he still needed to do.

"Good afternoon, Seth, or I guess it's still morning in Arkansas?"

"Almost afternoon," Seth replied. "Corey, we've finished our investigation of Sarah's death, and I didn't want to just send you a copy before talking with you first."

"As always, you have been extremely thoughtful. Is there anything I need to know before reading it?" Corey asked, sensing that there was something Seth wanted to tell him.

"No, we found nothing that would indicate anything other than an accidental fall. The coroner's report, the autopsy, the conditions at the site, all seemed to support the same conclusion."

"That's pretty much what I expected," replied Corey with a note of resignation. "Though I still have trouble reconciling it with her years of mountain hiking. Was there anything else?"

"Not really, I was hoping that you might read all the statements and give us your thoughts when you are feeling up to it. Not that it's likely we'd reopen the case, but I would like to have a letter with your thoughts on file. There was one unfortunate hitch in the investigation. As you know, the rescue team went back to the bluff after you left to try to retrieve the easel and a painting that they had sighted earlier. About a week later, we got a fax from the state police lab that they had found a set of prints on the painting that didn't match either Sarah's or any of our rescue team."

"Whose were they?" said Corey, his investigative senses suddenly wide awake.

"They belong to a high school senior, a girl who was on that trail with a group of friends earlier in the day. She and a boyfriend were some distance behind the rest of their group hiking back to Steele Creek. She said that she found the painting on the rocks at the bluff and sent it sailing. It was just a lark, she said. Both groups of kids said that there was no sign of Sarah when they passed by the bluff. Both groups also said that the easel was standing at the edge of the bluff. But, as we know, when Lucy Duckworth, the naturalist, came along, which she estimates was about 5:00 PM, there was nothing there but Sarah's tote bag partially hidden under some bushes. We finally got the two youngsters to admit that they had a scuffle at the site and knocked the easel over the edge. We'd previously interviewed all the students. In fact, they came to us when things started appearing on the news. As near as we can tell there was no one else on that trail that day except the students and Lucy."

"And there was no sign of Sarah when the first group of students came by? What time was that?"

"No, no one ever saw Sarah at the bluff or along the trail. All the students agreed on their times at the bluff, about 3:00 for the first group of five, and about 4:00 for the two stragglers. They came in two cars, and had a picnic by the river after their hike. There's a little more to it with these last two, but it had nothing to do with our investigation. Just a case of raging hormones. You'll read in the report."

"Well, Corey said, I'll be sure to read the statements and send you a note with my reactions. Maybe not until the week after next though. Will that be soon enough?"

"No, rush, Corey. I hope we get to meet again under better circumstances. I'll call you after I get your letter."

"Oh, by the way, where is that painting now?" Corey asked.

"It's in the box that I sent a couple of weeks ago. Didn't you get it?"

"Oh, yes, I got it; just haven't opened it. Thanks for calling."

9

VISITING THE SCENE

Looking through the box of Sarah's belongings when he got home, Corey thought that her unfinished watercolor of the bluff was really very good, in spite of the damage. Sarah had so perfectly captured the colors staining the bluff over the millennia that Corey felt as laughably insignificant looking at the painting as he did when he first saw them across the meadow at Steele Creek. The forest above the bluff was open and inviting, with still another bluff rising behind it into a cloudless sky. He decided to have it framed; after all, it was Sarah's final work. Perhaps, the frame shop could work Sarah's flute into the frame somehow. The bag still contained her cell phone, digital camera, and, hidden in a side pocket, her wallet. Sure didn't look like anyone was out to rob her!

Finding their father's old binoculars in the bag brought a sudden twinge of regret as he remembered Sarah's final phone message. He idly scanned through the dozens of digital pictures, noting the dates and times at the bottom of each. The last few were taken on Sunday. Was there some significance to the absence of photos on Monday? The last one was a picture of the bluff across the valley. Clearly it was the same scene as the one in Sarah's painting. He recognized it from having seen it on the day that he and Seth had climbed up to the overlook. In fact, there were three photos of the bluff, each identical. He got the painting and compared it with the photos. There was something puzzling about those photos and that painting. What was it? Why had Sarah taken three shots of the exact same view, when one would do? What was she seeing that he wasn't, or couldn't? Was there something more to the painting than just the challenge of the subtly blending colors?

Corey didn't sleep much that night, his mind kept trying to unlock the secret he felt sure was captured in the three photographs and in Sarah's watercolor. He got up and paced the floor, looking at the pictures, replaying Sarah's phone messages from June, and wishing he had Seth's final report in hand. He became aware that the grieving brother had again smoothly morphed into the experienced and objective investigator. It felt good. Not a closure. In fact, it was more like a beginning. He knew that he would be returning to the Buffalo. Soon!

Seth's report arrived two days later at Corey's office. A not very thick, but very official-looking tan envelope, marked "U. S. National Park Service, Buffalo National River, to be opened only by addressee." He told Jen not to disturb him and closed the door to his office so he could study the report undisturbed by the constant hum of office noise beyond his door.

With the detachment of an investigative professional, Corey read through the statements and conclusions of the Park Service's Official Investigative Report No. BNR-04-01, Subject: Sarah Pingree, dated 07-09-04, with the exception of the detailed autopsy report. The latter was not something he intended to ever read, and the last thing he wanted right now was to slip back into the useless morass of the grieving brother. It was enough to know that Sarah's injury to the side of her head would have rendered her unconscious if not immediately fatal.

The statements of Lucy Duckworth and Homer Stankey were less than half a page each and straight to the point. Lucy thought she had told Homer that she found the bag at the overlook, but perhaps in her hurry she had not and was sorry if she had failed to mention it. She'd been hurrying to an Audubon meeting in Fayetteville, and was thankful to run into Homer, so she wouldn't be delayed. She hadn't given it another thought until she got home late the next night and found her message light blinking. Out of sight, out of mind, as she said. It was heavy, and she knew someone would be missing it. And, since Homer was driving into the campground, and she had assumed the he would ask around for the owner, her job was done. No, she hadn't bothered to look inside the bag, she added indignantly, in response to a question from the investigator.

Homer, also in a hurry, said he should have asked Lucy where she found it. It just didn't seem important at the time. He was particularly apologetic for his failure to do anything about the satchel until sometime Tuesday morning. He'd simply dropped it on the floor on the passenger's side of the pickup and forgotten all about it. "Poor Homer." Thought Corey, he really set himself up to be the fall guy if the Park Service was looking for one.

The names and ages of all seven youths had been blacked out on Corey's copy of the report. The statements of each were almost identical except for the two that had trailed the pack. Not one had considered it unusual to find an unattended easel sitting on the rocks. All assumed that the owner had simply gone off the trail for a moment of privacy. Even later, during their picnic and bonfire in the meadow, when all seven were talking about their day and realized that they had found the artist to be absent at 3:00 PM and again at 4:00 PM, it hadn't triggered any curiosity as to why. "Kids!" thought Corey "Totally wrapped up in themselves." He tried to remind himself that he, too, had once been young and hormonally driven. But, it just didn't work for him. It's this new generation, he grumbled half aloud.

But, the fact that the trailing two also reported the easel to be present at 4:00 while Lucy Duckworth saw no sign of it an hour later hadn't escaped the notice of the investigating officer. He decided to call them back in. Only this time he reversed the order, boy first, then the girl. The boy was visibly nervous and immediately said he wanted to add something to his statement. He said that he'd forgotten to mention that he and the girl had inadvertently knocked the easel over the edge of the bluff.

"You didn't really forget to mention that, did you?" the officer asked, drawing out each word very slowly. The boy's already red face turned crimson.

"No," he replied.

"Now why was that?' asked the officer.

"I was told not to mention it."

"I wonder why she wouldn't want you to mention such an important fact?" mused the officer.

"I don't know," the boy replied.

"Oh, I bet you've got an idea though, don't you?" pushed the officer.

Suddenly the boy had blurted out: "She said she'd say that I raped her. I didn't, Officer, honest, I didn't, I couldn't do that!"

"Okay, son, I believe you. Now, why don't you wait outside while I have another talk with your young lady friend?"

Once confronted with the realization that her statement was clearly inconsistent with both that of her companion and that of the person who found the artist's satchel at 5:00 PM, the girl admitted that she had attempted to steal the painting, the boy had stopped her, and in the ensuing scuffle the easel fell over the cliff.

It was clear to Corey that the youngsters had nothing whatsoever to do with Sarah's demise, and that the park authorities had handled the situation with appropriate discretion. It was also clear to Corey that he needed to go back to Arkansas if he was ever to find any sense of closure, as a brother, and as a professional investigator who knew the importance of responding to his sixth sense. Things just were not adding up the way they should. He tried making a mental checklist of just what it was that didn't add up. But, it didn't help. He couldn't get beyond the first couple of items, namely that Sarah was an experienced mountain climber, and that she was fundamentally a cautious person. In fact, she was, by her own admission, somewhat scared of heights. On their climbs together, Sarah was probably what anyone would call super cautious. No, there was something more. He couldn't put his finger on it, but it was there. It was there, just like her presence was right there in the room, encouraging him on.

"Seth, this is Corey Pingree. I was wondering what the chances might be of my spending some time at the Steele Creek apartment in the fall?"

"Good to hear from you Corey. That should be no problem at all once the season is over. Those folks owe me big time!"

"No, no, I want to pay for it!" Corey replied.

"That would be way too much paper work. Can we just let it be on the U. S. Government?"

"Sure, even better! I've finished your report. Read it twice as a matter of fact, and I think your people did a very professional job of it. I just need to come down and find some kind of closure. For Sarah as much as for myself."

"Something in the report troubling you, Corey?"

"No, it's more like something that's not in the report is troubling me."

"I know what you mean, I've had that same feeling. Let me call you in a couple of days and give you some dates, okay?"

"That would be fine. Anytime through November would work for me."

"Good, let's plan to spend some time together. I've got a few questions for you, as no doubt you do for me."

10

BACK PACK ZACH

A blow to the back of the head with a rifle butt can be a life changing event. It doesn't really matter that it's an M-14, in the hands of one of your own search and destroy squad. It doesn't matter that it was done because you tried to stop your buddies from their mindless shooting of civilians, children, women, old men, in a remote jungle village. Give a kid a gun, and he'll shoot it, especially if he's already frightened half out of his wits. But, Zach remembered none of that.

Others had left behind their blood, their body parts, even their lives in the jungle. What Zach left behind was himself. Another patrol had found him, hours after he'd been left for dead by the boys he'd trained with, bonded with, trusted and loved. A year and a half later, he still remembered nothing. The once ruggedly handsome football player, the young man who had put off his first semester of college and joined the Marines because he needed the money, was gone forever. That Zach, or his ghost, probably still walked the jungles of Cambodia, reveling in the wildness of it. In his place was a gentle soul, a wild creature himself, who only knew that he was safe in the wilderness. The so-called civilized world was too dangerous a place to live, too violent, too unpredictable, and too noisy. Along with his memory, he left behind almost everything he ever knew about living in polite society. Zach was just one of many forgotten heroes of an easily forgotten war.

Zach was an odd mixture of childlike wonder, wisdom of the ages, and a healthy fear of anything complex. He remembered all the old obscenities from his youth, but not as obscenities, they were just words and gestures. This once well-read, well-liked, young Marine was now a hermit, a recluse, a curiosity. He, who had once dreamed of following in the path of his namesake, that distant relative, "Old Hickory," the twelfth president of the United States, this Zach Taylor looked like he had come right out of the pages of history, an authentic 1860s mountain man. We humans require social contact in order to grow and blossom, like a plant needs soil and water. Zach had been denied the chance to blossom and grow for most of his adult life.

Among the hills and deep valleys of the central Ozarks, no one knew anything about Zach's former lives. Known, for years, simply as "Backpack," because he carried everything on his back, Zach was just a local oddity. Rarely seen in town, sometimes seen walking the local roads, he was almost a wraith, a living legend. He seemed to be able to disappear, to just melt away into the trees. No one knew where he lived, or how. But these hills were full of old abandoned cabins, any one of which he might have adopted as his home. The only people he'd ever exchanged more than two words with were the postmaster and the clerk at the general store, the two places he visited when he'd make one of his rare appearances in the little town of Ponca, in north central Arkansas.

In a region of the country where minding your own business was as much a religion as the local brand of Christianity, Zach was just one of countless interesting characters. Put him in a crowd with any of a dozen other local eccentrics and he might stand out, but not that much. Local teenagers over the years learned that if they honked their horn at Old Backpack, he'd respond with a vigorous waving of his middle finger and what looked like a grin under his bushy black beard. "He doesn't mean anything by it, it's just his way," most folks concluded. It was, perhaps, their Christian charity, but it did seem to be his way of saying hello! and good bye!

In the years since leaving the VA hospital in Oregon, Zach had walked much of the country west of the Mississippi, leaving a number of carved walking sticks along the way with people who'd been kind to him, ending up in the Ozarks, where he took to the deep woods nearly a quarter of a century ago. Of the many rides he'd been offered, he'd never accepted one. Always thanking their generosity with his cheery middle-finger wave, prompting an accelerator blast and screeching tires, Zach was understandably leery of being in confined quarters with another human being. Cars and trucks were anathema to him. Losing physical touch with the earth tended to make Zach severely agitated. And, he knew he needed to be able to think clearly in order to survive whenever he came into the human jungle.

Much to the consternation of the doctors and nurses, he spent most of his convalescing time outdoors, or on the enormous open porch of the VA hospital in Portland, Oregon. He loved to climb the big old cottonwood in the middle of the hospital grounds, clear to its top. But, like an obedient child, he always came down when called. His hours were spent whittling, and he was very good at it. He particularly liked to work with the cottonwood limbs that he found high in the enormous old tree. The wood was soft and it yielded easily to his two-bladed penknife. He often came out of the tree with a newly carved walking stick adorned with a face at the grip. The faces were usually those of small children, open-eyed and fearful. By the time he had been discharged, Zach had whittled a walking stick for every member of the staff on his ward. Everyone assumed that he'd left messages whittled high up in the cottonwood, but no one ever dared to check it out.

Before leaving the hospital, the VA had set up an account for him at a bank in Oregon, into which flowed his monthly government check. It was small compensation for what he'd lost, but far more than his simple life style would ever need. They'd shown him how to get money from his account wherever he might be. The numbers were easy to memorize. Miraculously, his brain had developed, or sharpened, skills he'd never much called on before Cambodia, before the jungle, and before the ever-present headaches. In addition to an easy memory of things since the event, Zach had an almost primitive sense of survival.

Melting into the woods didn't really describe the change that came over him whenever he stepped off the traveled roadway. He became a part of the woods. He belonged not just in the woods, but to the woods. Anybody can make a home in the woods, but Zach was at home in the woods. The woods welcomed him back on every return.

He'd spent several months exploring the hundreds of thousands of acres in an around the Ozark National Forest and the Buffalo National River when he first arrived. He knew it was where he belonged. The growth of lush grape vines, as big around as his arm, disappearing into the tops of giant oaks and walnuts was comforting to him. Looking down the steep ravines to see a thread of shining water far below, was pleasantly reminiscent of something, he couldn't quite recall what. All that mattered was that he needed it. But he still had to find his place. He knew he would. It was just a matter of time. And he did.

On the edge of the Ponca wilderness, Zach stumbled upon an entrance to a cave hidden among jumbled boulders on a natural bench separating two massive bluffs. The lower bluff soared more than a hundred and fifty feet straight up from the floor of the Buffalo River valley. The bench itself, covered with a scattering of ancient oaks, was no more than two-hundred feet wide with its back against a second near-vertical bluff rising another hundred feet to the extensive plateau country surrounding the Buffalo. Nearly inaccessible except at either end where the bench trailed off as it followed the flow of the river, it was the No-Man's Land that Zach had been in search of for months. At the west end, the bench narrowed to what amounted to little more than a deep seam in the face of the bluff, a foot hold, extending to a series of difficult steps to the top of the upper bluff. At the east end, the bench narrowed to perhaps thirty feet in width while steeply ascending to the top of the bluff. Too inaccessible for logging, the bench had probably not been visited, even by hunters, for generations.

The tight squeeze of the cave entrance led down a gradual slant of twenty feet to a small room that was more of a widening in the passageway. To the north of the small room, tucked almost underneath the upper bluff was a larger room, one that had clearly been lived in at some distant time in the past. To the south, the entrance cave led along a brightly lit passageway to an opening overlooking the Buffalo and a beautiful meadow where there were campfires and horses grazing. At first, he thought they must be Indians, but then he saw their shiny vehicles. He could sit back from the long narrow slit of an opening in the bluff face, out of sight of the campers, and watch the campground for hours through the tree tops. It was the ideal distance for Zach to "socialize." He liked to watch but was uncomfortable being watched himself. By day, the bluff face warmed to the intensity of the sun, and the warmth penetrated all the way to the back of the cave. He realized that the warm air could be conserved by curtaining off the entrance to the middle cave with one of his army blankets in the winter.

He returned to the larger room and found that its dim light came from two long chimneys opening somewhere onto the upper bluff.

There was bright sky shining above. Ancient Indians had clearly used the room and its chimneys, a fact well attested to by the limestone encrusted skeleton that sat at the base of the farther chimney beside a small pool dripping of deliciously fresh water. Zach, respected the rights of the long-time resident, asking for permission to stay. Over the ensuing years, the two would have many conversations about the rewards of the solitary life.

The cave had an almost constant temperature that was about that of a warm refrigerator. Comfortable enough. On the rare occasions when he felt the need for a fire, he would light one at night, the smoke curling up the chimney into the night air, as invisible as Zach himself, and indistinguishable from the smell of the wood smoke emanating from the campground in the meadow below.

One day, at the approach of winter, during his first year in the cave, an old she-bear came waddling down the sloping entrance tunnel looking for a winter den. Squeezing her massive bulk between the entrance rocks must have been interesting to watch. Zach guessed that she'd been here before, and he thought that he might like to have the company. Maybe even the added warmth. The bear checked out every part of the cave as though making sure she was in the right place. She lethargically snorted at Zach, lay down, and commenced snoring. After only one night of her grunting and snoring, Zach managed to convince her that spring had come early. He prodded and pushed her back up the slope and through the squeeze. Squatters do have some rights! He wedged a pair of logs across the entrance to discourage her returning, and then walked for hours showing her suitable alternatives among the many that he'd discovered nearby. His occasional prodding from behind was met with a muffled snort and impatient head turn. Zach was a natural at hands-on wildlife management! In a different world, Zach might have been a very successful real estate agent. His salesmanship finally paid off when she crawled into a more appropriately sized cave at the far eastern end of the bench and didn't come out. He crawled in and listened to be sure she was snoring, and then headed for home, arriving well after dark, having crossed some of the most treacherous terrain in the Ozarks.

In recent years, one of Zach's favorite pastimes was shadowing Lucy Duckworth, well off the trail but closely watching her every move. Lucy was a grazer; every few steps she'd grab something and pop it into her mouth. Zach learned a lot about wild edibles from observing Lucy's diet. In just the first couple of shadowings he'd greatly expanded, and remarkably improved, the tastes of his own diet, going well beyond his mainstays of endless roots and shoots and nuts and berries and mushrooms in every season, Zach was now enjoying sumach tea and lichen tea, and just about every blossom in the woods except cherry and May apple. Lucy told the trailing bands of chattering children that were always with her that "some blossoms can make you very sick!"

His occasional forays into Ponca, or over the hill to Jasper, for a bag of cornmeal and a jug of sorghum were getting less and less frequent thanks to Lucy's teachings.

Zach was particularly fond of Lucy's hikes with youngsters. He'd learned to identify her Jeep in the Steele Creek Meadow. And, when it arrived, along with a yellow busload of kids, he'd slip out of the cave and head for one of her favorite spots along the River Trail. Lucy always had a difficult time keeping the children quiet, so that they could hear "the sounds of silence." Lucy's own strident voice made her constant shushing at the kids almost laughable. But, that voice actually warmed Zach. It was, perhaps, some distant long lost memory of his youth.

Despite the miles they had walked together, not once in all those many trips had Lucy or her charges ever discovered Zach's presence. Except one time when a little girl with especially sharp hearing broke the silence rule to say: "Ms. Duckworth, "I heard something over there in the woods." Zach froze. Lucy said: "Of course you did dear. You heard Nature breathing. That's the gift we get for walking in silence. Now, let's see how many of you can hear what Emma heard."

Zach's ability to glide through the woods noiselessly, though he could often hear his own footsteps, allowed him to get within touching distance of many animals and birds as they fed. The whitetail deer were as curious about Zach as he was about them.

When he slept in the woods they would nudge him 'til he awoke. When he ran with them, they would stop and wait for him to catch up. It never occurred to him to try to feed a deer by hand, although he could have easily done so. He found his own food. They found theirs. He watched the does give birth to spindly legged fawns that could get around on their wobbly legs immediately after birth.

Zach knew a kinship with deer that he couldn't recall ever feeling with humans. Somehow they sensed his wildness and the total absence of threat that they associated with others of his kind. The fact that he never killed another creature, never ate a bite of meat, probably meant that he lacked the essence of his kind, the aura of burger and beer and stale cigarette smoke that preceded those hunters and trappers who took great pride in deodorizing their clothing and gear before ever entering the woods.

For some of those "expert trappers," Zach had been a source of sport during his first years in the Ozarks. Tracking Back Pack had become a form of orienteering for them. Discovering exactly where Zach lived would be the equivalent of winning the Oscar for Ozark Wood Lore. But it never happened. It was never a contest, even for those who used dogs. Eventually, they tired of the chase concluding that Zach didn't live in the woods at all, but somewhere in one of the many abandoned buildings in and around town.

With his ability to be as wild as any of the forest creatures, Zach never lacked company. However, for the last several years, he had had Pup. To the extent that you can ever own a wild thing, Zach owned Pup; at least he felt responsible for him. Pup was the perfect companion. Gone, sometimes for days and weeks at a time, he fed himself and, once briefly, he even fathered a family of his own. Sometimes, if Pup happened to be around, Zach would take him along on one of his shadows with Ms. Lucy. Pup caught on to the game right away. One day, Pup sensed that Zach was about to be discovered, so he dashed across the trail in front of Lucy's kids to distract them. Ms. Lucy had been unable to stifle the hollering and chattering that ensued, all the way back to Steele Creek.

Zach had found Pup stretched out alongside the highway staring soulfully between his outstretched paws at what was left of his mother and sister in the road. Zach had talked to Pup softly while he lifted the remains of Pup's family gently from the roadway and carried them into the woods for a proper disposal. Then Zach left the road and started walking home, looking back from time to time. Sure enough, pretty soon along came Pup.

Zach knew he'd been adopted. And, with that knowledge, he knew that he had to teach Pup everything he knew about survival. He taught him to avoid humans, and to stay away from roads. He taught him not to panic at the sound of gun, and how to know when there were trappers around. He got down on all fours and showed Pup how to spring a trap with a stick held between his teeth. They wrestled together to build Pup's muscles. But, when it came to teaching Pup how to get food, Zach had a puzzle to solve. He wouldn't kill, not even for his little friend. Pup needed more than the ground berries and nuts that constituted Zach's mainstay. Lying on his back above the bluff, looking into the unblemished sky, the answer came to him in the form of circling buzzards.

From that day on, Zach and Pup watched for buzzards together. Then came the race to beat the buzzards to the lunch cart. Unfortunately, most of the meat came in the form of road kills, and Pup knew that roads were to be avoided. So, Zach taught Pup to lie in wait in the ditch until there were no sounds of vehicles on the road. Then, he taught Pup to look both ways before dashing onto the road to grab a piece of the carcass and scurry back to the ditch. Pup was a good student. And, Zach was a great teacher. If Zach saw that the carcass was that of a coyote, he avoided taking Pup near it. Either Pup understood or he completely trusted Zach. The bonding was complete.

Now, however, Pup was growing old and gray in the muzzle, and staying away longer and longer, as though not wanting to trouble Zach. When he came to the cave, Pup would spend much of his time lying in the sun on the rim rock, warming his aging bones. Zach knew that someday Pup would not come back. It was the way of wild things. Death should be natural, dignified, and private. After death would come the celebration of returning. The animals are wise.

Death was not something that Zach ever thought about. He'd seen death during his stay at the VA hospital, and he'd seen death many times as he walked the highways in search of where he belonged. If anything might have forced him to think about death, to jog his memory back to Cambodia, the carnage along the roads would have done it. It was mostly wild creatures with a few domestic and farm animals thrown in. But, twice he'd walked right on by deadly vehicle accidents that had just happened. They were just another natural event.

To Zach, the skeleton in the cave wasn't dead so much as it was silent. Silence! Now, that was a quality that Zach could cherish, like sunrises and sunsets, like the calm before and after a violent storm. Why do we prize the things we do? Perhaps if the last thing heard before receiving a life-changing blow to the head was the din of battle, the screams of the dying, and the roar of gunships overhead, silence might replace fame and fortune as life goals. Death, to Zach, was the ultimate silence. That made it a good thing, not something to be concerned about.

11

A DAY ON THE RIVER

"Fall in the Ozarks is every bit as beautiful as it is in the Northeast," Corey exclaimed, shaking hands with Seth at the airport. When Seth offered to pick him up, Corey asked if he would mind doing it in Sarah's Honda. The car had been sitting in the Park Service's impound lot for over three months and needed to be driven. Corey had gotten the title and license transferred and was hoping he might be able to sell it in Arkansas rather than drive it back to Saratoga Springs.

"I've never seen a New England fall, but I hear it's pretty colorful," Seth replied. Seth guided Corey to Steele Creek where he picked up a Park Sevice vehicle for the short trip back to Harrison. Before departing, he apologized for the Spartan appearance of the apartment, quickly qualifying the apology, adding, "I'm told the artists like it this way." Receiving Corey's assurance that he would come for dinner tomorrow night in Harrison with his wife, Dana, Seth left Corey to his thoughts, knowing that they might be overwhelming.

"Sarah, talk to me," Corey said softly. You were here, in this very spot just weeks ago. Here and full of life, full of excitement, finally starting your own life, eager to capture the Buffalo and all its life with your paints and brushes, and your imagination. He opened the refrigerator door and found an icy cold six-pack of Cuervo, one bottle missing, and a note:

"Sarah left this, and I tucked it away, knowing that you'd come some day."

Corey stared at the open refrigerator feeling lost. Knowing Sarah's liking for Mexican beers, and realizing that she'd bought this very six-pack, he struggled with his emotions, slowly closing the refrigerator door, saying "Okay, maybe later, Sis." He walked across the small room sinking at once into the leatherette couch and into a dismal funk wondering. Why had he come to this place? A place he desperately wanted to erase from his memory! His eyes came to rest on the tattered loose leaf Artist's Log on the coffee table. "Open it" a voice said so clearly that he glanced around the room for its source. But, he already knew no one was there, because it was Sarah's voice.

The entries started four years ago. Most were a page in length, written at the end of the artists' three-week residency in the form of advice to future residents. He read a few, than rapidly flipped to June of this year. He knew Sarah would write a daily entry if she wrote anything at all. She was too excited not to, and he had not been available for her to talk with, what with the quirky cell phone connections. Sarah had written two entries. On Saturday, the day before Father's Day she wrote:

"I have fallen in love with this valley. I know the bison were wiped out two centuries ago, but I can see them in the meadow's morning mist. I can't wait to paint them."

The next day, Sunday, she wrote:

"Took the Steele Creek trail up to the top of the bluff and found the spot, so many before me have raved about. It is truly an Artists' Bluff, an inspirational view of the valley. Don't miss it. And, don't let Old Mr. Griz across the valley scare you! Going back tomorrow."

"So, why did you want me to read that?" he said to the empty room.

Shifting into his investigator role, Corey decided he'd have that Cuervo now. Then he sat back down to reread the entries. What did she mean? Is Mr. Griz a rock formation? Obviously, there are no grizzlies in Arkansas. Not the first beer, or the second, helped to shed any light on the mystery. But, inexplicably, he no longer doubted himself for coming.

Corey had decided, before leaving New York, his first visit would be to Artist's Bluff. It wasn't just that Sarah had fallen from there; it was where the photos were taken from, where the damaged painting was made, and now this enigmatic note from Sarah. He had no idea what he was looking for, but maybe Old Mr. Griz was a clue? If nothing came from his visit to Artists' Bluff, step two would be to try to visit with those kids. Maybe they had seen something, anything, particularly those last two. Maybe they'd remember something now that they were not as stressed at having their indiscretions exposed.

Finally, he planned to talk with Lucy Duckworth. She'd been in a hurry that day, but people like Lucy were good observers. They often saw things that most other folks would miss. Why, for example, had she, in her hurry, seen the satchel that those kids apparently missed?

By noon, Corey had been sitting at Artists' Bluff for more than four hours. Only two hikers had come by. Exchanging a brief "Hi" they moved on down the trail. The Equinox sun was blazing hot even if no longer directly overhead. The air was still and the rocks were warm to the touch. He'd brought the enlargements that he'd made of the three digitals of the opposite bluff, and he'd brought Sarah's small painting protected in bubble wrap. He'd brought a magnifying glass to study them with, and their Dad's 7x50 binoculars that he'd found in Sarah's satchel.

In four hours, the only thing he'd seen on that slope above the bluff was a lone coyote walking the rim rock as though he owned it. He was getting the direct sun and obviously enjoying it, even lying down with his tail draped over the bluff. He'd studied every inch of that bluff looking for a formation that might imaginatively be seen as Mr. Griz. There were a lot of images over there, but nothing remotely close to a bear. There was a cave entrance below the rim rock, right where the coyote's tail lazily pointed, But, it was obviously inaccessible, too dark, and at the wrong angle to see inside more than a few feet. Interesting, but hardly a bear's den.

All his morning outing had provided was a sunburn, and a change in plans. He studied the wilderness map for trails on the opposite bluff.

There were none. That's okay, he thought, even better! Corey knew that he was a better-than-average bushwhacker.

That evening, as he arrived at the Greer's for dinner, Corey was surprised to be introduced to Lucy Duckworth. "I told Lucy you were coming to dinner, and she wanted to meet you. I hope you don't mind?" said Seth making the introductions. Dana, Seth's wife, was a peach. Her parents had lived in New York, Saranac Lake, to be exact. And, Lucy had attended Syracuse University, so, the table talk centered around things other than Sarah, like wildlife and the Adirondacks. Corey was quickly at ease with the small group. He found everyone so interesting, that he decided to say nothing to Lucy about Sarah. It could only spoil the evening for all, yet he couldn't help thinking how Sarah had brought them all together, and how much she would have added to the evening. As he was saying his good byes, he did mention to Lucy that he'd hoped to take a canoe trip on the Buffalo before heading for home, Maybe she'd like to be his guide he suggested idly.

"Oh, my boy, you simply must. But don't rent a canoe, we'll use mine. Would tomorrow be too soon?" Lucy asked.

Corey hesitated momentarily; his exploration of the bluff country could certainly wait another day, especially since he didn't know what he was looking for. "Tomorrow's good," he replied with muted enthusiasm.

"Okay, shall we say eight o'clock? Not too early, I hope." Lucy didn't wait for an answer. "Good, I'll bring a thermos of coffee and some of my famous cinnamon rolls and, of course, the canoe," she effused, taking his outstretched hand in her own.

Before slipping the canoe into Buffalo at the edge of the meadow, at precisely 8:00 the next morning, Corey glanced up at the towering bluffs above them, and asked Lucy if any of those rock formations had names, like Old Griz for example.

"None that I know of. People are always putting names on them though. The whole formation is called Roark's Bluff, named after an early settler. Come to think, there is one just around the corner that reminds a lot of people of the Sphynx."

"So, where are we headed this morning?" Corey asked.

"That depends on what you're up for. There's a couple of places where we can hitch a ride back to Steele Creek. You've done some canoeing, I take it?"

"Some," Corey acknowledged.

Though ostensibly his guide, Lucy graciously gave Corey the stern seat, and, within a minute, was assured that Corey had spent a whole lot more hours in a canoe than she ever had, or probably ever would.

"Water's always low this time of year—we're probably going to spend as much time carrying as paddling," Lucy commented.

"Done some of that, too," Corey offered.

About a mile downriver, Lucy called out the name of the formation dead ahead. "That's Big Bluff, and there's a gravel bar on this side if you want to pull in. I'll tell you about it."

The Big Bluff story, and its famous Goat Trail cutting across its middle like a vertigo sufferer's worst nightmare, was way too brief. It was just Lucy's big bluff to stop for a coffee break. Corey was suitably impressed with both the coffee and Lucy's famous cinnamon rolls. She sat in the canoe as he lay on the gravel bar looking up at Big Bluff, neither of them saying anything, just enjoying the peacefulness of the moment.

After a while, Lucy got up and walked around behind Corey.

"Time to go?" he asked.

"Not yet," she answered. He could no longer see her, but he heard the sounds of her steps in the gravel as she circled him. When he next saw her, she was carrying a large cottonmouth in one hand, taking it down to the river to release it.

"I didn't want to surprise you," she said, "but you were right in his path."

Controlling his surprise with some difficulty, Corey got up hastily and walked down to the river and watched it glide effortlessly away to the other side.

As they turned around to walk back up the bar and to their canoe, Lucy asked, "Do you see anything up there in the woods?"

Feeling like he was being tested, Corey looked in the direction that Lucy was facing. Squinting through the slanting rays of sunlight he was able to make out the dim outlines of an ancient half-collapsed cabin, well hidden by trees and vines.

She could tell he saw it. "That's the cabin the kids mentioned in their statements," Lucy said. "And that slope behind the cabin takes you right up to the Artists' Bluff trail. The rangers call it a 'bootleg' trail, and they keep trying to obscure it with brush and logs, but a lot of people know about it and use it. I've used it myself. It's a great way to appreciate the differences in the vegetation between river bottom and bluff top."

It was Lucy's first mention of anything connected to Sarah's death, and Corey just listened. He wasn't about to start asking questions concerning Sarah's satchel, when she had just saved him from an encounter with a cottonmouth. Lucy was his guide. It was okay to just listen to your guide. Silences were good.

They pushed the canoe back into the middle of the stream and Corey found himself looking around for snakes. Lucy smiled. "You were asking about a rock formation named Old Griz; does it have some connection to why you're here?" Lucy asked as they started paddling below Big Bluff.

"Lucy, I'm not sure why I'm here. Something to do with closure I suppose the psychologists would say. I doubt that Old Mr. Griz has anything to do with Sarah's death. It's just an interesting entry that she made in the artist's journal on the night before—" He didn't finish the sentence. Lucy didn't push for what the entry said, instead wisely changing the subject.

"There's a lot more of the Buffalo to see. We might cover a tenth of it today if we get as far as Kyle's Landing.

The eight miles to Kyle's included several carries through water that might have floated a kayak, but not two in a canoe. Those shallows just happened to coincide with opportunities for Lucy to expound on the natural wonders of the country they were passing through. Corey was a good listener, and Lucy was a good talker, in fact an almost obsessive instructor, at least on her favorite subject, the Buffalo. During the course of their short trip, Corey figured he'd learned more from Lucy than he could recall having learned from any of a dozen or more training sessions he'd been through.

At Kyle's, Lucy quickly proved her mastery of not just wild nature, but human nature as well, as she easily secured their ride back to Steele Creek. The canoe outfitters in the area clearly were eager to be in Lucy's favor, perhaps being in her debt for more than one guided trip of their own; trips that yielded a nice bit of change for the outfitters.

On the ride back to Steele Creek, Corey sat in the back of the pick-up with the canoe, while Lucy sat up front. They'd offered to squeeze three in front, but Corey liked the idea of not having to answer any idle questions the outfitter might have. Besides, something was troubling him. With Lucy loving to talk as much as she did, and being the curious person she obviously was, why had she not followed up on Sarah's entry in the artists' register? Was she just being considerate of his feelings? Giving him the chance to talk? She, had had an almost physical reaction to his mention of Old Mr. Griz, didn't she? Or was it just his imagination?

Back at Steele Creek, Corey helped load the canoe onto Lucy's little custom-made trailer. He thanked her for the wonderful day, and as she got into the Jeep, she, unexpectedly took his hand in both of hers, saying, "No, it is I who should thank you. I count every day on the river as a blessing. We really must do this again before you leave! Now, just when is that?"

"I'd like that." Corey admitted. "I'm thinking I may drive Sarah's Honda back to New York, in which case, I'll probably leave later this week."

Corey stood in the Steele Creek parking lot waving at the thick cloud of dust stirred up by Lucy's Jeep, his intuition shouting, "Lucy knows something or at least she thinks she does!" Walking back to stables, he paused several times to study the rim rock of Roark's Bluff. He found the Sphinx, but no Mr. Griz.

12

CONNECTING THE DOTS

Lucy Duckworth wrestled with her misgivings knowing that time was what she needed and that time was running short. Writhing and wriggling snakes she could handle with ease. Snakes could be saved one at a time. But, this was different. These were two people that she cared about. One was as wild as the Buffalo country she loved. It was the wild country that had given her new life five years ago, The other was tamed but, in every way, represented the arch enemy of the first. One thing she knew, with the certainty of her years of observation, was that the people who are entrusted with the care of wild things all too often lacked a fundamental understanding of the meaning of wild. Corey seemed different somehow. She needed more time to figure out just why she thought so.

She smiled as she thought about Zach. She never called him "Back Pack." To do so would have been like calling one of her hundreds of students by something other than their own name. And, Zach was as surely one of her students as if he'd been sitting in class. One of the best, and one she had committed herself to protect, to save his wildness from all who wanted to take it from him. And that, she sternly reminded herself, is what civilization is obsessively committed to do, whether it's the hunter seeking the trophy that will make him master of the wild, the wildlife professional who needs to believe the wild is his to scientifically manage, or the developer who can't abide seeing a patch of land that isn't earning money. Lucy's view was much simpler: the wild is something you leave alone. Corey didn't seem to fit any of the patterns. He was different. He was committed to protecting wild creatures from those who would exploit them. He, quite obviously, knew his way around in the woods, but in the woods was not where Corey really operated.

Lucy had done her homework well over the past three months. She was a stickler for homework as any of her students could attest. Thanks to the Internet, she knew quite a lot about Corey, and about Zach. Getting herself invited to Seth and Dana's for dinner with Corey hadn't been the idle curiosity that everyone presumed it was.

She was determined to meet the wildlife agent who had managed to infiltrate the big business end of an international smuggling ring specializing in elephant ivory from Mozambique and South Africa, then selling its wares in a few very pricey New York antique shops.

Accomplishing that feat, while ostensibly an up-state investigator of small-time poachers, was no small accomplishment. Lucy was a big contributor to the World Wildlife Fund, and $100 a month for a retired school teacher is big. So, people like Corey were her heroes! And, she particularly liked the intrigue of being the only one in the room, aside from Corey, who really knew all this. Two or three times, during the evening, she had expected the conversation to drift in the direction of rare and endangered species. But, it never did. She decided that to push it in that direction might set off Corey's alarm system. She had a better idea.

Lucy's research on Zach was a much different story. He was one of several Zach Taylors on the Internet, eclipsed by the nation's twelfth president. The Internet did, however, seem to confirm the local suspicion that he had been a wounded Vietnam era vet at the VA hospital in Oregon. End of the line. Not long after she settled in the area, Lucy had caught a glimpse of Zach in worn and filthy fatigues, loaded with a bulging pack on his back. It was a fleeting glimpse that she was not at all sure she had really seen, for the figure had immediately disappeared into the woods alongside Route 43. A few days later at the general store, she mentioned what she'd seen, getting the stock terse reply that she'd probably seen "Old Back Pack," Zach Taylor, a local hermit who'd been around the area for a couple of decades. From time to time, after that first encounter, she'd hear rumors of Back Pack being seen as far away as Buffalo Point, at least fifty miles to the east. Nobody really knew where he lived and, to most, he was a subject of either mild sympathy or cruel ridicule.

Lucy hadn't thought much about Zach for two or three years. Then, a year ago, she was sure that she had glimpsed him again. This time, it was while she was hiking the River Trail with a group of youngsters. It was a fleeting image, so fleeting she rubbed her eyes and looked again, in vain. But, Lucy, always a woman of strong convictions, knew what she saw. And, for some unknown reason, she knew that she had no reason to be afraid of what she saw. But, she was curious. She assumed Zach, if it was Zach, was simply curious too.

Over the ensuing months, she realized that she could tell when he was nearby. And, she quickly learned that if she didn't look in his direction he would often follow along at a discreet distance. She felt sure that they were both playing different versions of the same game. But, she realized that Zach was too unsophisticated, too wild, to know that she was playing a game as well. In her wild plant talks along the trail Lucy took to raising her voice, not just to get her group's attention but to be sure that Zach was also learning all the possible uses, and dangers, of each species of plant. Days later, when passing a spot where she'd emphasized a particularly useful root, she might notice that the soft soil had been disturbed in just the way she'd taught so as to minimize damage to the plant. She smiled the smile of a satisfied teacher.

Only once, did Lucy come close to letting Zach know that he'd been seen. That was the day when one of younger girls piped up with "Miss Duckworth, I heard something over there!" And she was pointing right at the rock where Lucy had last glimpsed a branch move all by itself. Lucy's heart sank. But then, as if by a miracle, everyone's attention was diverted by a coyote running across the trail. It wasn't the first time that Lucy had observed a coyote when Zach was nearby. That day, Lucy smiled the smile of a contented student. She was learning things about Zach that nobody else knew. The good teacher is always learning, and Lucy was very good!

Corey's arrival on the scene had the effect of speeding up Lucy's heretofore leisurely learning process about Zach. She had sensed immediately that Corey, like herself, was not one to ignore his hunches. In a rapid-fire sequence of conclusions, Lucy reasoned that she had to make a decision. She was caught right square in the middle. And, it was a most uncomfortable feeling.

Obviously, Zach had chosen the wild way of life for himself, and he was very, very, good at it. Like any wild creature, Zach didn't need the interference of any person, or any government agency, however well-meaning, to make his life better. Zach had made the mistake with Lucy of thinking that he was invisible. That mistake had made him vulnerable. He might do it again, with someone less caring than herself. The frequency with which she had either seen or sensed him made her realize that he lived somewhere near Steele Creek where she did the majority of her guided tours. Steele Creek was on the edge of the Buffalo Wilderness, which meant that Zach certainly lived on government land and at a place where he had a good view of the comings and goings at Steele Creek. Lucy didn't want anyone to know just where he lived. She didn't even want to know herself, for that would be the beginning of the end of Zach's wild way of life. While some folks might not like the idea of Zach, or anyone else squatting on government land, Lucy felt that was a small enough compensation for all he had given up for his country. And, finally, if the Park Service ever found out where he lived, there was no question in Lucy's mind that they would evict him.

Lucy was dead certain that somehow Sarah had seen Zach. Maybe the sighting scared her? Maybe she'd panicked? But, Lucy was also dead certain that Zach hadn't harmed Sarah. Lucy knew Zach better than any other living soul, and she knew he was incapable of harming another being. She held no doubts about that. Whatever he'd seen in Vietnam must have rendered him incapable of hurting another living being.

She hadn't figured Corey out yet, but she knew that she liked his quiet, unassuming ways. She particularly liked his answer to Dana, the other night at dinner, when she asked him how he liked being a wildlife manager. He'd said, without the least hint of correcting her, that he didn't manage wildlife, he just tried to protect them by managing people. It was the perfect opportunity for Corey to talk about greed, and the black market in endangered species. Instead he deftly diverted the conversation back to Dana, by asking about growing up in Saranac Lake. Lucy warmed to how Corey could guard information about himself while being disarmingly social.

Maybe, he could be trusted? With a twinge of regret, she knew that she didn't have a choice. But, she should go slow, and use the time to win his trust. She needed to see if he started connecting the dots on his own, without jumping in unless she had to, and not until she could be sure of his respect for the wild and for Zach's freedom to choose the wild. Lucy decided to call on Corey tomorrow and ask to see that register entry of Sarah's. "Old Griz" had to be Zach! She was sure of it.

13

COYOTE DAYS

Zach hadn't seen Pup for several days; it was not an unusual absence, except that Pup was getting deaf. Wild things need not just all of their senses, but all senses finely tuned. Survival depends on having that hair-thin edge in hearing, seeing, and smelling a predator seconds before that fatal lunge, that unexpected blow. In his early years, the learning years, when he first came to the Buffalo Wilderness, Zach started shadowing trappers as they made their rounds. Once, watching a trapper from a safe distance as he approached a coyote caught in a leghold trap, he saw the animal holding out his ensnared paw to the trapper, as though begging to be released. The trapper walked boldly up to the animal, holding a piece of meat in his outstretched hand. He dropped the meat to the ground and, as the coyote dropped his head to sniff the morsel, the trapper delivered a lightning-swift blow to the back of the unsuspecting creature's head.

Zach felt that blow. He could still feel that blow, all these years later. Even now, as he thought about that day, his hand unconsciously rubbed the back of his head.

Zach wasn't worried about Pup. In fact, the ability to worry about anything had ceased being a burden long ago. But, he cared. The chances of Pup being run over on the road were next to zero. Getting caught in a leghold trap was even less likely. Not only did Pup know more about traps than most trappers did, all trapping in the area had ceased years ago. Although the Park Service's public relations folks were quick to take the credit for the abrupt decline, it probably had more to do with the mysterious disappearance of any trap set within twenty miles of the upper Buffalo. Several deep fissures became the final rusting places for scores of steel-jaw leg-hold traps, their rusty red death stain trickling underground to eventually reappear as joyous streaks of orange on the face of the bluffs. Zach and Pup had made the woods safe for their friends for miles around.

It was one of those perfect October mornings in the bluff country, heralding a day when just knowing you're alive and knowing you're awake doesn't come close to all that you're seeing and believing about your world. It was a day to be celebrated by a long walk in the woods. Somewhere, far, far, away, yet as close as the back of his mind, Zach could hear Pup calling him to join in a romp for a little puppy play. Grabbing the walking stick he'd carved with Pup's eager face on it, Zach headed off through the giant oaks and nut trees, through a forest that had never known the bite of an axe. Its monarchs could have been cut, but getting the logs out would have been impossible. Not that that had ever stopped the loggers before. There just wasn't enough here to bother with. Eden has never been off-limits, just off-target!

Zach's senses were finely tuned, not only to the sounds of the forest, but to what each of those sounds meant in the life of the forest; for the forest's life was his own. Ahead and to his left, the hammering of a pileated woodpecker meant the destruction of one of his favorite bee trees. But the bees would move on. The remains of the grand old oak would crumble to the ground, already too rotted to burn.

Fire in the forest was one of only two things Zach feared. It wasn't simply that fire would bring firefighters and destroy his cover, fire would kill the trees, destroying the nesting places of hawks and owls, possums and raccoons. His home was fireproof while the homes of his neighbors were not. But, like the deer and the elk and the bear, Zach would flee the forest ahead of the fire. It was not a worry. Zach knew that fire, like the eagle, like himself, like all those campers in the meadow, was just a visitor.

Fire was a rational fear. You should fear fire. But, Zach's other fear seemed totally irrational. His reaction was immediate, intense, and uncontrollable. Whenever he heard the sound of a helicopter Zach instinctively dropped flat on the ground and placed his hands over his ears. They didn't fly over the wilderness very often, but when they did, he had no more control over his reaction than he could avoid blinking when a bug came toward his eyes. He didn't understand it; he didn't fear helicopters, and afterwards he would laugh at himself.

It was a reaction that Pup copied the very first time he saw Zach do it. When the helicopter had passed by, Zach looked up to see Pup trying to melt into the ground with eyes closed and paws over his ears. His laughter must have echoed for miles. Pup had seemed immensely pleased with himself to get such a reaction, licking Zach's face and running round and round him as he sat on the floor of the forest convulsed in laughter. Zach and Pup had had many laughs together over the years, but none better than the helicopter.

It would be a ten-mile hike to the abandoned old fields in the Ozark hills where Zach figured he might find Pup, and another ten rugged miles back to the cave. But, it was that kind of a day, a day wasted if it didn't lead to a good walk. And, if he didn't get back by nightfall, the woods offered lots of lodging places. The leaves were just starting to turn a pale yellow, and the early fall harvest would be far more than his backpack could hold. He looked forward to the crisp, if stunted, apples from abandoned orchards, spicy red sumach heads, juicy wild grapes, and some easily dried hen-of-the-woods mushrooms. His pack would be heavy, but this day's excursion would provide food for weeks.

Zach approached the field with caution even though he knew this once populated farm country was rarely visited, except twice a year to harvest its abundant sweet smelling hay. The woods surrounding these high country fields were once pastures. Today they hid a long-gone civilization of collapsing barns, crumbling foundations of ghost houses, rusted old hay rakes, plows, and skeletal farm trucks and tractors.

Cemeteries, deep in the woods, with their adjacent small white churches, doors and windows standing open, floors rotting, interiors vandalized, seemed to add a statement of finality to the scene. Even God had forgotten the generations who plowed their hopes into the soil of these hills.

Zach stood in the shadow of a giant walnut, eyes scanning the field. And then, he saw him, crouching low to the ground, inching forward with infinite patience, to finally pounce upon his hapless victim, a field mouse. Zach watched the performance repeated three or four times, feeling the swell of pride that any parent does in their youngster's success. Suddenly, Pup sensed Zach's presence, the subtlest shift in the wind, and he looked straight at Zach, without seeing him for a while in the shade. Eyesight failing too, thought Zach. Taking pity on his friend, he lifted his arm to wave. Then Pup saw him and came bounding across the field like the puppy that still lived inside him. Zach jogged to meet him, and Pup leaped and danced around him. Zach fell to the ground and they wrestled as they hadn't wrestled in years.

Zach got up and started walking toward home. Pup took a couple of wistful looks back at his mousing field, and then trotted along crisscrossing back and forth in front of Zach, playing the scout as he'd done for years. Watching Pup's playful game, Zach remembered two winters back when Pup came running to him from just such a game, whimpering and acting very much afraid. Curious, Zach back tracked Pup's trail in the new snow until he discovered a cougar's fresh track. The cougar had been shadowing them, silent and unseen, filled with curiosity, just as was Zach when shadowing Lucy along the river. Curious, Zach led Pup on a great circle to see if he could trick the cougar into becoming the hunted instead of the hunter. Gradually shrinking the size of his circle, the cat was forced to take to a tree, snarling his fury, and causing Pup more than a little anxiety. Curiosity satisfied, Zach once again headed for home.

All in all, it had been a very good day. For Zach, every day was a good day, but some were better than others. Even those days when ice storms prevented him from leaving the cave, were incredibly beautiful. On such days, when ice, or lightning storms, and winter blizzards howled, he would go to the outer of his three caves and sit on the rock shelf watching nature turn the meadow into a fantasyland, At those times, when nothing moved except a few elk pawing away the snow to get at the grass stubble underneath, Zach was filled with all the wonder of a child on his first birthday.

Over the years, he'd added to his stock of blankets and he'd even rescued a couple of abandoned tents that he used to curtain the winds from entering the inner cave. On the coldest nights, a very small fire kept him comfortably warm. But, not tonight, tonight was a night to sleep under the stars with an old coyote for a pillow, dreaming of shared adventures like hiding from helicopters, stealing traps, and hunting field mice. When the cougar screamed in the dark of the night, Zach felt Pup tremble beneath his head. Or, maybe it was just undigested field mice having their last revenge. Off and on, Pup would let out a little yelp in his sleep.

Throughout his months at the VA hospital, Zach would often shout obscenities in his sleep. It wasn't something that endeared him to his ward mates, but when they woke him he could never remember having done it. The doctors tried hypnosis and a battery of drugs, finally settling on a little green pill that the nurse gave him every night.

When Zach finally left the hospital, they had given him a vial of the little green pills, which he left on the table by the door, very much aware that the pills were not for him, but for the others in the ward. One night in northern Idaho, a farmer had awakened to the sound of loud cursing in his cornfield and called the police. By the time the troopers came, sirens wailing from five miles away, Zach had awakened and was an hour down the road. Zach remembered those little green pills as he lay smiling at the night sky wondering if Pup would benefit from one.

14

FINDING "OLD GRIZ"

Corey Pingree needed to get his hands on a good topographic map of the area. The Park Service maps were good enough for the casual tourist, but he needed more. Sarah's journal entry clearly referred to something across the valley, something that might frighten the unprepared. And yet, if it was across the valley, how could it frighten anyone? And why had she taken three photos of the same spot atop Roark Bluff? Her unfinished painting seemed to suggest that there was something hidden in the trees above the cap rock of the bluff but, unfortunately, that exact spot had been damaged when the painting was thrown over the cliff.

Since he didn't have detailed maps to study, he decided to look at the digitals one more time. The color enlargements he'd made from downloading Sarah's pictures back at Saratoga had showed nothing unusual, so he'd left them behind. But, he still had the originals in his laptop, and he had brought along a small black and white printer.

While the laptop was printing the pictures, Corey fixed his second cup of coffee, and mused about Sarah having been right here, fixing her coffee, planning her day, eating her solitary breakfast. For the hundredth time, he wondered what he was doing here, yet he knew why he had to come. He'd convinced his sister to come here. Surely he owed her something, even in death. And, that something was an absence of lingering questions.

When he returned to the table to look at the pictures, he saw it! There was a human form in those woods, a human in camouflage clothing. He wondered why he hadn't seen it before, and wished he had the colored prints for comparison. Obviously the camouflage had blended with the foliage and done its job. The black and white prints were blurry, but there was definitely a human form there, bent over, back to the camera, and moving away from the bluff. That human form had to be the mysterious Mr. Griz. That settled it, maps or no maps, he was going for a hike in the wilderness.

Because there was no way to get to the top of Roark Bluff from the meadow side, Corey headed out to drive around the valley and into the Ponca Wilderness from north side. Maybe, with luck, he'd find a good topographic map along the way. He remembered seeing a visitor center in Ponca along with a general store and a couple of river outfitters. One of them should have a USGS sheet that he could at least look at. Corey's experiences in the Adirondacks had taught him that the surface terrain could tell you a lot about what lies underground. That observation could be even more revealing in the almost vertical valleys of the Ozarks.

Pulling into the parking lot at the General Store, Corey noticed Lucy's Jeep parked across the street at the canoe livery. Lucy was coming down off the long porch of the log cabin office. She waved to him, and headed across the street, so he waited for her.

"Good Morning, Corey," Lucy called from the middle of the street. "You've saved me a trip down to Steele Creek!"

"Good to see you, Lucy. I was hoping to get another chance to thank you again for yesterday. How about a cup of coffee?"

"No, thank you anyway, I have to limit myself to one cup a day, otherwise, I might never stop chattering," she laughed. "But, I'll sit with you, if you're having one."

"You wouldn't happen to have a USGS sheet of this area in your Jeep, would you?" asked Corey.

"Of course I do, dear boy, I wouldn't leave home without it. Would you like to borrow it?" Lucy replied.

"I'd really appreciate the loan." Then, responding to the inquiring look on Lucy's face, he added, "I'm on my way to explore the wilderness above Roark Bluff, and I don't have a really good map."

"That's an area I've never visited. I don't suppose you'd like a companion?" Lucy asked, adding, "that would give us a chance to visit. Canoes aren't very congenial places to talk, and I've been wanting to follow up on something you said yesterday about Old Griz. Is that why you're going in there?"

"Uh huh," replied Corey, getting his coffee and feeling a little embarrassed that he really didn't want the company, especially after Lucy's generosity yesterday. He just knew that he could cover more country if he was alone. On the other hand, Lucy seemed to want to talk, and he didn't want to rush her.

"Okay, tell you what, leave your car here, we'll take the Jeep, and you can have your coffee while I drive. We've got a few miles to cover and some pretty rough country to hike through, so we'd best not dawdle!"

Lucy drove, mercifully silent, as Corey sipped his coffee, wondering just how much to share with her about the figure he'd discovered in Sarah's photos. A few miles up the hill out of town, Lucy broke the silence. "Maps are in that old ammo box by your feet," she said.

Of course, thought Corey. Where else would you keep your maps, but in an old ammo box. Secure from the rain and if Lucy had to ford a creek at high water, the box would float and the maps stay dry. Sharp old gal!

"I've got an idea who your Old Griz might be," she suddenly blurted out." And, it's possible that Sarah might have thought him scary. But, I can assure you that he would never deliberately scare anyone. In fact, he is extremely shy," she continued.

"Lucy, I think you may be right, and I don't think Sarah was really scared. But, whoever he is, he may know something, anything that might help explain why Sis, an experienced mountain climber, would fall off a cliff," Corey replied. "In fact, I think I may even have a photograph of Old Griz on the bluff, taken by Sarah. Does the person you have in mind happen to wear camouflage?"

"Camouflage and a back pack is all he ever wears. His name is Zach. Locals call him Back Pack. He's a real hermit. Nobody knows where he lives. But, I have every reason to believe he lives somewhere near Steele Creek, Maybe exactly where you're going today. And, I'd like you to reconsider trying to find him."

"Why?" asked Corey.

"Well, the local story, and I tend to believe it, is that Zach is a damaged Vietnam vet. On the rare occasions when people pass him on the road he usually gives them a wave of his middle finger. That makes folks think he's angry. I prefer to think it's just part of the damage he's suffered. He has chosen the wild as his way of life, and whatever his reasons are, I respect them. I just don't think it would be fair to intrude on that life. Frankly, I doubt very much that you can find him. Some of the best trackers in five counties have tried, and they all failed. On the other hand, I suspect if anyone could find him, you could. I'd guess, however, if you did, it would only be because he wanted you to."

"No doubt you are right. But what do I do, just turn around and go home, when this is the only lead I've got. You see, Lucy, I got Sarah into this. If it hadn't been for me, none of this would have ever happened. Sarah would be alive, probably driving up to Saratoga to have lunch with me right about now. Tell, me, what do you think happened to Sarah?"

"Corey, she fell, she slipped, she got distracted, or dizzy. Maybe she fainted. Did she have a history of fainting or dizzy spells? Was she taking some new medication? Could she have been skipping meals in her excitement to paint? The investigation found no hint of foul play, so what else could it be?"

"Look, Lucy, logic says you're right, but try to see it from my point, Old Griz, or Back Pack, or Zach, may well be the last person to see my sister alive. What would you do? Wouldn't you want to talk to that person?"

"Please, Corey, his name is Zach, not Old Griz, and not Back Pack!

And, yes, I'd want to talk to him, if I were you. But, I'm not you. You don't need my protection. Zach does. So, please don't expect me to take up for you. I respect the wild too much to interfere with any part of it, including Zach's life."

Corey sat silent for the next few miles, until Lucy pulled off the road, through the leaves, and into a barely distinguishable overgrown drive that quickly ended at a collapsed old tarpaper shack.

"Roark's Bluff is probably two miles southeast from here. Go, if you must, but take the map, and I'll come back and pick you up around six o'clock. And, if you're not back, I'll check every couple hours or so. Just in case you get invited to sleep over," she said a little jokingly. "So, don't worry about me, and I promise not to worry about you."

"I am sorry Lucy. I thought that you wanted to see this area too? I promise I will not do anything to disrupt Zach's life. If you're not coming, would you mind just telling me how you came to have this protective concern for Zach?"

Corey and Lucy sat in the Jeep for more than an hour as she told him about Zach's shadowing episodes, and how she'd gotten to know him without ever meeting him. When she told the story of how Zach's coyote had saved him from being discovered by a horde of shouting schoolchildren, Corey whistled.

"So, Zach has a pet coyote?" he asked.

"I wouldn't call it a pet, but there has been a coyote that was clearly accompanying him on a couple of occasions," Lucy answered.

"Well, that clinches it!" Corey exclaimed.

"What do you mean." asked Lucy.

"That day I spent up at the overlook, I watched the area above the bluff that Sis had photographed, and I saw a coyote walking the rim rock liked he owned the place. I'd be willing to bet that Zach lives pretty close to that spot. And, Sarah had three pictures of the top of the bluff in her digital camera. One of them seems to show a human form moving away from the rim."

"If he does, he's discovered a quick way down off the bluff and into the meadow. A way nobody else has ever found," Lucy replied.

"How so?" asked Corey.

"Well, whenever I have a school group to take on a nature walk, we always meet in the meadow around midmorning. And, by the time I've taken them a mile down river, I can usually tell if he's shadowing us. And if you think he's swinging on vines like Tarzan, how do you explain the coyote being with him?"

Corey sat still for a long minute, wondering just how far to push this. "Lucy, thank you for all you've told me, but I get the distinct feeling that there is still something that you're not sharing with me. And, I respect that. But you do know that I'm terminally afflicted by the curiosity bug, don't you? Before I head out, could I ask you just one more question?" Without waiting for an answer, Corey continued, "How come you were never scared by the knowledge that you were being shadowed?"

Now it was Lucy's turn to sit silent, staring straight ahead, hands gripping the Jeep's steering wheel, fingers turning white from the pressure, as Corey waited, staring straight ahead on the off-chance that maybe Lucy had sighted something in the woods. Corey was about to ask if she was all right when Lucy said, "There's nothing frightening in these woods that comes, even remotely close, to what you might find in any major city. I suspect that you've never taught in an inner-city school, but when you do, you learn to not be afraid, or you get out. It's all I ever did, and I retired six years ago, so you can assume that I learned how not to be afraid. Would you like to know how I did that?" she asked.

"Only if you'd like to tell me," Corey said.

"Yes, I think I would like that." Another long pause, followed by a deep breath, for it was a story that Lucy had never told before.

"I think the most frightening thing in the world is discovering yourself, discovering that what you are capable of doing can be both a rewarding and a devastating experience."

Another long pause as if she was unsure of where to begin.

"It all seems like such a long time ago, another era, another person even. I promise not to bore you though. I'll stick to the short version, but you'll have to bear with me. I've never told this to anyone before. You see, I transferred to an inner-city high school, from the job I'd always loved. I needed the money, or I thought I did. There was this big kid, a junior, and I was really scared of him. The principal and the rest of the staff had told me to watch out for him. He glared at me endlessly, never did his assignments, never responded when called on. He had no skills, he'd just been passed along year after year because nobody wanted him. Somehow he knew I was different, that I wasn't going to do that. One day he followed me to the apartment building where I lived with my invalid mother. I was so afraid of him, the very next day I bought a gun to protect us, now that he knew where I lived. I carried that gun in my purse. We hadn't installed metal detectors in our schools back then.

"His name was Corey, the same as yours. Only my Corey was black, big and black. He must have weighed 250 pounds. The next time he followed me, I turned right around and walked up to him with my hand in my purse. He said, Miss Duckworth, are you going to pass me?

I looked him in the eye and said, Probably not.

To my horror, he started crying, saying, You've got to pass me.

And is why is that? I asked.

'Cause I need to get into the Marines, he almost whispered.

I had relaxed and taken my hand out of my purse, and I said, Corey, I cannot pass you, only you can do that.

Whadddaya mean? he asked.

I said, You pass your tests and I'll pass you. And, furthermore, I'll help you. Can you stay after school every day for an hour?

Corey agreed. And, he lived up to his bargain. The very first day he stayed after school, I asked him why he needed to get into the Marines.

And he told me his brother was missing in action in Vietnam and he had to get over there and find him.

"He passed, barely. A year later, Corey graduated, lost some weight and got into the Marines. He wrote to me twice, once from boot camp, and once from Hawaii on his way to Vietnam. He lived exactly one week in Vietnam. The poor boy never had a chance. I still have both of his letters."

"For a very long time, I would wake in the night shivering with the nightmare of having pulled the trigger that day, out of sheer fright. I took the gun back to the gun shop the week after my encounter with Corey. The dealer apologized, saying he could only give me half of what I'd paid for it. I've always thought that was a pretty cheap price to pay or the education it gave me!"

Now it was Corey's turn to sit and stare and say nothing.

"So, you go ahead and do what you have to do. I'll be back between five and six. But, I suspect it's going to take you a lot longer!"

"Okay, sure you don't want to come along?"

"Very sure," Lucy replied. "I've had all the Vietnam connection that I can bear for one day. Besides, I'm getting way too old for bushwhacking in this country."

15

WILD CLOSURE

Corey took his water bottle, insect repellant, Lucy's topo sheet and a couple of energy bars that she pressed on him, and headed into the wilderness feeling quite guilty about the excursion he was embarking on, but knowing that it was something he had set in motion before ever leaving New York. Corey was, if anything, not a quitter. He knew himself, and what he knew was that if he didn't pursue this to some conclusion, he would feel even worse than he felt right now as a result of letting Lucy down. He salved his conscience by convincing himself that she understood his dilemma. If anything, Lucy had made his determination even stronger.

Just knowing that Zach had shadowed Lucy and her charges along the trail, not once but several times, suggested that it wasn't impossible for Sarah to have been shadowed and, unlike Lucy, it would have scared her. Hell, she'd seen "Deliverance"! He doubted it happened that way, but he could, at least, eliminate the possibility.

And, now, he understood Lucy's earlier reticence. She, too, had suffered a profound loss. She, too, had asked herself over and over again: Why, and what might she have done differently to change the outcome?

He didn't need a compass, his inner one had never failed him. He headed straight for where he knew the top of Roark Bluff would be. And, when it was time to come back, he would simply retrace his steps. Before the first hour had passed, he knew that he had badly misjudged the country he was entering, and he was overwhelmingly grateful that Lucy had bowed out. The jumble of fallen and broken trees left by the ice storms of past winters, made traveling in a straight line impossible. What should have been a one hour hike to the bluff country was already stretching into twice as long and he hadn't covered half the distance according to the map. He wondered as he crawled up and over huge blow downs, how anyone, any creature, could survive the cold and the winds that must envelope this country in wintertime. Then, he remembered the winters of up-state New York!

For as long as he could remember, Corey had, taken pride in seeing himself as an outdoorsman. In less than a couple of hours, the Ozarks had humbled him in a way he'd never have believed possible. He ached, his leg muscles were cramping, he was bone weary, and he hadn't even arrived at his goal. He still had to search the area and return. His body was failing him! But, quitting was not an option.

Two hours later, badly scratched, bug bitten in places he hadn't believed they might find, and exhausted beyond his own belief, Corey arrived at the rim rock. The sun was well over the ridge behind him. But now, he was, at least partially, out in somewhat open country. He could see Steele Creek Meadow below. And he recognized his present location from the hours he'd spent studying this bluff top through binoculars from across the valley. His inner compass hadn't failed him. This was where he'd seen the coyote. Just to be sure, he scanned the opposite bluff across the meadow and, even without binoculars, he could make out artist's bluff poking through the trees.

The realization of having achieved his goal energized him, and he began searching the forest above the bluff for signs of habitation. The forest was open and mercifully free of windfalls. He felt energized by a freedom he hadn't felt on the way in. Without a concern for the waning light and his own fading strength, he searched and searched through the giant red oaks and the field of immense boulders that had tumbled from the upper bluff in the last ice age. There was nothing! He tried peering over the rim to where he'd seen what looked like a cave entrance, but he could see neither a break in the face of the bluff or any possible way of getting down the bluff without risking his already shaky life and limb.

After a second search of the entire bluff top, extending several hundred feet in each direction, he realized it had gotten too dark to attempt the hike out. Settling into a comfortable niche among the boulders, and looking up at the first star of the evening, his exhaustion took over and he fell soundly asleep.

Zach and Pup returned from their long excursion to the fields just as the first hint of light began to color the eastern sky. They'd slept for a while under the light of a moon so bright that it caused the stars to hide. Refreshed, Zach awoke to the brilliant moon unable to ignore its pull on him. His movement aroused Pup and the two of them set off for the bluff, Pup proudly taking up his accustomed role of advance scout. When they got within a few hundred yards of the cave, Pup came running back to Zach with the softest of whimpers.

'What's the matter, boy?" Zach said, recognizing Pup's concern. Pup ran ahead again, shortly coming back to whimper a little louder. Zach figured there was something ahead, very likely a big cat or a bear. And, whatever it was, it had to be still asleep, or Pup would have provoked at least a snarl or a growl from it.

Zach decided to circle the area and come in from the other side. Pup clearly approved, falling in behind. In no time at all Zach too sensed the alien presence. Assuring himself that the rock hiding the cave entrance had not been disturbed, he walked to within twenty feet of Corey and sat down to study this unwanted visitor. Pup whimpered softly at his side until Zach reached down and put his hand on the old coyote's head. Zach's senses told him the stranger was not one of the locals. A tourist then? But, he didn't look like a tourist. The stranger reminded him of someone, but he couldn't remember who.

He had the look of the rangers he'd seen from time to time. But, he wasn't dressed like one of them. Besides, he'd never seen rangers this deep in the woods. Zach and Pup sat staring at the stranger as the morning light spread softly over the eastern horizon until the hint of the red-gold disk started to peek over the treetops. The stranger stirred.

Corey was always a sound sleeper, even in an uncomfortable and unfamiliar bed. Taking advantage of opportunities to sleep had given him an edge on the job many times when just a little rest could make a huge difference in the risky business of undercover work. He'd also retained his boyish habit of waking up with a hugely vocal yawn to greet the new day. Today's greeting might even have been a little stronger than usual as a result of yesterday's muscle aches now compounded by sleeping in the cool open air. It certainly surprised Pup into releasing a yip, immediately followed by Zach's "You lost?"

Not yet fully awake, Corey had been facing the rising sun, and the unexpected question, and the sharp yip coming from somewhere behind him, took a moment to register. Momentarily wondering if he might be still asleep, Corey spun around to confront his questioner with an agility that surprised even himself. He instantly recognized, first the bearded, cammie-clad image of Old Griz, and then the coyote. He studied both for a full minute before answering, "I guess not, if your name is Zach."

"It is. Who are you?" replied Zach in a voice so deep and soft that it surprised Corey.

"My name is Corey Pingree. I've been looking for you."

"Seems you found me." The note of sadness in Zach's voice was clear, along with his obvious disinterest in knowing why.

Corey was, at that moment, overwhelmed with an understanding of Lucy's need to protect Zach's wildness. "I'm sorry to have intruded. I just want to ask you a couple of questions and then I'll leave."

The resignation in Zach's eyes was profound. He simply wanted Corey to leave, and he didn't know how to make it happen. So, he said nothing, just continued to stare soulfully at Corey as if this was the worst day in his life. Corey was at a loss, recognizing Zach's disinterest and apathy. There were a few times in the past when he'd spoken to deer in the wild, and even once to a bear. But, he'd never felt foolish doing so.

Now, all at once, he felt both foolish and the chagrin of feeling foolish. He knew how a burglar must feel when getting caught in the act. His reasons for being here were suddenly reduced to trivia in the face of the enormity that he was imposing on Zach.

In the lengthening silence that hung between them like an unpleasant memory, Corey found himself remembering something he'd read years ago about the discovery of Ishi in northern California. Ishi was America's last Stone Age Indian, found in the early 1900's. It was a sad story, but Zach's story seemed even sadder because Ishi needed help, while Zach emphatically did not! Zach wasn't looking for anything. He was simply living and, if the stories were true, he'd certainly earned the right to do it. Especially on US government land, the people's land!

At length, Corey stood up, saying, "Perhaps my questions can wait until another time. I think I need to leave." He wanted to start walking toward the road, but he realized that to do so, he'd have to walk right toward Zach and the coyote, a move that might be mistaken as threatening. He hesitated, turning to take one last look at the meadow, still filled with the soft morning fog. He could see the tops of a few trees sticking up above the fog like islands on the opposite bluff. Artist's Bluff just peeked out through the fog, and he let out a small groan as he stared at the last moments of Sarah's life. His eyes fixed on the spot for long moments, and then, as before, the deep soft voice behind him said, "You're lost." Only this time it wasn't a question.

The sun had stopped peeking. It had made up its mind, time to get to work and burn off that pesky meadow fog. Corey made his decision with the sun. He too had some fog to burn off.

"No, I've lost someone. It's a lot worse than being lost." He said it flatly, matter-of-factly, his own mood reflecting what he'd read in Zach's eyes. When there was no answer, he went on.

"I lost my sister early this summer. Right over there," he said, pointing to Artist's Bluff. "She fell from that rock," Corey explained in almost a whisper. The silence that engulfed them was almost like a prayer, a requiem for Sarah. Finally, Corey let out a sigh, knowing it was time to go. The interview was over.

"She didn't fall." Zach's voice was low, the words electrifying!

Corey steeled himself against turning around. He wouldn't be able to control the reaction on his face, in his eyes. Instead, he waited a bit, then, slowly, repeated what Zach had said:

"She didn't fall? You saw what happened?"

"Red Tail hit her," Zach said by way of explanation.

Corey's mind was racing. He remembered reading, in the Park Sevice's search and rescue report, that the rescuers had found a destroyed nest of a red-tail hawk in a large oak below the bluff. Their report concluded that Sarah had, in falling, hit the nest and then bounced back onto the shelf below the bluff.

"Where did the Red Tail hit her?" Corey asked, now more the investigator than the brother.

"Hit her head," Zach replied. Pup had wandered off a few yards to stretch out in his greeting to the sun, no doubt bored by more talk than he'd heard in a lifetime.

"What was your sister's name?" Zach asked.

"Sarah," Corey said idly, trying to piece together the parts of a story that had suddenly had its blanks neatly filled in. The red-tail was simply protecting its nest. It certainly hadn't meant to hit Sarah, just a miscalculation or a sudden shift in the wind. The blow had, very likely, killed the hawk as well. Corey hadn't read the autopsy report, but he'd be willing to bet that it mentioned hawk feathers in her hair. It certainly mentioned severe head trauma. Sarah must have already been unconscious by the time she went over the edge and broke her neck either on the tree or when she landed on the rock shelf. The incident report had simply discounted the feathers in Sarah's hair as having come from hitting the nest during her fall. Mystery solved. He'd have to find a way to explain it to Seth without mentioning that he'd talked to Zach.

"I liked her," Zach said. "She waved at me."

Corey looked at his wrist watch: 7:15; it would be close to noon before he could get back to the road. Lucy would be getting worried. She promised not to worry, but that was yesterday noon. The gratitude he felt toward Zach for lifting the burden of doubt left him feeling indebted. And debt is not a burden that a Yankee carries lightly or willingly. "I think Sarah liked you too, Zach. She mentioned seeing you in the notes she left behind. In fact, she told anyone who might see you to not be afraid."

Zach hadn't been this close to anybody in months, not since the last time he'd gone to see the mailman and the store lady. He looked into Corey's eyes, and he liked what he saw. "Sarah," he said it slowly, softly, drawing it out and giving it life. Zach was clearly as intrigued with the situation as was Corey.

Impulsively, Corey asked, "Would you like to see her picture?" He pulled out his wallet where he'd secreted half-a-dozen photos of Sarah just in case he might need them when trying to refresh local memories of anyone that might have seen or talked with his sister.

Zach took the picture, glanced at it, and stuck it in the pocket of his fatigue jacket. He seemed confused for a minute, as if he was expected to give Corey something in return. "Come," he said turning his back on Corey and striding toward the woods and into the boulder field that Corey had searched so carefully yesterday. Corey followed obediently, enchanted by the utter simplicity of the fellow. He glanced back to see the coyote watching the two of them from his place in the sun.

Zach easily shifted a large boulder from its resting place against the bluff wall to reveal a crawl-sized opening in the wall. He motioned for Corey to go first. Zach, for some reason unknown to him, had an aversion to having anyone behind him. Corey examined the boulder closely, and then crouched to accommodate his six feet into a four-foot passage. After going ten or twelve feet he found that he could stand up and walk down the remaining incline into a small, dimly lit room. Zach indicated that he should turn to the right into another passageway that led to a much larger room. He could hear water running down the far wall of the cave. Light filtered in from two chimney-like cracks in the roof. Looking up he could see the sky through a few leafy branches.

He knew that he was in Zach's home. He felt honored, sure in knowing that no one else had ever been here. As his eyes became accustomed to the dim light, he looked around the room in growing amazement. Bathed in reflected light from the farther chimney, sat a skeleton by a pool in its yellow-white wetness, locked in place by the calcification of eons of water dripping through limestone. Across from the macabre sight, on the opposite wall, he could just make out the outline of a bison scratched deep into the stone, perhaps by a flint spear point. The combination of the two ancient images gave the impression of an old Indian sitting and admiring his art as he prepared to set off on his final hunting trip.

Almost at his feet was what must be Zach's bed, piled high with thick moss, and covered over by an old, mouse-chewed, army blanket.

Along the wall, beyond the bed, was an extraordinary collection of shelving made of gnarled driftwood, no doubt carried up from the river, held together by knotted vines. The uprights had all been embellished with intricate carvings of leaves, owl faces, soaring birds, and snakes. Next to the pool with its pleasantly dripping water, Zach had placed a table and chair made of old boards that he'd probably salvaged from one of the many abandoned cabins throughout the forest. Zach was an artist in wood. Not just a primitive artist—he captured the essential details of his subjects. "If Sarah could've seen this!" Corey said to himself.

He turned around to see Zach standing by the entrance watching him with obvious satisfaction. To Zach's right was an enormous collection of walking sticks leaning against the wall. Zach carefully selected one, and handed it to Corey. Carved in deep relief on the handle was the image of a woman, with her face turned away from a hawk about to strike her head. Zach had captured Sarah's final moment of life.

Wordless, Corey looked at the collection and saw that most of the sticks had carvings on the handles. One had a very distinct and flattering image of Lucy. Some were carved the full length of the stick. He turned back to try to look into Zach's dark eyes in the dimness. Zach patted the photograph in his shirt pocket, and, pointing to the cane, he said, "For you." and turned back into the passageway, indicating that Corey was expected to follow him.

Zach led Corey to the outermost cave, now bathed in the full morning light, where they both sat to admire the view across Steele Creek Meadow. Because of the upward slant of the cave floor they could not see the meadow, and could not be seen by anyone in the meadow or beyond on the opposite bluff. Corey drank in the view of leaves just beginning to turn color, the last wisps of morning mist scattering from the searching sun, and felt himself slipping back a thousand years. How many ancient ones had sat right here to greet their own new day?

The two of them sat wordless for what must have been close to an hour. No words were needed. At length, Corey stood, saying, "I have to go," and handed the walking stick back to Zach. Zach seemed puzzled and reached almost reluctantly for the photo in his shirt pocket.

"No," said Corey. "Keep Sarah's picture. May I pick another stick?" he asked.

They went back to the inner cave, where Corey picked out the walking stick with Lucy's face carved on it. Zach looked even more puzzled.

"This is Lucy," Corey explained. "She is waiting for me, so I must go. But, I'd like to take this to her. As a gift from you?"

Zach now understood and vigorously shook his head in approval.

"Lucy is your friend," Corey explained. "If there is ever anything that you might need, all you have to do is ask Lucy."

Zach had heard the students call her Miss Lucy. So, he immediately corrected Corey. "Miss Lucy is my friend too," he said.

Zach and Corey left the cave. Corey automatically extended his hand to say good bye. And, Zach grabbed it, roughly yet gently.

Corey looked back, before disappearing into the woods, waved, and saw Zach vigorously waving his middle finger at him. For the next hour or more, he had the distinct impression that he was being shadowed, but he never did catch sight of Zach or pup. When he was about half-way to the road, he heard Lucy hailing him. He hadn't seen her, but she'd seen him. He was annoyed with himself for not having seen her first. But, then, she'd been looking for him, and he wasn't expecting to see her. She was breathless when they met up, and he silently thanked the fates, that she'd seen him, or it would have been a very long day for both of them.

"How was Zach?" she asked light heartedly, not really expecting that there had been any contact.

""He sent you this," said Corey, extending the walking stick to her, handle first so that she'd be sure to see the image.

Lucy's eyes widened and moistened. She said nothing. The carving said it all.

Over the next two hours Cory related the entire encounter including a detailed description of the cave, punctuated by Lucy's insistence every time he stopped for a breath, that they had to find a way to protect Zach's sanctuary. Most of all, it had to be protected from the National Park Service. The bureaucracy's definition of wilderness was that it is a place where no permanent human habitation exists. Humans are the antithesis of the wild, except, perhaps, for certain indigenous populations. "Which, incidentally," Lucy observed, "was the very reason behind the first proposal for creating national parks, back in the 1840s!"

"Anyway," Corey added, "Zach wouldn't fit any definition of

indigenous that would fly with the Park Service. Not really wild because he doesn't believe in killing."

"Not really civilized for the same reason," Lucy retorted. "I suppose you could make a case that he's not really permanent," she added half-heartedly.

"Without that little genuflection to the camping industry, wilderness would have never made it through Congress," Corey observed.

"Imagine," Lucy said, "without Congress there would be no wilderness. If Joyce Kilmer was still around, he'd have to rethink his conviction that only God can make a tree!"

The ride to Ponca was made in total silence, lost in their own thoughts and finding no happy scenario for Zach, or any measure of comfort for each other. Lucy and Corey both knew, with the crushing certainty of a train that has already left the tracks, that Zach and his wilderness were destined to be separated.

16

MOVING ON

The night before Corey left for Saratoga in Sarah's Civic, Lucy had given a farewell dinner for him, inviting the Greers. It was, at least in part, Lucy's way of saying thank you to Seth and Dana for having invited her to meet Corey last week. But, in fact, Lucy and Corey had orchestrated it as a way of convincing Seth that Corey had found the closure to Sarah's death that he was looking for.

A convincing explanation was clearly called for. Both of them saw in Seth the kind of person who would go on looking for an explanation if Corey failed to provide one. Officially, Sarah's case was closed, but good investigators keep trying to tie up the loose ends. It's a hobby with them, and Seth was a good investigator! The last thing that either of them wanted was an unanswered question that might lead to Zach. Sooner or later, Seth would get promoted and move on. He was clearly destined to be a park superintendent someday. But, that was a gamble that neither Lucy nor Corey were willing to take.

"So, it's your thesis, Corey, that a diving red-tail hawk hit Sarah in the head in defense of its nest?" Seth had asked.

"Actually, it was Lucy who came up with it because she knew the nest was in that oak below the bluff. She'd been quietly keeping an eye on it for weeks," Corey replied easily, knowing that it was at least half true.

"It never occurred to me at the time," Lucy interjected. "You see, I knew that the fledglings had already left the nest. I suppose the adult was instinctively continuing to defend its territory."

"And, until then," Corey said, "I had never read the coroner's report. I just couldn't bring myself to it. But, once I did, in light of Lucy's idea, I realized that the blunt trauma was not caused by Sarah hitting the nest. She was already unconscious. And, while some of the hawk feathers in her hair may have come from crashing into the nest, I suspect most came from the impact of the adult bird."

"One missing piece of information, and everything comes together. How many times have we seen it happen?" Seth added with an air of finality.

Everybody was eager to change the subject, and the rest of the dinner conversation focused on Dana and her passion for teaching English as a second language to the area's growing Hispanic population, and her volunteer work investigating reports of animal cruelty over a wide area of northern Arkansas and southern Missouri. After dinner, Corey and Dana sat by the hearth sharing investigative stories, while Lucy used every tactic she'd acquired during forty years of teaching to persuade Seth that the Park Service needed to do much more in the way of environmental education.

That evening, two weeks later, provided many warm memories for Lucy sitting now on a backpack and leaning against a huge old sycamore beside the Buffalo. She was about a mile below Steele Creek meadow where she'd left her Jeep in plain sight. In fact, as she'd hoped would be the case, it was the only vehicle in the parking lot. The week before, she'd bought an old camouflage backpack at the army surplus store in Harrison and stuffed it with a couple of new army blankets, a couple of field guides, *Edible Plants and Wild Mushrooms*, a couple boxes of wooden matches, a couple of sharp pen knives, and a real fine Arkansas sharpening stone. She couldn't think of anything else that wouldn't interfere with Zach's lifestyle. As an afterthought, she threw in a large box of doggie treats for the coyote and another of raisins for Zach.

Lucy sensed he was out there, probably watching her even now. She decided to give it another half-hour and, if he decided not to come in, she'd leave the backpack in the abandoned cabin and head for home. Lucy had never exchanged a word with Zach, and she wanted it to happen today if at all possible. But, if Zach wasn't comfortable for whatever reason, maybe the backpack had put him off, she'd try again in a week or so. Her mind kept checking off items from the endless list of things that she could have brought to make his life easier. Things like twine and rope. But making life easier just wasn't a wild idea. If you wanted life to be easy, you wouldn't choose to live in the wild! Corey had mentioned Zach's old beat up binoculars, and she'd thought of getting him a new pair. But, she realized that his old ones probably meant more to him than just something to look through.

"Miss Lucy."

The voice was so close behind her, Lucy jumped, but quickly regained her composure. Corey had told her that Zach's voice was soft and rich, but it was still unexpected. She turned slowly, deliberately, and said, "Hello Zach."

Zach's appearance was also startling. For a man who had to be at least in his midfifties, he looked more like someone who was no older than their midthirties. She found his eyes so fascinating that she failed to notice, at first, that he was thrusting something toward her, saying, "For Corey."

When she looked at it, she saw the likeness of a young girl on the handle, a likeness that she immediately recognized as Sarah, from the picture that Corey had given her, she gasped. "It's beautiful!" she said as she looked it over. "I'll send it to him." Then it was her turn. She bent over to pick up the back pack and handed it to Zach, saying, "This is for you."

He took the pack, opened it and dumped it on the ground, going through the contents as a child might. The pen knives and sharpening stone caught his immediate attention. The look in his eyes as he transferred them to his pocket, told Lucy she'd done exactly the right thing. Zach gathered up the blankets the books and the treats, stuffed them in the back pack, shouldered the load and headed back into the woods. He turned once, beckoned her to follow, saying, "Come Miss Lucy."

Lucy stepped off the trail and followed obediently behind. She quickly made a mental note to leave him some new camouflage trousers and wool socks on her next visit. She smiled wryly realizing that men just don't care! Was he actually going to take her to the cave? And, if so, he'd have to take her by his secret route to the top of the bluff, wouldn't he? Lucy was intrigued, yet, it wasn't something that she wanted to do. Corey's description of the cave was enough. She still believed that the gap between the wild and the civilized could not be breached without ultimately damaging the wild.

If Lucy had any remote interest in seeing Zach's cave and secret trail, they were dashed when he stopped at the base of a broken and hollowed old sycamore. He pointed up to where a few lethargic bees were buzzing around a large hole in the broken stump about twenty feet off the ground. Zach was sharing his bee tree with her. It was a true gift, his way of saying thanks for the backpack and contents. In Zach's world, a bee tree was infinitely more meaningful than showing her his humble quarters. And, being totally spontaneous, it brought a tear to her eye.

Lucy turned from the tree and looked quizzically at Zach. Did he expect her to find a way up that enormous trunk and harvest some honey? Zach smiled, and through his black beard, Lucy saw it to be a handsome smile indeed. He reached over and gently lifted her ribbon-adorned pith helmet from her head, put it on his own head, grabbed a nearby grapevine and scurried to the large hole near the top of the trunk. With the hat he shooed off the few bees, then reached into the hole and extracted a large chunk of the comb dripping with honey. He was back on the ground in front of her in less than a minute. "For you," he said. handing the dripping hat back to her. He turned, licking his hand, and headed on his way. For the first time, she noticed the coyote, as he ran up to Zach to share in the hand licking. Had she thought to turn around as she headed thoughtfully back to the trail, she'd have seen Zach waving at her with his trademark middle finger wave. Probably no one but Lucy would appreciate the veiled significance of that wave, like a statement for all things civilized.

On her hike back to the Steele Creek parking lot, Lucy kept a sharp eye and ear for anyone else who might be coming down the trail. How would she explain a hatful of honey in her hands to a ranger? Honey does not transport well in a pith helmet, even one that's lined. But, despite the honey that smeared Lucy and the Jeep seats, she ended up with enough to seal in a pint bottle to be used only for very special occasions. It had, indeed, been a sweet day!

SAVING THE WILD

Tomorrow was Thanksgiving Day. It was not a day that Corey had been looking forward to. Every few years, Thanksgiving just happened to fall on the same day as Sarah's birthday. This was one of those years, and it was a double whammy. It was exactly a year ago, that he and Sarah had Thanksgiving dinner together and he'd shared the announcement about the Buffalo artist-in-residence program with her. Unfortunately, right how he didn't have an ongoing investigation to lose himself in. In fact, since coming back from the Buffalo, Corey hadn't been to work more than one or two days a week. He couldn't seem to keep his mind on his work. Jen made up a folder of reports for him to work on at home.

The simple fact of the matter was, and Corey knew it, he missed the Ozarks. He missed the Buffalo and its endless mysteries. He missed the interesting people, Lucy, Seth, Dana, and, of course, Zach. He even missed the challenge to his outdoors skills that had exhausted him that day in the Ponca Wilderness. Corey was nursing his second gin and tonic when the doorbell rang.

"Who is it?" he called.

"FedEx delivery," a female voice answered.

"Thanks, just leave it by the door," Corey replied, trying unsuccessfully to bring back the warm daydreams of his Ozark friends.

Corey was sound asleep on the couch, steeped in a dream about chasing wildlife poachers through the tangled Ozark wilds, when an insistent phone awakened him. Damn, he thought groggily, and in a not too friendly voice, answered it.

"Hi Boss, it's Jen, we were just wondering what you're doing for Thanksgiving?"

Corey was awake enough to know that he didn't want to caught up in anyone's sympathy invitation.

"Hi Jen, thanks, but I've made plans to go up to Boston for a long weekend," he lied.

"Okay, well you know we'd love to have you join us if your plans should change!"

It was an okay lie, he thought putting down the phone. Then he remembered the FedEx delivery and went to the door to find a long cylindrical package. He shook it. It rattled. He looked at the return address. It was from Lucy. Opening the cylinder he found, carefully packed, a beautiful spiral-carved walking stick, surmounted with a perfect likeness of Sarah on the handle. There was no message. It didn't need an explanation. He held it carefully as his eyes filled and a tear dropped on Sarah's face. Then he knew what he wanted to do for Thanksgiving. He'd have a long talk with Lucy about some wild ideas that had been bubbling to the surface ever since the drive back from the Buffalo.

Lucy was genuinely pleased to hear Corey's voice when she answered the phone. In fact, she'd been thinking of him, knowing what a difficult time for him this Thanksgiving must be.

"Corey, how delightful to hear from you, and on Thanksgiving Day no less!"

"That's exactly why I called Lucy, but you must have plans and I thought perhaps we could set a time to visit later if this isn't convenient?"

"Not inconvenient at all, my boy. I am a having a few of the garden girls over this evening, but we have plenty of time. Let's do visit now, I'd like that."

"I wouldn't be honoring the spirit of Thanksgiving, if I'd failed to thank you for your friendship. I know how difficult it must have been for you to cope with my insistence on finding Zach," Corey began.

"Oh, you were a tough case, but I've dealt with a lot of tough cases in my day," Lucy replied cheerfully. "I have to tell you though I was secretly hoping that the two of you might meet. I just felt that you were the right person for Zach to feel comfortable with. And, as it turns out, you were!"

"Meeting Zach was unforgettable. I can't seem to get him out of mind. I suppose that's the real reason for my call. I am endlessly thankful that you are there for him. The walking stick tells me that the two of you have talked. Tell me about it, please."

"It was brief, but something I know I'll remember until my dying day! We actually exchanged gifts. When you come back, we'll have some of his wild honey. Of course I am here for him, but there's really nothing I can do without interfering. And that I cannot do," Lucy said with a note of sadness.

"Actually, Lucy, there is something you might consider. That evening at your home, Seth mentioned that there is going to be a wilderness review team set up in Harrison to look at their goals and procedures for managing the wilderness areas within the park. Lucy, you need to invite yourself onto that team, just to keep an eye out for anything that might disrupt the status quo for Zach."

"I could do that, but tell me, what kinds of things would I be on the watch for?" Lucy eagerly agreed.

"I really don't know. I guess you'd recognize a threat when you saw it though. I'm afraid that wilderness managers will always err on the side of management rather than on the side of wilderness unless there is a constant reminder. 'Less is better' needs to be their maxim!"

"Thank you, Corey. You're obviously feeling the same anxiety that I am about Zach's ability to stay there undisturbed for as long as he wants to."

"That's actually the easy part of my concern," Corey explained. "Driving back to New York, I realized that Zach is part of a much larger issue, one that I've been wrestling with for days. I admit that I don't have an answer, but it just seems to me that there is something terribly wrong with sending young people off to a war zone, and saying that they can't live, and recuperate, in the peace zone of a designated wilderness area. You know there's a lot research that documents the healing properties of nature. Don't we owe them that much?"

Lucy exhaled a long sigh. "Of course we do! But, one person living in the wilderness is not what you're talking about is it? There must be hundreds, maybe thousands, just like Zach! What's the answer for them?"

"I wish I knew, Lucy. But, for now, perhaps the park people need to officially look the other way — if they ever do suspect he's there."

"A little administrative discretion could go a long way. But, it's the bigger problem that Zach personifies, that I can't get out of my mind. Maybe Zach should be found? Maybe in that way he could become a national issue? It isn't just Zach who is living on the edge of a bluff because of war, we've all become cliff dwellers staring into the abyss. In an odd sort of way, Zach may be one of the lucky ones."

Lucy thought about the positives of Zach being found, and asked, "What are you going to do with yourself now, Corey?"

"I don't honestly know, Lucy. All I can tell you is that my life is changing as a result of all of this. I don't know where it's headed, but I do know that going back to where I was is not an option! I suppose that someone else could just ignore everything and go back to trying to figure out the minds of poachers. It's dangerous work, not something to do unless you've got a clear focus on the job. How do I do that when my own mind is so preoccupied with what seems like messages?"

"Can I help, Corey? What do you mean, messages?"

"Well, perhaps 'messages' may be a little strong. But, I can't help thinking that all these edges must add up to something. I pushed Sarah right up to the edge of Artist's Bluff in a way. Now, I feel as though she is pushing me to do something, but what? And, here I am pushing you to do something that only you can do. The hawk that pushed her over the edge was the wild that she hoped to devote her life to. She was on the edge of starting a new life. Zach is not just living on the edge of a bluff, he's on the edge between wilderness and civilization. He's on the edge of being discovered and pushed out any day. You figured out that he was somewhere in the area. I figured it out from Sarah's pictures. How long do you think it will be before someone in the Park Service figures it out?"

"I know you're right, Corey. And, frankly, when that day comes, I hope I am no longer here. I don't know what I would do, or could do. We both know he would leave if he was discovered, but that's not something I want to see happen, ever!"

"Lucy, what do you think Zach wants?"

"I told you about that other Corey in my life, all he wanted was to find his brother alive. I think all that Zach wants is to someday join that other fellow that sits in the cave by the pool. And I want that for him. But, what is it that you want, Corey?"

"Sarah and I had a brother-sister pact. We talked everything out whenever either one of us was facing a difficult decision. I guess what I want right now is to talk with Sarah."

"Why don't you do just that," said Lucy.

18

COYOTE MOON

If there was anything that Pup enjoyed more than a long walk with Zach, it was a long run by himself, and maybe, once in a while, finding something dead to roll in. The walks and the runs he understood. He continued to look forward to them, even though they tired him out. They also made him feel young again. But, the rolling, that was something else entirely. He didn't understand it. He didn't look forward to doing it. It was just something that happened. It was like the sun coming up, or like playing one of his tricks on Zach, hiding something and watching him search. Dead things are there to roll in. He knew that whenever he did it, Zach wouldn't let him back in the cave. But, he really preferred sleeping outside anyway.

One spring, a couple of winters after he'd chosen to come live with Zach, he'd rolled in the still ripe carcass of an elk that had died during the winter. He'd been on one of his long runs when it happened, and before he'd gone a mile from the carcass, he became aware that he was being followed by a another coyote. At first, he charged at her, but she just rolled over instead of running away. He sniffed her. She smelled good. When she just stayed on her back, he ran off a ways and looked back. She got up and followed him at a distance. He'd run, she'd run. He walked, she walked. It had been a very good day for Pup. They played and ran, and rolled together for hours. They mated. It was another one of those things that just happened. In that moment, Pup forgot all about Zach, he'd found a purpose in his life, a purpose that pushed his past into some deep abyss.

Then, without warning, another, bigger, stronger, coyote had charged Pup and knocked him rolling. Pup fought bravely while his new mate just watched impassively. It was never a contest. She may have saved Pup by just walking away, a move that prompted the big coyote to stop mauling Pup and follow her. Pup was badly hurt. More dead than alive, he'd dragged himself back to the cave.

Hours later, Zach returned from one of his rare trips to Ponca.

Pup's eyes were swollen and closed, but he knew Zach's smell, and he whimpered at hearing him approach. Pup didn't just look bad, he smelled terrible. But, Zach picked him up gently and carried him into the cave after feeling him all over for broken bones. Once inside, Zach cleaned Pup as well as he could with fresh cold spring water, then he carried him outside to lie in the sun. Emma, the store lady, had pressed upon him a jar of her famous Newton County Fair prize -winning apricot preserves. This he smoothed onto all of Pup's wounds, hoping it might get him to start licking them and healing them.

Within a week, Pup was looking almost like his former self. But, he'd changed. He didn't run for several more weeks. And, when he did, he ran stiffly, favoring his rear left leg and his right front paw. Pup came away from his near-death experience with a distinct fear of all others of his species, and a powerful liking for apricot jam.

While Pup was mending, Zach had found a short cut for getting from the top of the bluff down into the Buffalo River Valley. It was a deeply recessed vertical crack in the bluff about quarter mile east of the cave. The recess ran back into the bluff in places forty feet or more. At its deepest point, the crack split in two, forming a set of natural steps that got him down the steepest part of the descent with the help of an enormous grape vine. Part of the way down the dark and slippery steps, he found another deeply incised outline of a buffalo, identical to the one in the cave. At the foot of the steps there was a long talus slope that delivered him to the upper edge of the forest and, eventually, to the valley floor within a few hundred feet of the welcoming waters of the Buffalo.

In his eagerness to share his discovery with Pup and get him down to the river for a good bath, Zach had attempted to carry the coyote under one arm using the other to guide himself down along the grapevine. But, Pup would have nothing to do with it, snapping at Zach to let him know that the hurts were still there. Pup limped off to find his own way down the slope and was at the bottom waiting when Zach appeared out of the crevasse.

Obviously, Pup had found a better way and, between the two of them, a whole new world of river bottom opportunities had opened up. Where the bluff top had its abundance of nuts and mushrooms and grapes and wild apples every fall, this new Eden was overflowing with its spring and summer harvests of berries, and roots and shoots, and honey and an endless supply of cool running water during the hot days of summer.

Just as Zach had delighted in showing Pup his discovery, Pup was no less proud of sharing his better route back up the bluff. Zach wasn't so sure it was any better, but he didn't want to hurt his friend's feelings so he put up with a lot of unnecessary scrambling on hands and knees. It was, most certainly, nice to have a choice.

Pup undoubtedly had pups of his own that year, but if he ever saw them, it would have been from a distance. He may have even fathered other litters in the years that followed, but that first lesson had been well learned. No long-term commitments. He could fight if he had to, but there were lots of better ways to spend his days!

One of those better ways had always been to lie in the sun on the rim rock and watch all the interesting goings-on in Steele Creek Meadow. The camper's cars and trucks and the horses and horse trailers provided endless hours of study for a curious coyote. And the smells that wafted up from evening campfires were almost too much to resist. Once, when the aroma of hamburgers overpowered him, he ventured down to investigate and was rewarded by the campers throwing bits of food to him. When two large white German Shepherds appeared on the scene

Pup had visions of being mauled again. They gave chase, but urban dogs were no match for a coyote in coyote country. By the time they got back to the meadow, tongues hanging out and footsore, there was little doubt as to who had been taken to school!

Lately, Pup had taken to spending more time lying in the sun. He knew that something was happening to him. He'd lost his appetite, and was losing weight. His once beautiful coat was shaggy and matted. He'd go for walks in the woods with Zach, but, he wasn't interested in long runs or rolling in those things he used to roll in. In fact, they'd lost their appeal for him. Pup's world was changing, and he didn't understand it.

He woke one morning, about a year after the stranger had come to visit, dusted by an early September snow fall. Something was calling him. He tried to make out where it was coming from, but he couldn't seem to put a direction to it. So, he just started walking. First, he checked out the cave entrance for signs of activity from Zach, but there were none, so he kept on walking. The snow was not very deep, and it actually felt good on his tired old paws. The snow on his face was refreshing when he licked it off. After a while he no longer recognized the country he was walking in. It all seemed very strange. But, whatever it was that called him kept on calling. He didn't seem to be getting any closer.

Ever since that first winter with Zach, Pup had loved the snow. They'd rolled in it. Zach had thrown the stuff at him, and he tried to catch it in his mouth. The snow was his friend. The snow was falling in big soft flakes and it was getting thicker. It was getting harder for Pup to see ahead of him, but he kept on walking, feeling warm inside his new white coat.

After a while, he heard a sound that was vaguely familiar. Somewhere in the past he'd heard it before. The sound grew louder, as two bright lights pierced the blizzard. At the last moment of his life, Pup remembered that sound. He remembered his mother and his sister. He could almost see them through the snow. His mother had run back into the road to snatch his sister in her jaws. He had barked at that truck. Now, he just wailed softly, the sounds of truck and coyote mingling, dying, in the night.

19

RIVERSIDE RELAPSE

It had been almost two years since Lucy Duckworth had been able to walk the Buffalo Trail, let alone canoe the river. Her vintage Jeep was up on blocks in her garage back in Ponca. She hadn't set eyes on it for months, not since moving into an assisted living apartment in Jasper, following her massive stroke. The doctors told her that she could expect more strokes if she didn't slow down. She'd almost fully recovered, but the experience had taken a lot out of her. For the very first time, since that day so long ago when she'd bought the gun, Lucy felt scared.

The apartment was nice, but it had not been an easy transition for Lucy. Her life after teaching had been the nearest thing to a dream she might have had, if she'd ever taken time to dream about her future. The aches and pains of old age had caught up with her, but she'd always found that they were bearable whenever she could get out in her garden, or go down to Steele Creek in her Jeep and walk along the river. Months of confinement had taken years of toll.

Today was Lucy's 75th birthday. It was a very big day. The Friends of the Buffalo were throwing a birthday party for her in the meadow at Steele Creek. A very big tent had been set up in the middle of the meadow. In the middle of the tent was a very big birthday cake in the shape of a vintage 1952 Jeep. The decoration included a replica of Lucy's personalized license plate: WILD—ONE.

The wife of the new park superintendent had insisted on picking Lucy up at her apartment and driving her to Steele Creek. It was Dana. The Greers had recently returned to the Buffalo after a stint at Arches National Monument where Seth was the assistant superintendent. The two of them had a wonderful reunion on the ride over, reminiscing about the tragedy that had brought them together those many years ago. Neither of them had heard a word from Corey since that Thanksgiving call he made to Lucy back in – she couldn't remember. At first, Lucy had tried to check up on him via the Internet, but he seemed to have dropped off an edge somewhere.

They arrived ahead of most of the guests, so Lucy asked Dana if she would walk with her down to the river. She couldn't remember when she'd last been here. But, she remembered the last time she'd seen Zach. It was down the river at the bee tree, where they'd met three or four times after that first contact. Zach had been alone the last time. Pup had simply gone off into the wild, in response to some inner calling, some new adventure. But Zach was not lonely. He did seem to walk a little slower and his jet black beard was starting to show streaks of gray. Pup, in a very special way, would always be with him. How could he be lonely? Loneliness, like an easy life, had no relevance to Zach. Lucy had cried at the loss of Pup, and after that, Zach had stopped coming to meet her. It was a bitter pill for her, but she knew it was for the best. She'd always suffered at letting her students go. And Zach was certainly her most memorable student.

At the river's edge, Lucy sat and looked up to where Corey told her Zach's cave opened to a view of the meadow. She once hoped that he'd always be there sitting beside the old Indian. But, she knew he was gone. The recent news that some local youths had found, and vandalized, a cave thought to have once been occupied by Backpack Zach pretty much closed that door forever. Zach was gone, and apparently had been gone for some time. She closed her eyes and smiled.

Dana sensed that Lucy needed to be alone, so she walked up the nearly dry river bed, picking up pebbles, examining them, and idly tossing them back to the stream. The riverbed was known for its "holy rocks," rocks with holes in them. Everyone collected them for luck, even park employees and their spouses. Local legend says that if you peer through a holy stone at the North Star on the darkest night of the year you will see eternity. If you carry it with you, it will ward off bad luck and evil spirits. If you give it away you will know true love. And, if you return it to the Buffalo you will become endowed with great wisdom. Lucy always returned her holy stones, giving them back, already wise with the knowledge that love easily trumped longevity, wisdom, and riches.

When Dana returned, Lucy hadn't moved. She appeared to be asleep. Leaning against a silvery gray driftwood log, Lucy Duckworth seemed to have joined the wild she so dearly loved. Her faint smile seemed to suggest that she was off on another grand adventure. Dana gently lifted her left arm from its awkward position on the ground, to place it onto her lap, and Lucy fell over. She seemed to be breathing, very faintly. Dana yelled for help.

II
VANDALS, POACHERS, AND PREDATORS

20

HIGH ADVENTURE

For several long minutes, the two boys gazed speechless at their discovery, knowing no words to match their amazement. They gawked, open mouthed, unable to take it all in. Inseparable friends for the past four years, Paul Purvis and Randy Speaks had shared many firsts in their young lives: first time shooting the rapids in a canoe, first turkey hunt, first deer kill, first bear sighting. But, nothing quite as wondrous as this!

The cave had unmistakably been lived in, but certainly not for some time. It looked and smelled more like an animal den. It was full of stuff, interesting stuff, a lot of it well chewed on by its more recent occupants. The droppings of mice and bats, mixed with those of larger animals, were everywhere evident. The skeleton, encased by translucent wet limestone, startled them at first. Then, realizing its great age, it captivated them. More than anything else in this mysterious place, this ancient guardian gave the two of them a profound sense of humility which, when added to their awe, had them whispering in reverent disbelief. Somewhere in the dimness behind the skeleton, water was dripping into the pool. The clock-like drip and their own excited breathing were the only sounds. They couldn't both be dreaming? Could they?

But, being practical-minded young lads, once they'd reassured themselves of being awake, they knew that they couldn't leave without taking something, anything, with them. Without something tangible, they might never be sure that it wasn't a dream. And, how else could they possibly convince their peers that it wasn't a lie? Convince, not prove! They had no intention of showing the cave to anyone else, ever! It would remain their secret, another knot in the rope of their avowed life-long friendship. So, helping themselves to a couple of carved, mice-chewed, walking sticks from the pile in the corner, they reluctantly headed for home, but not before making a complete exploration of the cave and its three separate chambers.

Hiking out of the wilderness, Paul and Randy, reaffirmed their secrecy pact and made plans for an early return to their "Indian Cave." It would just be another of their many camping and fishing trips to their parents. But, for Paul and Randy, camping and fishing had suddenly become too tame to even consider. They had catapulted themselves into high adventure. Indiana Jones had come to the Buffalo River Valley!

Over the next few months, Paul and Randy made three more visits to the cave, each time sleeping over and bringing back another memento of the visit, a carved gallon jug stopper in the shape of a wolf's head, a carved belt buckle, a wooden comb, a finely braided head band made out of dried grass, all museum pieces that, sooner or later, would be bound to attract attention. On each visit, they approached the cave with utmost caution, expecting to find the owner returned, in residence, and fearfully angry at their intrusion.

Gradually, word spread among their friends that Paul and Randy had, indeed, discovered a secret cave somewhere in the bluff country of the Upper Buffalo, an Indian cave containing ancient artifacts . They enjoyed their newfound popularity, particularly with the girls, and they didn't worry about attempts to follow them into the wilderness. They knew their colleagues well, believing that even if one or two had the ambition to try it, none of them shared their own ability for getting in and out of the back country with relative ease.

But, what Paul and Randy didn't realize was that communities abhor a secret as much as nature abhors a vacuum. And, the community of their peers was bound to include some whose jealousy of the friends' popularity was ample motivation to discredit them by exposing their secret. The two became careless. They didn't know that they were being watched and followed. And, predictably, it was just a matter of time until, one day, they arrived at the cave to find it vandalized.

The vandals were not content to just let them know that their secret had been discovered, they had proceeded to demolish whatever they couldn't haul away. Dozens of beautiful carvings had been dumped over the brink of the bluff, along with everything movable in the cave. Even the ancient skeleton, having for so many centuries sat by the pool, had been pounded by rocks, the skull removed, and broken bones scattered over the cave floor. The creed of the vandals hasn't changed in over seven millennia: Vanquish your adversary by destroying whatever your rival cherishes. To complete their work, the vandals spread the word that they had found the cave, very easily. And, that they were surprised to find that it had been so badly treated by Paul and Randy. They freely told others how to find the now not-so-secret cave, and see for themselves. In a matter of a very few weeks, others found the cave and completed the job of looting and destruction. Of course, word spread throughout the larger community like wildfire, first of a momentous discovery of ancient artifacts, and then, of their destruction. Most incomprehensible of all was why such an atrocity would have been perpetrated by the son of a respected park ranger.

Responding to widespread public outrage, the normally lethargic bureaucracy swung into high gear. The Park Service investigation quickly determined the truth of the matter. But, by then, it was too late to do much more than seal the cave entrance, to prevent further damage. Laboratory research was ongoing to determine the age of the calcified skeletal remains found in the cave, however, preliminary estimates pegged them to be at least 500 years old.

One of the official findings established that the cave had apparently been used within very recent history by a hermit, most likely the one known in the local area as Backpack Zach. Backpack had not been seen in the area for perhaps two years, coinciding nicely with evidence of decaying food materials in the cave. A few items were recovered from where they had been tossed over the cliff, along with those curios that Randy and Paul had pilfered. An exhaustive search and public appeal for the missing skull had so far proven fruitless.

One unmentioned casualty of the affair was the end of a youthful friendship, at parental insistence, along with the abrupt end of the age of innocence for the two friends. The price of parental embarrassment is ever the restriction of freedom, somewhat like paying for education by dismantling schools.

A second, personal and private, casualty of the final report was the relapse of the now feeble Lucy Duckworth, who had just begun to regain a modicum of speech following her second stroke at the birthday party on the Buffalo. A well-meaning nursing home attendant had read the news item to Lucy, knowing of her patient's interest in the Buffalo. It was a relapse that Lucy would not recover from. Nor, did she want to. Lucy knew that there was only one way she would ever see the Buffalo and Zach and the two Coreys again. She was eager to start the journey.

21

ON THE ROAD AGAIN

Zach had been on the road for the better part of a year when he decided to head for home. He knew that it wasn't just the solitude of the cave that had started to pull him back. That was only part of what he longed for. It was the sanctuary from the ever-present noise of humanity, the honking horns, the high-pitched whistling of tires on pavement, the yelling and catcalls from passing cars, and the ever-present odors of exhaust fumes, asphalt, and road kills. And, it was the futility of trying to go back, to find answers from another life that surely couldn't have been as good. Zach's travels hadn't been all bad. There had been a few good moments, but it was time to go home.

The number of dead creatures along the highway saddened him. He'd given up trying to move their carcasses away from the kill zone on the very first day. Unless it was a coyote carcass, and there were lots of them. These were things that he'd forgotten from his trek east years earlier. Cave life had afforded him the ability to be friends with live creatures, not just mourn the countless dead ones. He missed the assurance of living creatures in his life, their touch, their steamy breath on cold winter mornings, their smell. Pup had taught him that the nose was as powerful as the eyes and ears. He missed his birds, not that there weren't birds along the roadways, they just didn't seem the same, didn't talk to him, didn't seem to be enjoying life as much. He missed the old oak that shielded the cave entrance, he missed the grape vines that he held onto when going down the bluff, and he missed the top of the sycamore with its bird's nests that he could almost touch from the cave's overlook onto the meadow.

Long before he left the Buffalo, he'd known it was time to move on.

For months after Corey's visit, he hadn't slept well. His nights were filled with dreams, something he hadn't experienced for how long? Years! Corey's visit seemed to have triggered something that lay slumbering beyond that wall in his memory. He didn't know what it was, but he knew that he was remembering things, dreaming things, that had no connection to his present life. And, they had no connection to each other. There were people in his dreams that he seemed to know, faces that were vaguely familiar, events that seemed to be important in some obscure way. It was as though he was looking through breaks in a brick wall. And, the breaks seemed to expand and contract and run together.

Hs headaches had come back. It was all very confusing, but the doctors had told him it might happen and, if it did, he should call them. But, he had no interest in talking with anybody, except, perhaps, Corey. Corey had come to him, asking for help. There was nothing in all of Zach's fractured memory that came close to Corey's need for help. It had been a good feeling. It was good to be needed.

Perhaps, more than anything, more than finding his lost memory, that's what he'd left the cave in search of?

Pup's disappearance had served to make up his mind. He had no idea where he was going, only that it was time to go. Still, he lingered on, unsure of why he should go, untrusting of the alien urge to leave.

Perhaps Corey had the answers? But, how could he? Zach didn't know where to begin. Miss Lucy! Of course, Miss Lucy would know how to contact Corey. For weeks he watched for her Jeep to appear in the meadow, weeks during which the urge to move kept growing stronger. Finally, he packed what he needed in the new backpack that Miss Lucy had given him, shouldered the pack, and headed out. He hadn't gone more than a few steps when he stopped, took off the pack, and went back inside the cave. It occurred to him that he could leave a message for Miss Lucy.

Picking up his old backpack and a carving of Pup that he'd made years earlier, Zach made a quick trip down the side of the bluff, then downstream across the river to the old shack where Miss Lucy had often left things for him. He hid the pack and the carving in a dark corner of the cabin beneath the partially collapsed roof, for Miss Lucy to find. Sure that she'd know their meaning, he was back up the bluff and on his way.

The first few nights away from the cave, and all it had held for him, were difficult for Zach. The decision to leave felt wrong from the start, but turning back seemed impossible. It didn't help matters that he'd finally chosen to leave in October when the freezing rains already held the hill country in their slippery grip. This was the time of year that he and Pup had reveled in the warm dry cave. It was home! During the rest of the year, the cave was simply a place to come back to after enjoying the wonders that surrounded them.

The leafless days of winter when you could finally see through the forest, particularly when there was a new snowfall on the ground were their favorites. Those were the days when they could follow the trails of deer and elk, wild cats and cougars, even the occasional coyote to get Pup singing. Sometimes the new snow would be stained with blood and bits of fur, signifying the final moments of a rabbit or a squirrel, or a grouse, or the efficient killing capability of an owl. Zach was having feelings that weren't exactly new to him, but he hadn't felt in years, sadness and loneliness. Uncomfortable as he was with his feelings and his wet clothes, he couldn't go back. Something inside him wouldn't allow it. Not yet, anyway.

On his tenth day from the cave, he started to cough. His chest hurt, way down deep. He hadn't covered much more than a hundred miles. The road signs told him that he'd left Arkansas, and was about to leave Oklahoma and enter Kansas. That night he shivered in an abandoned barn, sleeping in the powdery dust of ancient hay and not-so-ancient coon and possum droppings.

The next day, the cold rain finally eased up and, though aching in every part of his body, he was able to make decent progress under the warmth of the first weak sun he'd seen since leaving the cave. Because he'd been able to eat from the abundant leavings of farm and orchard crops along the way, his pack was still nearly half-full of dried fruit and nuts he'd gathered for the trip. But, his canteen was empty. He longed for the sweet cool water of the cave's pool, and the excellent company of its long-silent guardian.

He'd turned down half a dozen offers of rides. Finally, after nearly four weeks on the road, Zach accepted a ride. He'd been standing at an intersection trying to read the confusion of direction signs. He still hadn't decided where he was headed, but he felt as though he needed to follow the sun. The cold rains had returned during the night. He was feeling very weak, otherwise he wouldn't have considered getting in when the big truck pulled up alongside.

"Where ya headed, Bud?" asked the bearded, heavyset, driver.

"West," shivered Zach, struggling to get up the steep steps of the semi while putting his backpack and walking stick in ahead of himself.

"Well, I'm headed for Wichita. That west enough for ya?" asked the driver, sniffing and looking a little uncomfortable with his new passenger.

"Thank you," smiled Zach with a courtesy that belied his appearance.

Not a mile down the road, the driver said, "Name's Dwayne Capp." Getting no reply, he glanced to the side and saw that his passenger was sound asleep. From time to time, over the miles, Dwayne looked at his sleeping companion. Each time, his glance caught the head of Zach's beautifully carved walking stick. He tried to study the face beneath the beard, wondering if it was the same. He finally decided it was, but the carving was a much younger version burnished by years of handling.

Dwayne Capp and his small family turned out to be one of only a few happy experiences of Zach's trek west. Dwayne had pegged Zach as homeless, so when he pulled up in front of the family's small farmhouse south of Wichita, with a still-sleeping Zach in the cab, his wife, Donna, insisted that the poor guy just couldn't be left in the truck overnight.

"Well, I have to warn you, he's a mite pungent!" said Dwayne.

"He can stay in Buddy's old room over the garage. Now you just go get him, Mr. Capp. You both can sit right down to a hot meal just as soon as Becky get's home from babysitting."

Dwayne and Donna Capp and daughter Becky had welcomed the stranger into their home, knowing nothing about him other than he was in need. After finally learning each other's names, Dwayne convinced Zach to stay the night, and got him ensconced over the garage, explaining it was their son, Buddy's, room, who wouldn't be needing it. Buddy was a casualty of the Gulf War, he explained.

Zach nodded a silent understanding. While Zach was showering, Dwayne had dropped a pile of old clothes on the bed, obviously not Dwayne's, they must have been Buddy's farm clothes. As they gathered around the aged oak table, Becky and Donna reached for Zach's hands. He watched, as with bowed heads, they listened to Dwayne asking for the Almighty's blessing on their home, their guest, this meal, and Buddy. Becky lightly squeezed his hand.

Donna apologized for the small meal, explaining that they never eat much on the day before Thanksgiving. "You must stay with us, Mr. Taylor, for Thanksgiving!" she said.

Zach didn't answer; he was lost in thought about the hot shower he'd just had, the nice soft bed in Buddy's room, and the long-forgotten smell of potatoes whipped with butter, homemade bread, fresh baked rolls and pies. Besides, being called "Mr. Taylor" just didn't register, until Becky touched his arm. "You will stay for Thanksgiving, won't you, please, Mr. Taylor?" she implored.

Zach looked at her, slowly, smiled, and said, "Yes. Thank you."

Dwayne looked across the table, saying, "Zachary Taylor is a most unusual name—could you be related to the one who was president?"

"I don't know," Zach replied with honest sincerity.

"But, how could you not know?' Mr. Taylor. Oh, I hope you are. It will be such fun to tell my friends that we had Zachary Taylor at our house for Thanksgiving!" Becky bubbled.

"Remember, Rebecca, pride goeth before a fall," admonished her mother. "And, don't pester Mr. Taylor; he said he didn't know!"

"Sorry, Mother," apologized Becky.

Zach surprised himself, and won a smile from Dwayne, by immediately saying, "I don't know, Becky, because I lost my memory in a place called Vietnam."

It was an answer that evoked a score of questions in Becky's mind, some of which seemed to be worth risking another maternal rebuke. Dwayne could see the questions rising in his daughter's eyes. He knew she was about to take the plunge, so he quickly changed the subject.

"I need to head out right after dinner tomorrow for the Oklahoma panhandle. I'll show you on the map. You're welcome to ride along, if that's where you want to go, Zach."

Buddy's room over the garage was something more than just a room! Photographs from high school football days and from his days in the Marines adorned the dresser top as well as two shelves of the bookcase. Buddy's dress uniform and cap hung proudly on a wall hook of polished brass. The jacket was adorned with three shiny medals and their colorful ribbons. A framed letter to the right of the door told of his heroism. It said that Buddy had been nominated for the Congressional Medal of Honor, and was signed by the Commandant. To the left of the door a matching frame held his Eagle Scout certificate.

Zach studied everything at length, staring at the uniform, wondering, puzzling, knowing something, but he couldn't remember what it was that he knew. His eyes grew moist as he stared at the dresser where three books stood bracketed by simple unadorned wooden blocks serving as bookends. One was Buddy's bible. It was signed from "Dad and Mom, Christmas, 1975"; another was The Boy Scout Handbook, 9th edition, and the third was *Fields of Fire*, by James Webb. Each contained numerous earmarked pages and underlined passages.

His hands were drawn, as if by a magnet, to the wood blocks yellowed with age. He picked one up and ran his calloused wood-carver hands reverently over each side. Almost mechanically, he dug out his pocket knife and started freeing an image from the soft pine. Wood chips quickly covered the rug beside the bed as the first image began to appear. It was an exquisite replica of the Marine Corps emblem. He rubbed the anchor, globe, and eagle as though trying to push them back into the wood. Then, turning the block, he began working a second image out of it. It was Buddy's face copied from the family photograph over the bed. Before falling asleep, the two pine blocks had been turned into a Capp family portrait gallery, complete with an image of Dwayne's Eighteen Wheeler!

The Capp's Thanksgiving feast, a brunch to accommodate Dwayne's schedule, turned out to be largely wasted on Zach, a light and infrequent eater at best. Zach was clearly uncomfortable and eager to leave. Dwayne's attempt to lighten the situation with his "Good morning Mr. President," had fallen flat, and when Becky added, "and please give Mr. Taylor back his memory," to her father's ritual blessing, her mother had frowned. Becky's calling attention to the fact that Zach had passed up the meat platter for two meals in succession hadn't helped things with her mother. But, Zach had become fond of Becky, and tried to answer her question as best he could.

"When I was in the hospital, Becky, I saw something on the television about animals getting hit on the head before they were killed. After that, I couldn't eat meat. They told me that's how I lost my memory, by getting hit on the head."

"Oh, I'm sorry," Becky murmured.

Dwayne and Donna both noticed that Becky didn't finish the turkey on her own plate. Donna's plan to pack a couple of turkey legs for the men to eat on the road quickly got revised to a couple pieces of apple pie. Becky and Donna stood on the tiny porch waving until the semi disappeared around the bend. Later, when Donna went to the bedroom over the garage, she found the bed had not been slept in. Buddy's clothing was neatly folded and piled at the foot of the bed. Propped on top of the pile rested Zach's walking stick. Idly picking it up to examine the carved face more closely, she found the back side had been flattened and bore a freshly-carved relief of two clasped hands, one larger than the other. Donna knew that Zach had not forgotten it.

Then, puzzled by the huge pile of wood chips on the rug, she looked around the room, her eyes falling on bookends neatly in place on the dresser, newly adorned with her family's images. Donna wiped away two tears, one for Buddy and one for Zach. She brought the walking stick to Becky, saying, "Zach left this for you."

"For me? How do you know?" Becky asked.

"I just know!" her Mom answered softly, never mentioning the fact that Becky's usual twenty dollar bill for babysitting the neighbor's twins was missing from the kitchen cork board at just about the time she'd finished bagging the men's lunches.

Dwayne and Zach parted company in Guyman, Oklahoma, but not before Dwayne arranged a ride for Zach to go on to El Paso. The idea of leaving a homeless vet on the frigid Oklahoma plains in late November, wasn't something Dwayne wanted to live with, any more than he wanted to pay the penalty for ignoring Donna's whispered instructions: "Don't you dare leave that poor man without finding him a warm place to stay!" Fortunately, Donna and Becky missed seeing Zach's final middle finger wave as he climbed up into the cab of Dwayne Capp's Peterbilt 379 tractor.

El Paso was a frightening place. But, certainly a much warmer place for a homeless person with not one bit of body fat to protect him from the wintery blasts. The trip, and the driver, couldn't have been more different from his ride with Dwayne. Ray, who hadn't felt it necessary to share his last name, never stopped talking, even when Zach was asleep, apparently preferring to believe that Zach was just resting his eyes. Ray's hero and role model, was Charlton Heston. So, Zach was treated to a blow by blow recount of every movie ever made by the NRA president. "Sure, he'd never been president of his country, but he could have been if he'd wanted to! And, wasn't being Moses better anyway?"

Ray seemed to have a girlfriend in every roadhouse along the way, and he insisted on sharing their most intimate assets and flaws with a usually sound-asleep Zach. Ray's deep understanding of highway politics was far and away his most sleep-inducing theme. Eisenhower built the Interstates for trucks, and the country would be a damn-sight better off if cars were restricted! Two-and-a-half very long days later, arriving at the El Paso airport, Ray had thoroughly exhausted his companion, though he hadn't begun to plumb the depths of his own encyclopedic mind.

Ray hadn't stopped for breath, even as he pulled off the highway to let Zach off. Over the noise of the diesel, Zach could hear Ray's voice trailing off: "Watch out for them airport cops. They love to hustle you guys off their grounds. Did you see that guy they dumped off back at Wilson Road? Looked like you, as a matter of fact! And, stay the Hell out of Juarez. With a name like yours you might never come back!"

22

"GRINGO GABE"

Gringo Gabe was a Silver City enigma, just another drifter who had become a familiar fixture on the streets of just another small southwestern city. One more added responsibility for the local police. His ragged clothing was the same in the shivering cold of winter as in the high desert heat of summer. His kind had been around since long before the Big Depression. The difference was that vagrants back then had been pitiable. Now they were a faceless nuisance.

Lacking any visible means of support, Gabe had spent more than a few nights in the local jail, and had more than his share of escorted rides in a police cruiser to the city limits, two meals under his belt, and a bed, courtesy of the good citizens of Silver City, New Mexico. On more than one occasion, the cops had thrown a bundle of thrift shop clothing after him, often with a MacDonald's breakfast burrito tucked inside. Whoever thought that cops don't have a heart had obviously never spent any time on the streets of Silver City!

Part of the landscape of the Southwest, like the cactus and the tumbleweed, drifters are tolerated as long as they don't cause a problem for the merchants, or offend the more genteel element in town with public drunkenness. If the line between vagrancy and drifting exists anywhere, it is in the minds of bored night court hearing officers. But, drifting is not a crime, and there is no need to identify a drifter, unless, of course, you have nothing better to do. Usually, all jail keepers have something better to do, like playing solitaire and sleeping. Besides, if you should fingerprint a drifter and send the prints off to the FBI, your drifter would be released long before the report came back, not to mention the fact that you'd end up pissing off the FBI. Of course, that could be fun in itself, but pissing off the sheriff was a whole different matter. He might just need those feds some day. You are expendable, the feds are not! However, had anyone ever bothered to take the prints of this particular drifter, they'd have been in for a big surprise!

Gringo Gabe's deeply tanned and sunburned features, what little could be seen of them beneath the matted beard and tangled black hair, revealed nothing of his ethnic background. If it weren't for the label Gringo, he could just as easily been Hispanic or Indian. He spoke rarely, only when absolutely necessary, so his voice and any possible trace of an accent provided no clues. But then, nobody really gave a rat's ass about Gabe anyway. And the few who did simply wished that he'd go away and stay away. Gabe was like the nuisance bears that came into town every spring looking for a handout. The bears got baited into a culvert trap, ear-tagged, and hauled a hundred miles out of town. If the same bear came back a second time, it got a tag in the other ear. That's all folks! No bear ever came back a third time unless, of course, it had three ears! Some folks might have liked to ear-tag Gabe and his cohorts, but nobody ever mentioned it. There were more of them than bears.

This time, there was no bundle flying out of the cruiser after him, and no flying burrito either! Just a terse, "Don't come back!"

Like so many times before, Gabe sat beneath the big log sign welcoming folks to Silver City on one side, and saying "Hurry Back" on the other. He smiled, though who could ever tell, as he waited patiently for the ride he knew would come, and wondering if it was all worth the effort. After about an hour of waiting, wondering, and coming to no useful conclusion, the gray half-ton New Mexico Fish and Game truck pulled up at the sign. Gabe vaulted into the back of the truck and lay down amid the assorted paraphernalia of wildlife law enforcers everywhere, spotlights, winches, ropes, pulleys, cables, a four-wheel ATV, and assorted waterproof duffle bags filled with emergency gear of all kinds. There were no other vehicles in sight, and the truck took off, having stopped for less than two seconds.

Ten miles down the road, the pick-up pulled into a barely visible side road, overgrown with weeds and a few courageous clumps of switch grass, stopped, and the driver got out to open an aluminum cattle gate. He got back into the driver's seat and drove over the cattle guard, pulling to a stop while his passenger vaulted out, closed the gate and got into the cab. Again, the driver had been careful to be sure that no other vehicles were in sight in either direction on the highway. The small bullet riddled sign on the gate read:

New Mexico Fish and Game Department
Research Area — No Trespassing!

For the next six miles into the distant mountains, the wagon road often disappeared for a hundred yards or more. The driver was careful to avoid running over the occasional sage or creosote bush. The oversize tires left little in the way of tracks on the baked and rocky ground. Gabe reached into the cooler chest at his feet and pulled out an ice cold Starbucks cappuccino, offering it to Denny, his driver of nearly two years. Denver waved it off, saying nothing, so Gabe greedily downed it and then a second. The silence between them was strictly protocol. In addition to his unidentifiable features, Gabe had another valuable asset for his job, a truly photographic memory. On their trips out of the back country the two had developed a strong friendship, but on the trips in, he had insisted on complete silence until he'd had time to finish writing up his report and purging the mental photographs.

Denny would stay overnight, or as long as it took, for Gabe to finish his report, seal it and hand it over for the trip out. Most times, Gabe stayed behind, sometimes for as much as a month. Denny would return for Gabe when his boss told him to. Denny never knew and never asked what was in those reports. What he suspected, was that his life and the lives of his wife and family were a whole lot safer sticking with protocol.

Slowly, the great red sandstone bluff on the horizon inched closer. The old line shack finally came into sight at the base of the bluff. Gabe knew the shack would be well stocked with steaks and beer in the gas refrigerator, but his appetite would have to wait. Denver pulled the truck behind the shack and, before going in, waved as Gabe disappeared into the narrow break in the sandstone bluff. Denny went inside the line shack to wait. There was no telling how long he'd have to wait. Sometimes it was only an hour. Other times it could be several hours before Gabe would reappear at the back door, a sealed envelope in hand.

Originally, the plan had been for Gabe to live at the line shack when he wasn't on an undercover assignment that might be anywhere in a three-state circuit from El Paso to Tucson. Gabe was a guest of the New Mexico Game and Fish Commission. He was not an employee. A rather special guest. His job was to help monitor the black market traffic in rare cats: jaguar, jaguarundi, ocelot, puma, and margay, living or dead.

Arrangements had been made for his extended visit to the three states by the US Fish and Wildlife Service. He didn't seem to work for the feds either, in fact, no one in the three-state region seemed to know who he worked for or what his real name was. Instructions came from the feds directly to Phoenix, where they were immediately transferred to the Silver City office of the Game and Fish Department. On rare occasions, he might get a direct order by way of a visit to the line shack from an unmarked private helicopter. And, he had a signal device well hidden at the shack, that, should he ever need it, would bring that helicopter to him in less than an hour. Snakebites and broken legs were a distinct possibility in this country.

The periods between assignments could be as much as a month, sometimes more. Between assignments, Gabe rarely lived in the shack, preferring to explore the maze of steep-walled canyons bisecting the miles of red-stone bluff separating it from the mesa a hundred feet above.

He'd either sleep somewhere in the canyons or, most frequently in the old cliff dwelling ruin securely hidden in the folds of the canyon behind the shack. It wasn't exactly an authentic cliff dwelling. That is, it wasn't built by the Ancient Ones, the Anasazi. According to Denny, the simple little dwelling had been built into a natural recess in the bluff by the rancher who'd owned these lands back at the turn of the twentieth century. He had plans to build several more and rent them out to tourists who wanted to stay in an "authentic" cliff dwelling. At the time, cave dwellings were a hot news item in the eastern states, with new discoveries being made almost monthly throughout the Southwest.

Unfortunately, or not, depending on your point of view, the project was never completed, World War I came along, the rancher died, and it turned out that the bluffs were not on his land anyway. The 4,200-acre ranch couldn't support anything except, perhaps tourism, so the property languished for decades until the Game and Fish Commission acquired it for back taxes in the 1960's, adding it to their abutting acreage.

Gabe could get to the dwelling in five minutes from the line shack, and it made an ideal study for him. If he tried to write his notes while Denny was bustling about the place having a beer, cooking a steak, or just engaging in his incessant humming of Golden Oldies, it would have been difficult to concentrate.

The cliff dwelling was all but impossible to spot from the old ranch because of the way it blended into the bluff, making it a perfect lookout spot to scan the landscape all the way back to the road without ever being seen. So, Gabe had spent hours in it, observing the stars and the fantastic weather patterns that emerged across the high desert, studying his growing collection of dessert artifacts, and writing letters in his mind. Letters he could never commit to paper. If he left them here, someone might find them, and once he passed them along in one of the sealed pouches, there was no assurance that they'd be secure. Anyhow, mailing them would necessitate some explanation of where he was and what he was doing. Not a good idea! Besides, keeping his few contacts in his head was a sort of comfort. It was a way to avoid the reality that he was a man lacking family and close friends. Did he prefer life that way? Maybe he did, but it was not worth thinking about. Not now, anyway. Being a loner was what made his work possible, work that he had a love-hate relationship with. But, it was all he really knew.

His mental letter to Lucy was now finely tuned, brief, thankful for all she had done for him, and, of course, inquiring about Zach. A most remarkable woman, Lucy Duckworth, he often wondered if his mother had lived would she have been like Lucy? He thought of Lucy as a mother figure, the best kind, the kind that gave her charges room to discover their own abilities. At times, his feelings of guilt at not having contacted her after their Thanksgiving talk, became overpowering. Lucy, and his sister, Sarah, had been two of the most positive figures in his life, a life dominated by the negatives of the criminal element and the aloofness of the bureaucracy. Memories of his mother were fragmentary, and of his father, fleeting. Marie, his mother, had died when he was still very young, and Tom, his father, spent every available hour working, whether to forget his loss or to provide for him and his sister, Corey was never sure.

He'd written other mental messages, to Jennifer, his loyal and worrying secretary, to let her know he was all right; to Seth Greer, the chief law enforcement officer at the Buffalo National River, thanking him for his patience and understanding during the months after Sarah's death; and to Theo Price, his brother-in-law. He knew he'd been less than fair to Theo. Theo's marriage to Sarah had been a mismatch from the start, but he'd been a perfect gentleman and very generous in the settlement. And, curiously, it was Theo who was responsible, though indirectly, for the past two years. What if he'd not been in the office that day when Theo called? He'd called on impulse, and probably wouldn't have called back or even left a message under the circumstances. How many times had he played that brief call over and over again in his mind: "Corey, glad I caught you. I know you don't get the Times, so you may not have seen the item, buried on page six, about your old friends, the Turners."

"No, Theo, I haven't heard a thing about them in years. What 'd it say?"

"Not much, really. Just that they're back in business. One of them got caught selling an ocelot pelt in the city."

"Hey, thanks. I'll check it out."

A few years earlier, Corey had been on the verge of busting a case wide open, involving Wes and Walt Turner, when agents of the US Customs Office stepped in and had him yanked off the case. Corey had been posing as a seller of black bear gall bladders, a hot item on the Asian market, and was just a day away from making a big sale. But, it seemed, the Customs boys had some bigger fish to fry with the Turners. Customs blew the case, and Corey was outraged. Theo had learned about it from Sarah. It was early in their marriage, and Sarah was trying hard. She just hadn't thought. She apologized profusely to Corey. But, Corey had become one less item in Theo and Sarah's strained repertoire of things to talk about in a marriage that had stopped providing comfort to either partner in its first days.

The Turner case had been a real sore point for Corey back then. It was even more so now. Theo was now high up in the State Prosecutor's office, and his call not only brought back a rush of painful memories, it had served to remind him of the inability of law enforcement agencies to work together.

Wes Turner was wealthy, owning homes in Saratoga and in Silver City, New Mexico. The slap on the wrist he received in federal court, only served to anger Corey more. He decided the moment he'd hung up from Theo's call, that he needed to talk to his contacts in the US Fish and Wildlife Service. Three weeks later, Corey resigned his job, saying only that he needed a change and was going to travel for a while. After cancelling his lease, leaving his pick-up with his secretary in exchange for keeping it maintained, he put everything he owned including Sarah's Honda Civic, in storage at the farm that the two of them still owned in northern Vermont. Corey Pingree had hiked back out to the main road, thumbed a ride, and disappeared from the face of the Earth.

Five weeks later, a disheveled drifter stood at the perimeter fence of Mesa Airpark, outside of Phoenix, watching a private helicopter land. It was silver and it had the right markings. A tall, deeply tanned pilot, with the look of a cowboy, emerged and headed for the terminal. The walkway would take him within twenty feet of the ten-foot hurricane fence topped with three strands of barbed wire.

"Are you Ben?" the drifter asked.

"And, you are?" the pilot drawled.

"Name's Gabe."

"Been expecting you."

Thirty minutes later Ben and his passenger were a silver dot in a clear blue sky headed southeast. Gabe watched the scene below as the wheels of commerce roared across the desert like reincarnated giant Jurassic creatures in search of their next meal.

23

LONG TRIP TO NOWHERE

El Paso, and the ride with Ray, had been the turning point for Zach. The idea of heading west, based on some vague notion of maybe calling on Dr. Hugh in Portland, had gotten to be more far-fetched with every passing mile. He thought that if he slept enough, it wouldn't be so painful. But, now the urgency of getting back to his quiet home in the Ozarks had become overpowering.

He'd found the twenty-dollar bill in the lunch sack that Becky had insisted on giving him. After he'd finished his lunch that first day out of Wichita, he simply crumpled it up inside the paper sack and stuffed it in his shirt. He said nothing to Dwayne and, drifting back to sleep, promised himself he would find a way to return it to her. If he needed money all he had to do was remember the magic number that Dr. Hugh had given him. Maybe he would give Becky that number.

It was hot and it was dark, but Zach was walking again, it was what he did best. Walking was when Zach did his best thinking, and thinking drove away the headaches — headaches made worse by Ray's incessant chatter. Walking toward the far-off lights of El Paso, and all of the wonders that Ray had adorned it with, generated thoughts of only one kind: escape! By the time Zach had walked the few miles from the intersection where he'd been dropped, to the truck stop where Ray assured him he could find a ride to anyplace in the country, he'd made up his mind. He scanned the dozens of trucks in the parking lot, finally finding one with an Arkansas license plate. The truck was hauling farm tractors, but there were lots of places where he could crawl inside and not be seen. He went into the truck stop, made a visit to the men's room, bought two apples from a vending machine and returned to the truck.

Even with the best of planning, our lives are ruled by the Goddess Assumpta. Assumptions, whether right or wrong, propel us down life's interesting pathways. To assume, for example, that a license plate from Arkansas might mean a direct return to Arkansas can be a costly mistake. In Zach's case, that one faulty assumption turned into the real-life equivalent of a free ride to jail and three months on the Maricopa County work gang. By the time he'd realized his mistake, there was no getting off. When the truck finally stopped, it was a direct delivery to the work camp.

Another trucker had seen Zach sitting on a tractor draw bar and had radioed the "Arkansas Traveler," alerting him to his free rider. Somewhere, far off in the cosmos, Assumpta smiled. Saint Christopher might promise safe travels, but only Assumpta could promise interesting ones!

Good behavior was a promise of reducing his sentence by two weeks. For ten weeks, Zach Taylor was a model prisoner, and a good worker on every kind of outdoor project. A favorite of his fellow inmates and guards alike, Zach had volunteered for the duty so that he could spend his days outdoors. While he found the black and white striped suit to be uncomfortably large and a hindrance when the gang was picking up litter on the roadsides, he loved the work of building trails and stabilizing stream banks around the county.

Zach's quiet demeanor and dietary preferences won him a lot of friends among the other prisoners who shared, in turn, the fruit brought in by their loved ones.

"You do know they're going to try to keep you in here when your time's up don't you, Zach?" said Joe Figuroa, one night in the dark from the next bunk. Joe was doing his mandatory six days for DUI. He was the original barracks lawyer, a member of the Arizona Bar no less!

"Can they do that? murmured Zach.

"You bet they can, and you're just the kind they want to keep, the kind that works hard and keeps his mouth shut!"

"No, when my time is up, I'll just walk away," replied Zach. It would be easy to walk away from here at night, or even when I'm out on the riverbank, he thought.

"Uh, uh, don't do it. Sure, it's easy, they'd love for you to do it! You do that and you'll be right back in doing a year of hard time!" Joe exclaimed. "What's more, they're not even going to release you for the good time you've earned unless you can prove that you have a job or a sponsor waiting for you!"

Zach lay on his bunk in silence for so long Joe thought he'd gone to sleep.

"What happens if you don't have a job or a sponsor?" Zach finally asked.

"They're supposed to help you find a job, but don't count on it," Joe replied. "Tell you what, put down my name as your sponsor when the time comes. They'll have to accept it. Believe it or not, I'm a good citizen! I'll come get you and take you out of the county. And, you can bet that I won't be drinking, either!"

Zach remained silent for several more minutes, finally saying, "Thank you Joe."

"One more thing, Zach, you really should stop waving your middle finger at the cars honking at us when we're picking up litter. You've got the whole damn crew doing it now, and the guards are getting pissed off at you!"

Four weeks later, true to his promise, Joe showed up, signed the papers taking responsibility for Zach, and the two of them drove for hours to the California border. If Zach had been hoping to sleep, it didn't happen. Joe's lawyer mind wouldn't allow it, easing out every bit of information, however limited, that Zach could provide about his past, including his indecision over going on to Portland or returning to his home in the Ozarks.

"Look, why don't you let me take you to a VA hospital here, Zach? They can put you in touch with your Portland doctor."

Zach knew that Joe meant well, but he didn't like being pushed into a corner. He didn't like being driven to the California border either, but Joe insisted that there was no other place in the Southwest where Zach would be safe. Joe had given a whole lot of thought to Zach's problem, even providing him with hiking boots, a pack containing trail food, fruits, socks, and a set of brand new Triple-A road maps highlighted with alternate routes from southern California to Oregon. On the front of each map, Joe had written: In Case of Emergency call Attorney Joe Figueroa, followed by both of his telephone numbers. Inside the California map, Joe had tucked five twenty-dollar bills and a pre-paid Greyhound ticket from Yuma to Portland.

Over a simple meal at the Yuma bus station, Joe told him about the bus ticket and all the reasons why busses were the only way to travel these days, particularly if you wanted to have a little snort along the way, Finally, Joe hugged Zach and headed back to Phoenix.

Zach didn't think that he'd ever been hugged before. He wished Joe hadn't done it, but he guessed that Joe must have had his reasons. He also wished he hadn't bought that ticket, he wasn't that interested in going to Portland, despite all of Joe's urgings. It was spring, and all he thought about while he was on the prison work gang was the beauty of an Ozark spring. But Joe had been kind. He needed to do as Joe said. Assumpta was clearly not letting Zach out of her sight!

Zach stood looking up across the long rolling lawn in front of the Portland VA Hospital for nearly half an hour before deciding not to go in. He knew there was nothing Dr. Hugh could do for him. He hadn't had a headache for weeks, and he didn't want to delay his return to the cave. He knew the way now, even if it was all those years ago, and somehow it felt really good to be starting on that journey again.

Zach felt twenty years younger, with a spring in his step, as he hiked along the Columbia River. Not until he was south of La Grande, two weeks out of Portland, did Assumpta find him again. She showed up in the form of a battered old Ford pick-up with a coyote riding shotgun.

"Hop in back," the gray-bearded driver told him, in a thick accent, as he pulled alongside. He seemed to have an authority to his voice, making Zach hesitate, remembering the authority voices he'd had to respond to in the work camp at Tent City. Zach kept walking, and the driver kept pace alongside. It was the coyote in the jump seat that finally did it. The resemblance to Pup was at once reassuring and relaxing. Zach unshouldered his backpack and tossed it in the bed of the pickup, hoisting himself in on top of it, and the old Ford picked up speed. Zach had promised himself, no more big trucks! His record with long-haul truckers hadn't been that good after Dwayne. But, he was ready for a ride—not that he was tired of walking, he was just feeling a growing urgency to get home.

Another twenty miles and the Ford turned onto a gravel side road, stopping at the intersection alongside the prettiest woman Zach thought he had ever seen. The driver was about to tell his rider that this was as far as he was going, when the pretty face cut him off with an equally pretty voice:

"Hi!" she said, extending her hand to Zach. "I'm Mirin, Miro's wife. Give me your hand, I'll get in back with you. There's nothing down the road for forty miles, so you better have supper with us. I don't suppose Miro bothered to introduce himself?" Zach just shook his head, stupefied by this woman's dark beauty, long black hair, and a smile that erased the pain from his aching joints.

Three months later, Zach was still living with Miro and Mirin Kiraly, and Cody, their coyote, in their remote wilderness cabin. The Kiralys were mossers, filling their minimal needs for cash by harvesting moss from the forest and occasionally selling a pickup load to packing houses in and around La Grande. Miro had been, most recently, a US

Forest Service scientist who got fed up working for the bureaucracy. Before that, he'd been a student and a Freedom Fighter, a refugee from Hungary who'd escaped to the states and found that if he stayed in college and made himself valuable, he could remain and even become a US citizen. The university community was glad to have him as a part-time lecturer and part-time researcher. Mirin was a botanist and a painter of wild flowers. They'd met at the university where Miro still did occasional guest lecturing, and they discovered in their mutual love of all things wild a bond with each other that they gradually accepted as exclusive. Not only could it not be shared with others, it had to be lived intensely, day by day. Eventually, they found that it had to be lived in the forest. To leave the forest for more than a brief trip was almost physically painful.

That first evening, Miro and Mirin discovered the hermit in Zach, and encouraged him to stay for as long as he liked. They shared coyote stories, and Cody found a playmate in Zach. He slept in the moss shed, and helped with the collecting.

For the first several weeks, Zach almost believed he was home. Going to sleep with the fragrance of moss drove away any lingering trace of headaches as well as his once overwhelming desire to return to the cave. But, it was an interlude, and he gradually came to realize that he needed his cave in much the way his new friends needed to be with each other. Leaving Cody was, however, a different matter.

Mirin's face registered her disappointment when Zach raised the subject one night at supper. She had grown to enjoy their evenings together far more than she realized. From the first, she and Miro had been able to draw Zach out. First, by talking about Cody and Pup, later by asking about the cave. Miro was particularly fond of speculating about the limestone encrusted skeleton. Eventually, he found that his stories about hand-to-hand combat in the streets of Budapest, as a teenager during the Hungarian revolution, were being intensely absorbed by Zach, even though Zach rarely commented on them. Zach listened more intently than seemed necessary to every word. It was as though he was desperately trying to remember something. And, then, for no apparent reason, his eyes lost their focus and he was very obviously shutting out the words, once even clamping his hands over his ears.

That night in the darkness of their cabin, after Zach had left for the moss shed, Miro and Mirin talked for hours about what was becoming their mutual obsession: what to do about Zach? "He needs to stay here," Mirin insisted. "At least, we should drive him back to Arkansas!"

"The old Ford would never make it," insisted Miro; "and besides, he wouldn't want us to do that!"

"Frankly, I don't know how he's made it this far, he's so . . . "

"Vulnerable!" Mirin filled in with a catch in her voice.

"I believe that Zach has a powerful protective mechanism at work within him. He'll make it. And, you need to stop worrying!" But, it wasn't that easy for either of them. Sleep did not come easy that night, or for weeks to come for the two caring mossers!

For a scientist, Miro was certainly very antiscience. "You did the right thing, Zach. They may be nice and all, but their main interest in you is as a specimen. And, because they can learn from you, they will want you to try different kinds of treatments, drugs, to see if they can help you to recover your memory."

"And," chimed in Mirin, "most of the time, they have very little knowledge of what the real effects will be on you. Zach, you strike me as though you are doing just fine without those long-term memories. How can anyone know what's best for you?"

"Maybe those memories would just make you very unhappy," added Miro.

Zach had had long practice in being taciturn, ever since they'd told him in the hospital that he needed to be careful with his speech so as not to give people wrong ideas about himself. He knew that, in addition to profound memory loss, he'd lost the ability to pick and choose his words. Words were just words. But, Zach couldn't trust himself. One of his doctors had tried to be helpful by telling him to avoid four-letter words. So, when an answer was called for, he'd often think about it, and get rid of all the four-letter words. It had never been easy, and it was getting harder now that he wanted to talk with these two good people. It was particularly difficult on those occasions when the two of them would show up while he was bathing down at the hot spring by the river and join him. Zach found the nudity and the bonding that resulted, a remarkable experience. Mirin was obviously much the younger, but they were, by any standards, a beautiful couple, embracing in the pool, oblivious of his presence. But, whenever they would try to engage him in conversation, he could never find the right words. Everything was four letters: pool, heat, cool, cold, good, love, nice. In his frustration, he'd simply mutter "fuck," and walk back to the moss shed, usually with Cody running on ahead.

While nude bathing at the hot spring had been a bonding, though frustrating experience, moss gathering had been a solidarity celebration. Zach quickly became expert in identifying which mosses to pick and at just the right stage to ensure the survival of the parent plant. His collecting bag was always the cleanest at the end of the day, containing even fewer bits of bark and twigs than Mirin's. Cody reveled in running back and forth between the three of them, and whenever one of them would find a particular treasure of berries or mushrooms, the other two would come running.

Over the course of several evenings, the three of them sat around the table going through Mirin's collection of roadmaps, searching for the best roads to get Zach home, avoiding the interstates and marking the older highways that connected small towns and farms, places where he'd be likely to be offered rides by local folks, people who liked the slower pace of life.

The night before Zach left, he presented Miro with a carving he'd been working on. It was a Sitka spruce burl, the size of an orange, intricately carved and polished, with an image of Mirin on one face, Miro on another, and Cody on the third. It was the most beautiful and complex carving Zach had ever done. As he'd worked on it, his hands had darkened and burnished it to the point where it took on the appearance of antiquity carved by one of the great masters!

That night Mirin, dabbing at tears, painted a portrait of Zach almost hidden by the leaves and flowers of the abundant wild pink azaleas. It was the only portrait she'd ever done. The next day, when they dropped him off at the little city of Ponderosa, she tucked it into the flap of his backpack along with a dozen of her oatmeal cookies, and her collection of roadmaps, musty, old, and fragile, but enough to get him to Arkansas.

Zach was glad to be back on the road again. His feet were light under the pack, no doubt because his mind was filled with images of the past few months. At the parting, Miro had cried, Mirin had cried, Zach, unable to cry, or to find the right words, laughed. Finally, they all laughed. For days, Zach hummed the Hungarian love song, "Roses Love Sunshine," Mirin had sung with her deep throaty voice while collecting moss.

Going home! It was the thought of it that sustained Zach over the long months after leaving Oregon. It was the single thought that took his mind off the aches in his legs and burning heat on the soles of his feet searing through the ever thinner treads on the hiking shoes that Joe had pushed on him when he left Yuma. After a while, he stopped thinking about the going and just thought about being home, about his cave, about Pup, about Miss Lucy, and sometimes, about Corey. What was it about Corey that aroused his feelings of unrest and led to his leaving all those months ago?

His experiences with Joe, and with Miro and Mirin, had pretty well helped Zach get beyond his reluctance to accept rides, but he still wouldn't stick out his thumb, not after what Joe had told him about waving when he was at Tent City. It was okay, he liked to walk, and those who stopped on their own, like Miro had done, really wanted to help. There was the nun in the middle of Idaho who was going on retreat in her battered old Volkswagen bus, and the farmer south of Pocatello who invited Zach to ride on top of his load of hay. He had rides from Mormon missionaries, Seventh Day Adventists, a logger who'd served in Vietnam, an elderly woman on her way to a cancer clinic in Minnesota, an off-duty policeman, and a Korean couple looking for work in Nebraska. He'd also turned down rides, like the young people who went speeding past him, came to a screeching stop, and backed up to Zach with their radio turned up so loud that they had to shout, "Want a ride?" Zach answered by putting his hands over his ears and shaking his head violently.

Taking shelter in an underpass, from a violent Kansas shower, he was joined by a motorcyclist who offered him a ride on the back of his Harley. Zach made over a hundred miles that day, and went on his way with an extra poncho and a full belly courtesy of an unknown friend with silver beads on the back of his jacket that said "Hell's Angels"! By the time Zach left Kansas and entered western Missouri, he'd given up any thought of maybe seeing Dwayne and Donna and Becky again.

Now, it was mid-October; he was cold and exhausted beyond belief. He hadn't eaten much in weeks, and he knew he was sick, barely able to place one foot in front of the other. If he hadn't been nearly delirious, he never would have allowed those three young people to almost bodily pick him up and deposit him in the back of their van.

Five miles down the road, a rusty white van pulled to the side of the road, the back doors opened, and a barely alive shapeless form with an immense black beard flecked with gray and dripping with blood, rolled out. The namesake, and possibly remote descendent, of a one-time President of the United States, the back of his skull fractured, had been left to bleed to death on the gravel and litter of a nearly deserted country road in the nation's heartland. Zachary Taylor had lived well for more than two decades in the wilderness, but it took only thirteen months for him to become a victim of civilization.

A hundred feet down the road, the white van once more stopped briefly and all of Zach's worldly possessions, came tumbling out, accompanied by a volley of curses, scattering and rolling into the obscurity of the night. A small watercolor, on homemade paper, of a gentle, bearded man looking through azalea blossoms, was carried away by the night breeze.

One thing remained in the road, a now empty camouflage backpack. It was enough to attract the attention of a deputy sheriff going home for the night, who braked to a stop alongside Zach's inert body. He remembered the white van that he'd passed a few miles back, the only other vehicle on that deserted road, and cursed himself for being too much in a hurry to pull them over for having only one headlight!

Too late now, as he detected a faint pulse in the bearded man's neck.

24

MYSTERY MAN

To the nurses in the intensive care unit at St. Jude's in Springfield, Missouri, the comatose shape resting beneath their sheets for more than two weeks was nothing less than a national hero. One of them had smuggled in a pair of small flags, the Stars and Stripes and the Marine Corps' Semper Fi, and attached them to the metal frame at the head of his bed. X-Rays revealed that his skull had suffered another severe fracture several years earlier. He'd been identified, through his fingerprints, since the second day of his arrival.

All that anyone knew for sure was that he was an ex-Marine who'd served in Vietnam, who'd spent nearly a year in the Portland, Oregon VA Hospital, and who'd been officially listed as "whereabouts unknown." His medical records forwarded from Portland were over an inch thick, and the x-rays clearly matched the earlier skull fracture. They also knew, from the large note attached to the headboard written in red neon Magic Marker, that a Dr. Hugh Norton at the Portland facility was to be contacted immediately whenever the patient returned to consciousness.

Whatever was going on inside Zachary Taylor's head, on the outside he was being treated as a visiting dignitary; perhaps the object of an awakened social conscience that had, for so long, found it easy to dismiss all Vietnam veterans as carbon copies of one Lieutenant William Calley.

Zach's hospital bed, with its comatose patient, was smack in the center of a web, a network of filaments some of which extended two thousand miles. Zach's web of life was exceedingly tenuous. It lacked the reinforcing strength of all those intermediate connections that define most of our lives. If it were to be diagrammed, it would look like a very small spider web with lots of close connections, doctors, nurses, technicians, aides, electrodes, monitors of all sorts, and two very long, weak, filaments stretching in opposite directions connecting the inner web to VA offices in Washington, DC and Portland, Oregon. The long connections existed strictly for reasons of science and record keeping. That's what made them weak.

There was absolutely nothing in Zach's web to help explain the enormous gap between this unconscious being and who that same person was more than two decades earlier residing in the Portland VA hospital. It was such an obvious weak spot in the web that no one paid any attention to it. No one that is, except Amanda Cousins, freelance writer, featured columnist for the Springfield News Leader, and sometimes feature reporter on KSPR-33.

Amanda's web was far more complex than Zach's. Hers was strong in the very places that his was weak. Amanda had scores of intermediate connections. Those connections were how she made her living. Within minutes of the time that an unidentified drifter had been admitted to the local emergency room, Amanda knew. And, within seconds, she dismissed the information as not newsworthy. She also knew, within minutes, once he'd been identified as one Marine corporal Zachary Taylor, Vietnam veteran, and a patient of interest to a certain doctor in the Portland, Oregon VA hospital. Amanda was at the hospital administrator's office ten minutes later.

"Come on, Prudie, I understand that you can't let me see his records, and that I can't take his picture, but can't you just give me the name of the Portland doctor. Please!"

"Sorry, Amanda, no can do. Perhaps you'd like to tell me how you knew about Portland? No? I didn't think so. I'll plead your case at today's staff meeting. It's the best I can offer. Call me later this afternoon, okay?"

Prudence Waite was well named for her job. And Amanda held little hope for a staff meeting reversal of their gatekeeper's interpretation of the rules. But, Prudie was not the only, and certainly not the strongest, hospital filament in Amanda's web. Prudie was just a formality. The real connection was Ruth Ann Sculley, high school classmate, one-time soul mate, and ICU night nurse. Ruth Ann would be sleeping now, and she hated to wake her. On the other hand, if she waited until the staff meeting had put up a brick wall, any help from Ruth Ann could evaporate the minute she came on duty.

"Hey, Ruth Ann, It's Amanda, I didn't wake you did I?"

"O, Hell No, Amanda. You just interrupted the only ménage a trois dream I've ever had!"

"Oh, I'm sorry. Was I in it?"

"That would be your dream!"

"Look, I won't keep you from getting back to Mission Impossible, but I wanted to thank you for that message you left about the Vietnam vet in a coma. I don't suppose you'd happen to remember that doctor's name in Portland would you?"

"Uh, uh, sorry. Why don't you call Prudie?"

"I tried that, but no answer." Little white lies were stock in trade in Amanda's business.

"Sorry, I'll call you tonight when I get a break. Bye."

Amanda was still puzzling over her next move, when the phone rang.

"God damn you, Amanda, I couldn't get back to sleep, trying to remember that name. It's Morton, or Norton, or maybe Horton. Something like that." Click!

"Veteran's Administration. How may I direct your call?"

"Uh, Doctor Orton please." Amanda had practiced slurring over the first letter in hopes she wouldn't have to pin down one of the three names that Ruth Ann had supplied. Or, worse yet, maybe it was none of those. Could just as easily be Fortin.

"I'm sorry, could you repeat the name please?"

"Shit!" thought Amanda. She made a quick decision, and went with Morton.

"I'm sorry, we have no Dr. Morton on staff. Are you saying Morton or Norton?"

"Look, I'm calling long distance, and we seem to have a very poor connection. Can you hear me? It's Norton, N, as in nurse."

"Yes, I can hear you fine. Dr. Norton won't be in until Friday. Would you like to leave a message?"

"No. Thank you. I'll call back on Friday. Oh, by the way, can you tell me what Dr. Norton's specialty is?"

"Dr. Hugh Norton is a neurosurgeon. May I ask what this is about, please?"

"Oh, it's not important. But thank you anyway."

Amanda's inner signals confirmed what she already knew, she was on to something. And, she knew that a phone call on Friday would be a waste of time. Her next call was to book a flight to Portland. She'd make up a story on the way. It would have to be one of the darker shades of white.

Amanda had been sitting in the waiting room nearly two hours, when the receptionist asked if she'd like to go down to the cafeteria. She was famished, but declined, not wanting to miss Dr. Hugh Norton.

"Oh, you won't miss him, He knows you're here. He just buzzed to say that he'd be tied up another hour, and that you should go eat something."

"Thank you, how very kind of him," Amanda muttered as she headed for the elevators and the signs leading to the cafeteria. The wait had actually been a good thing, she realized. It gave her a chance to put a few convincing touches on her story. Amanda was not about to fly all the way to Portland at her own expense, and come away with nothing for her effort!

How do they manage to do it? she wondered. The broiled cod,

mashed potato and broccoli all tasted exactly alike. Glad I passed on the tapioca pudding, she mused. So much for her theory that fish get better as you get nearer the coast! She pushed her tray aside, got out her steno book and tried to compile a list of just what she had so far. Nothing! Zachary Taylor was real, and so was Dr. Hugh Norton. She'd learned from Gloria, his receptionist that Doctor Norton was retired and still came in two days a week to help out and keep in touch with his old cases. But, everything else was hunches. She even had a hunch that Doctor Norton was a bored, and boring, retiree who needed to find a life. Amanda's signals were letting her down. Had she let her hunger for a story get in the way of her better judgment?

Amanda returned to the waiting room with a sinking heart, and found Dr. Norton's office door wide open. Gloria waved her on in, and Dr. Norton rose from his desk and came to the door to greet her.

"How can I help you? Miss Cousins, is it?"

Amanda's practiced eye took it all in an instant. The worn and frayed carpet, the ugly office furniture from the '70s, or maybe earlier, rows of tired filing cabinets, all screaming the same silent message: No pretense here! And, that face! Dear God, how could anyone lie to that face. It was the face of her father combined with every Father Knows Best character she'd ever known, and a touch of Our Father Who Art in Heaven thrown in for good measure! Magnificent snow-white hair, and a smile to die for! Too bad, she thought, it was a damn good story too!

"Thank you for seeing me, Doctor Norton. Yes, my name is Amanda Cousins, and I'm a reporter from Springfield. Missouri."

"Aha, I thought as much. I'm afraid one of my obsessions is accents, and your accent is decidedly Ozarkian," he smiled. And, I did get a bit of a refresher recently talking to the folks at your hospital. I'm betting that you're here because of Corporal Taylor. Am I right?"

"That's right, Doctor." Amanda was starting to feel nakedly uncomfortable. It must have showed.

"Gloria told me that you'd gone downstairs to our world-class cafeteria. So, you've lunched?" He said it less as question than commiseration. "Let me guess again, could it have been the broiled fish?"

They both laughed. The good doctor's half-eaten peanut butter sandwich laying on his desk spoke volumes. He'd broken the ice for her. *If you have to be in the hospital, this is the only doctor you'd ever want!* Amanda thought.

"Doctor Norton, I'm keeping you from much more important work. I'd like to know anything you can tell me about Zachary Taylor. I want to do a story on him. But, he's a mystery."

"He is that. I'm afraid there is not much I can tell you. Of course I can't show you his records, but I can tell what little I know. Zach enlisted from a small town about 400 miles due east of here called Joseph, after Chief Joseph of course. His enlistment papers show him to be Nez Perce. We're not even sure his name is Zachary Taylor. I'm sure you could probably find a few Zach Taylors, along with a Franklin Pierce or two among the tribes. It was not uncommon for the Indians of his grandparent's era to have both an American name and a tribal name. In fact, some schools back then required it. But, he listed no parents, and no next of kin, when he signed up. He was probably orphaned, certainly of mixed parentage. Now then, what can you tell me about him? How does he look, have you seen him?"

"No, he's still in intensive care, and they won't let me see him. All that I know is that he's in a coma, but otherwise, his nurse says he looks strong. She thinks that he will come out of it."

"Good! Good!" Doctor Norton said enthusiastically, as he got up from the chrome and sagging leatherette chair, and walked across the small office. "I want to show you something."

He came back to her chair with a walking stick and handed it to her. "Zach carved this for me. It's an absolute work of art. Zach's an artist with a whittling knife. That's probably the one certain thing that I can tell you about him. Oh, there is one other thing. We had an account set up to receive his government checks here at a local bank. If you'd like, I can call and see what kind of activity the account has had. His account number is in his file."

"Oh, Yes, please do! Can you really do that?" Dr. Norton winked at her, as he opened the file on his desk and dialed the bank.

A kinder, gentler, Amanda left Portland feeling much less cynical about the condition of humanity, and a whole lot less comfortable with her own jaded practice of using little white lies whenever it served her purposes. She also had a renewed faith in her hunches. Zachary Taylor was shaping up to be a real story! In Dr. Norton, Amanda had acquired another strong filament in her web of life. His parting comments, as he walked her to the door, left her feeling a little shaken about her motives, "Remember, my dear, Zach is more than just a mystery, and more than just a story. And, please, call if I can be of help." Her mumbled "Thanks" as she ran to catch her taxi, seemed so damnably inadequate, but she wasn't about to look him in the eye just then, or into that face one more time! Amanda knew she'd be talking to Dr. Hugh Norton again.

Amanda left with something else. Zach Taylor had, apparently, been living in or near Ponca, Arkansas, according to the latest withdrawal from his account. But, that was way more than a year old. Ponca was less than half-a-day's drive south of Springfield.

When Amanda arrived in Ponca, two days later, she headed straight for the General Store to ask if anyone knew the whereabouts of Zachary Taylor. Before leaving Springfield, she'd thought about waiting another day. She'd find the Post Office open on Monday. But, waiting was not one of her strong points. Besides, her phone light indicated a whole bunch of messages that she didn't want to deal with. Better to get out of the city!

"You mean the guy that used to be President?' the diminutive clerk asked with a straight face.

"No, just someone with the same name. Is there anyone around here with that name?"

"Not that I ever heard of," the young clerk replied. "But, I'm just filling in today for my mom. You'd need to ask her."

"Where might I find your mom?" inquired Amanda.

"She's down at Steele Creek at a birthday party for Miss Lucy Duckworth. She's the one you really need to talk to. Miss Lucy knows everybody in the valley!"

"And how do I get to Steele Creek?" Amanda asked, in her politest tone.

"You just follow the highway two miles south and turn left at the big curve."

Big curve?' thought Amanda. This road is nothing but big curves!

Half-way down the entrance road to Steele Creek campground, Amanda had to pull over for an ambulance flashing its lights and wailing its siren as it came up the steep winding hill.

The story was short, shorter than Amanda would have liked. She wished she'd taken the time to go to Joseph, Oregon, before flying home. But, Dr. Norton had assured her it would be a waste of time. He'd done it himself, years ago, and ended up with nothing. "That is, if you could call some great fishing and some incredible scenery nothing," Hugh Norton had added. He obviously couldn't.

Furthermore, once he'd seen the country, it seemed to have the look of Zach, or, at least, it had the look of some of Zach's carvings.

She'd almost written Ponca off as another Joseph when she learned, at Steele Creek, that the person she was looking for had just been taken to the hospital suffering from what looked like a stroke. Purely as an afterthought, she'd asked at the distraught gathering if the Ponca postmaster happened to be there. Indeed, he was. And, sure, he knew the name. But, he knew it, as did most folks in the valley, as simply Backpack Zach, a local hermit who'd frequented the area for years, but nobody had seen him for months. In fact, the local Park Service officials believed that he'd been the resident of a nearby cave that had recently been vandalized by local youths.

It wasn't the story Amanda wanted, but it would have to do. Maybe it would get picked up by one of the nationals and she'd get some feedback for a second installment. One week later, it showed up as a small item in *USA Today*.

25

UNDERCOVER AGENT

Long after Denny's tail lights were consumed by the desert night, Corey sat on the front porch of the line shack, thinking, writing a mental letter to himself. His report had been boring, repetitive, unfulfilling, like so many others that he had filed. He'd precisely reported the comings and goings of every vehicle at the Turner compound on the hillside overlooking the university. It was the perfect spot for watching. Nobody ever gave a second look at some bum sitting up against a tree on college grounds, except for the one time when a grad student in sociology insisted on recruiting him for her study of The Forgotten Ones. He was finally able to convince her that he couldn't speak, not English, not Spanish, nothing!

He'd seen the Turners exactly two times in two years, neither time in Silver City. He saw Wes one day while staked out at the El Paso airport, and Walt once at the Tucson airport. On both occasions the Turner's appeared to be model citizens. No contacts, no drops. Thanks to the cluster of arriving passengers, he'd even been able to follow them into the men's room, before the airport police hustled him off to the outer limits of their jurisdiction. He knew the information that he provided was just one small part of a much larger picture that was being compiled, by someone, somewhere. But, it was losing all meaning for him. Wouldn't it just end up as another inconclusive court case? Another slap on the wrist? How many judges treated wildlife crimes seriously, unless a federal agent or a game warden got killed? The way Corey saw it, there was an endless supply of wardens and feds, but there were only so many ocelots left in the world.

He finished his beer, latched the screen doors on the front and back of the shack, and headed up to the cliff house for the night. He never entered his little sanctuary without thinking of Zach. He thought how much his life had become like Zach's. It was a good feeling! Zach embodied Corey's youthful dreams of living in the wild. He fondly remembered every detail of Zach's cave in the Ozarks. In his entire life, he had never coveted what another man had, until he met Zach. And, Zach had nothing!

Corey's whole career had kept him from really enjoying the nature that he'd grown up loving in Vermont. Nature was the reason he went to college and majored in wildlife management. Early on, he had gotten seduced into the excitement of law enforcement, and a promise of reducing wildlife poachers to an endangered species. But, it was a career of seeing the ugly side of nature, the greedy side, the side that some of his colleagues referred to as the human dimensions of wildlife. They were being academic, but to him it was beautifully sardonic as the unhappy side, particularly for the wild creatures.

Finally, in this remote sanctuary, he'd found the nature of his youth. He had spent days studying the lives of desert creatures. Often, he'd spend his nights reading about them in the line shack's small wildlife library. He would never have believed the richness of wild creatures and the beauty of flowering plants in such a dry place. He would never have believed that here is where he'd want to spend the rest of his life! Corey knew with each passing day that he was inching closer to quitting. But, he resented the idea of having to leave his unique paradise, a paradise that had become his alone. That old rancher of a century ago knew what a treasure he had! Corey had only seen the seasons go around twice, but he was hopelessly hooked! Knowing where you wanted to live, he'd concluded, was simply a matter of knowing where you wanted to die!

Corey also knew that his life had to change, and soon. Living two, such very different lives had put him through a metamorphosis that he found increasingly hard to live with. It just happened. At first, his days in the desert were like a cleansing agent for the seamy side of life that his undercover work exposed him to. Watching the desert unfold into bloom overnight after a sudden spring torrent, could almost make him forget his inability to intervene while drunks were being brutalized in back alleys for what little cash they might have. Attending the birth of an antelope whose mother's time had come, just when she found herself trapped in a corner of an old barbed wire fence, was so intensely absorbing as to drive out the images of young girls being pushed into prostitution in fear for their lives.

But, the catharsis of the desert had worn off. In its place was the desert's constant reproach. To go on swimming in filth just because there's a fresh water shower waiting is a sorry way to live. He was forced to accept his own inaction, time after time in city after city, simply because he had bigger fish to fry. The collective impact of doing nothing when he could have made a difference was taking a terrific toll on his self-esteem.

Even if he caught the Turners, and sent them to jail, wouldn't they just be replaced by others, and then others, in an endlessly sickening parade? Sure, the trade was obscene, but weren't the suppliers just fulfilling a function that is prized in a free enterprise system? Could he really make a difference for wild creatures, or was this just an ego trip, not all that different from the one that drove the people who just had to have an ocelot jacket? It was a trip that could cost him his life the next time he left this paradise. It was eroding his life, bit by bit, every single day! And, yet, wasn't it that same ego trip that had brought him here, and so profoundly affected his life that he now knew he could never leave the desert's ever-changing beauty?

It was hours before sunup, two days later, when he heard the copter come swooping in below the mesa. Damn! He wished he'd fired off that resignation with his last report. It was something he'd thought about doing with every report over the last six months. Too late now! Gabe slept in his clothes. It gave him that authentic drifter look!

He was out of his sanctuary and on the ground before the chopper had landed and switched off its lights. He was about to climb aboard, expecting the chopper to lift off before he could close the door, when the engine shut down. "No hurry," boomed the voice emanating from the dim shape of Ben Richardson, the pilot, exiting on the other side. "Let's go inside, we need to talk."

Ben helped himself to a Corona from the fridge, sat down on one of two creaky chairs, and casually dropped his sweaty Stetson on the flimsy old kitchen table with its scars and scratches revealing at least four ugly coats of enamel paint. "Jesus Christ, wouldn't you think the cheap bastards could at least provide you with a decent table? Okay, here's the deal. But, before I tell you, you need to know that everyone, all the way to the top, wants you to think about backing out of this. No one likes the way this is coming down. Least of all me!"

"You've got my attention, Ben. Go on!"

"The geniuses on both sides of the border think we can nail the Turners once and for all. But they need your help. A big sale is set up for fourteen hours from now at the brother's cabin on the Gila River. They'll both be there, along with their supplier from Mexico, a real bad guy named Arana Quintana, the Spider. They're supposedly all on a fishing trip. Customs is playing along with us, leaving Quintana alone, but they can't provide any help at the cabin. Neither can we, without arousing suspicion."

"Sounds good so far," said Gabe quizzically.

"Yeh, well here's where things get goofy. The boss wants you to show up as the mystery buyer from Canada. The brothers received half the money two days ago. Right under your nose, I'm told. So, they're not going to be suspicious. There's a silver Lincoln with Ottawa license plates waiting for you at commuter lot C-3, at the Tucson airport. I'm to take you to Tucson this morning. But, she wants you to get cleaned up, shave, and drop the Gringo Gabe look. I've got some pretty nice duds waiting for you in the chopper, along with your Canadian passport, charge cards, cell phone, and new ID."

Gabe blinked. His eyes were the only part of his face that Ben, or anybody, could read.

"She thinks the Turner's will recognize you, panic, and peel on out of there, smelling a sting. They probably will, they're not fighters, and we'll be waiting for them when they hit the intersection with US 6 at Gila Bend. The Spider is the unknown quantity, except for the fact that he is considered dangerous. You'll have to be unarmed. You'd never get past their flunky when he picks you up at Gila Bend on the way in. And, he's probably been instructed to see the money before bringing you to the cabin. So, I've got a briefcase full of cash for you, two-hundred and fifty thou! Our guys will start moving in as soon as their driver picks you up, but, they may not be in place in time to be of any help to you. I have to say this sounds like a sacrifice mission with you as the sacrifice!"

"I think the Director has it figured right. I've sized up The Spider on a couple of occasions. I think I can handle him."

"Well, the brains think it's a win-win for us. Either they recognize you and bolt, or they don't recognize you and you get out safely with their driver before we move in and catch them red handed with the marked cash."

"I agree," said Corey.

"Okay, but I'd feel a Hell of a lot better if you were wired, so we'd know what was going on!"

"I wouldn't! Let's go, I've been waiting two years for this, and I want to get it over with!"

"I'm sure you know that a helluva lot of planning and risk has gone into setting this up. Everybody seems to think that you can pull it off. I dunno what they know, so all's I can say is good luck! Any messages you want to leave with me? You know, just in case?"

They left the cabin half-an-hour later with a very surprised Ben staring at the wealthy, neatly-trimmed Canadian sitting beside him in the chopper, looking for all the world like a Russian count, and apparently eager to be delivered to the Tucson airport.

"Who in the Hell are you, anyway?" Ben blurted, not really expecting an answer.

"Just another citizen concerned about crime," came the reassuringly cool reply, with the hint of a clipped Canadian accent.

Ben Richardson shook his head in the dim light of the helicopter bubble. A ribbon of red was just outlining the eastern horizon.

"If it makes you feel any easier, I'll be coordinating the three teams when we close in on the cabin," Ben offered as they parted. Corey just smiled. But, behind the smile, years of experience had already told him that Ben was much more than a messenger and chopper pilot!

Walking through the Tucson airport, Corey picked up a copy of *USA Today*. It was partly for reading on the shuttle bus ride to commuter lot C-3, and partly to hide behind. Flipping idly through the pages, his eye caught the briefest of items, from the Springfield, Missouri, *News Leader*: "DO YOU KNOW ZACHARY TAYLOR?" Mystery man in third week of coma in Springfield, Missouri hospital." The three-sentence report lacked further details, except that a reporter by the name of Amanda Cousins had instituted a nationwide search for anyone knowing the person whose photograph looked vaguely like Backpack Zach sans the wild beard. Now, there's a coincidence, he thought. Hang on, Zach, I'll be there as soon as this is over!

Corey glanced at his fancy new gold Rolex President, and wondered if he'd get to keep it once it was over. No time to call Amanda Cousins or Lucy Duckworth. He wondered; maybe Lucy had already followed up with this Amanda Cousins person. But, what was Zach doing in a hospital in Springfield, Missouri?

He folded the newspaper and tucked it in the handle of his expensive alligator briefcase. It was unsettling, to say the least. Earlier,

Corey had felt good, shaping the beard, trimming his hair to a less wild look, and just becoming a bit more like himself again. He'd decided not to completely remove the beard. The trimmed look might give him a better chance at fooling the Turners. He really wanted them to stick around so he could be in on the arrest. Leaving the cliff house was not hard; he knew he'd be back. With time to spare, he'd stopped by the airport barbershop for a more professional trim, and a reassuring look at himself in the mirror. Suddenly, he wasn't sure of himself at all. As Ben had asked: Who in Hell was he, anyway? Right now, the last thing Corey needed was a distraction! The Zach Taylor mystery was a big distraction, bringing back a flood of memories about Sarah. All of a sudden, he was thinking about the little airport chapel he'd walked so easily by. He wished he'd stopped in for a minute and lit a candle, one for Sarah at least!

26

SHOWDOWN ON THE GILA

The tension in the richly appointed fishing cabin was in the air as much as in the lines of the drawn faces of Wes and Walt Turner. Corey stood looking at the pair impassively as the voice of the driver from somewhere behind him said, "He's clean, Boss."

Wes nodded slightly while Walt grinned his relief. Corey had long thought that Wes was the brains of the pair. Wes was clearly the one to watch if things started to get out of hand. Corey had used the drive from Tucson to practice his accent and his greeting, but he'd forgotten it all when the Turner's driver pulled over halfway to the lake and ordered him out at gunpoint while he did a careful job of patting down his Canadian passenger, and taking away his briefcase.

"Sorry if your first impression of us was a little rough, Mr. Benson," Wes said. "I'm sure you understand we have to be very careful in our business. How 'bout a drink?"

"Canadian, straight," replied Corey, hoping to sound aggrieved rather than relieved. Neither of the brothers had shown the slightest hint of recognition, So far, so good, he thought. He wasn't sure whether or not they'd ever seen him in New York.

"I'm Wes, this is my brother Walt. You've already met Gordie." Gordie had set down the briefcase on the pine trestle table and disappeared.

"Gordy could use a refresher in his PR skills. I assume your choice of hired help doesn't represent your taste in merchandise!" Corey said coolly, accepting the drink from Wes and studiously avoiding Walt's outstretched hand.

"As I said, we can't be too careful, Mr. Benson. But, let's use first names, shall we, Ken?"

Clever aren't you? thought Corey. A little test, perhaps?

"If we were to use first names, mine is Kent. However, since we don't know each other, and my visit must, regrettably, be short, let's keep this formal shall we, Mr. Turner?"

"Well, Ken," said Wes, sarcastically, "we've had a little shipping delay. Unfortunately, your package won't arrive until tomorrow morning. We have lots of room, and Gordie dishes up a fine breakfast. So, make yourself comfortable. You are our guest."

He's bluffing, thought Corey. "Well, that **is** unfortunate, because by tomorrow at this time, I shall be having dinner with my daughter in LA," he responded swiftly and decisively.

"Now, Ken, you really do need to plan these things with a little more leeway for error. You'll just have to call LA and change your plans. Gordie is checking out your cell phone at the moment, but feel free to use our phone if you like. Do sit down and enjoy your whiskey."

Goddamn it! thought Corey, I don't even know what's on that damn phone. His mind was racing. "No thanks, I'll have to wait for mine, I have no facility for remembering numbers," said Corey settling himself on the comfortable leather couch, which gave him a perfect view of Wes's shoulder holster.

Walt was sitting across the glass-top coffee table, his back to the huge picture window, with its magnificent view of the last rays of the setting sun over the Gila river. Corey noted that Walt wasn't wearing a shoulder holster, but he was looking curiously at him.

"I'm thinking we've met, Mr. Benson? Your voice sounds familiar, I think?" Walt explained a little stupidly.

"I rather doubt that we travel in the same circles, Mr. Turner," said Corey without looking up, and accenting his words to sound more Canadian than Bostonian.

Fortunately, Walt's attention was diverted by Gordie who'd come back and was whispering something into Wes's ear. Corey fought down the temptation to look at his watch.

"Here's your phone, Ken. Why don't you make that call now? said Wes as he tossed the cell phone to Corey.

Corey deftly fumbled the catch and the phone clattered to the polished pine floor, popping open, and spilling its battery. It landed squarely in front of Walt, who picked up the three pieces and set them on the coffee table.

"Gordie and I are wondering how it is that there are no numbers in your cell phone. Mr. Benson," Wes asked with mocking politeness.

"What?" said Corey reaching across the table to pick up the damaged phone. "Oh, Hell," he said studying the front of the phone. This isn't my phone! It's the one I bought for my daughter in LA. I must have picked up the wrong one when I left the car up the hill."

Corey was so pleased with his explanation, he almost believed it himself. But, just to settle the obvious doubts on the faces of Wes and Gordie, he quickly reached in his pocket and tossed the car keys to Wes. "Here, perhaps your man would be good enough to go back up the hill and get my phone? It's on the front seat. Even better, I'll go along and bring the Lincoln down."

"Sit down Ken! Walt, go with Gordie!" snapped Wes.

"Thanks," said Corey. Now, how about a refill?" He was feeling totally confident now. It was just himself and Wes. Of course, Wes had a gun, and time was on Wes's side. Walt was the only one who might have ever seen Corey, and he'd been diverted. And, besides, that was ages ago, when Corey was clean-shaven and wore a uniform. At best, he figured he had ten minutes before Gordie and Walt came back, having found no second phone in the Lincoln. But, maybe Ben's team would in place by then, or they might intercept Gordie and Walt. There had been no sign of the Mexican supplier. Had the Spider been here and left, or had the delivery really been delayed? He had to know!

"Look, goddamn it, Wes, let's stop the fucking games. You've got my money, and we both know that those pelts are here. You and I both have more important things to do. I need to be on my way to LA as soon as possible. You screw up my daughter's birthday, and I assure you this will be a one-time deal!"

"I don't like you, Ken! So, if it's all the same to you, we'll play this my way. You're right, the pelts are here. And, in a few minutes, Gordie will be back with your phone. You'll call your daughter in LA. Everybody will be happy and you can be on your way. And, frankly, I don't give a flying fuck if this is a one-time deal. The only thing that would make me happy right now is to smash this across your fucking face," growled Wes, pulling a snub-nosed 38 out of his shoulder holster and waving it menacingly in Corey's face. "So, just sit down and shut up!"

Corey sat down, but he knew if he shut up, he'd lose what little advantage he had.

"Will you just count the goddamn money while we're waiting, so I can get going when they get back. I don't like being around you any longer than I have to either!"

"I don't need to count the money! Wes hissed. "What you need to do is shut up, and start thinking about how you're going to look at the bottom of the Gila river in that Lincoln of yours if you don't have a daughter in LA! It's a goddamn shame the highway department doesn't fix that curve up by the dam. Can you believe it? We lose an average of three tourists a year on that fucking curve!"

At that moment, something came over Corey. He was actually enjoying this, despite the ominous muzzle of the 38 staring at his face. He'd spent the better part of two years waiting to bust this sonofabitch, and by God, he was going to enjoy it! Throwing caution to the winds, and relishing the stunned expression that came over Wes's face, Corey shot back, "Yeh, I can just see the headlines now: WES TURNER CONVICTED IN THE DEATH OF FEDERAL AGENT COREY PINGREE."

The blood momentarily drained out of Wes's face and his body went slack. And, then, just as rapidly, his pallid color was replaced by the flushed purple of apoplectic rage. "You! You, fucker! His body stiffened, and he raised his arm pointing the gun directly at Corey's face not three feet away.

"THAT WOULD BE A REALLY BIG MISTAKE!" came Ben's soft voice from the doorway. Wes wheeled toward the voice and fired. At that moment, Corey dove at Wes wrapping his arms around his chest, and felt a searing pain shoot through his left arm. Only then did he hear the second shot, or was it an echo? Ben had dropped and fired in one smooth motion, his single bullet taking a chunk out of Corey's wrist before tumbling on into Wes Turner's chest. Wes never had a chance to get off a second shot, after his first ineffectually tore huge splinters out of the knotty pine doorframe inches above Ben's head.

Ben was in a near state of shock, himself, as he wrestled apart the two bleeding figures staining the huge white bearskin rug. "Jesus Christ, man, are you all right?" he kept saying to Corey, who looked like he was ready to pass out.

"I think so," said Corey, thinly. "Thanks partner, your timing was beautiful! Mine was a bit slow."

Ben went to work on Corey's arm to stop the bleeding, while the rest of the team rushed in and roughly pried the 38 out of Wes's hand. But, Wes Turner was too far gone to have pulled the trigger again. Ben's single shot had apparently found whatever shriveled excuse the man had for a heart.

Corey looked curiously at the figure whose life's blood was staining the remains of a creature he'd either killed or had killed. Was it fitting or a sacrilege? He was feeling too woozy to figure it out. He strangely wished that Ben hadn't shown up just when things were about to be finally resolved between the two of them. He looked away, and saw the shattered Rolex on the edge of the rug. "Damn!" he muttered. Ben was still applying pressure to his arm, as Corey passed out.

Ben proved to be a thorough planner with an ambulance and an Air Evac helicopter standing by ten miles up the road at Painted Rock Dam. Corey woke up to a room full of every kind of federal agent, Customs, ATF, Fish and Wildlife, along with a few assorted State of Arizona law enforcement types searching the premises. Walt and Gordy were secured somewhere outside. Corey could hear the sound of a helicopter arriving, and vaguely wondered if it was for him or for Wes. One look at Wes, still lying on the rug, and he knew it was for him.

"Look, Ben, I'm okay, just a little dizzy, I don't need a helicopter," Corey was adamant. "Besides, I want to talk to Walt."

"Your dizzy because you've lost a lot of blood, Corey, and your arm may be badly damaged. So, I'm calling the shots here, and I say we've had enough heroics for a while. Oh, and by the way, thanks for introduction, finally. I think, however, that headline may have to be rewritten! I'll have to say that I'd sort of guessed who you were some months back. You're a pretty famous guy in this business. Just for the hell of it, I tried to find you once, and discovered that you'd quit your job and disappeared. It was fun thinking that you were right here with us, that the bureaucracy was serious, and that maybe we were really going to get these guys!"

The next day, Ben and Corey were sitting in the solarium of the Good Samaritan Hospital in Phoenix. Corey, his left arm heavily bandaged and elevated, and his right arm still receiving a transfusion, was listening to Ben's recap of the previous night's events. They'd found the pelts and Quintana at the boathouse. The Spider was out cold from booze or drugs, probably both. Ben ended by saying that he was putting Corey in for a distinguished service citation.

"You're either a damn fool or the coolest customer I've ever met," he said. "You know, I thought for a millisecond of not distracting Wes, just so I could see what your next move would be!"

"Ben, I didn't have a next move. Boy, did we misjudge him! I never figured he'd be wearing a gun, let alone pull it. I guess I was going to try to talk him out of it by letting him know that the cabin was surrounded. But, when I saw the hate in his face, I realized he was going to pull the trigger. I owe you, Ben."

"You don't owe me a thing;" it's the other way around. I've been replaying those two seconds ever since. I'm so damn sorry! I know they operated on your wrist last night and understand you may have to have another?"

"Yeh, maybe, it's a wait and see situation. Look, I know that you have mountains of paperwork waiting on all of this, but I wonder if you could do me a favor before you leave?"

"Just name it! You want some recovery time out at the line shack?"

"No, but that's not a bad idea, I'll take a rain check on it. For now, could you find a copy of yesterday's *USA Today*. There's an article in it that I didn't finish."

Corey's call to Amanda Cousins, at the *Springfield News Leader* was unproductive. He left a message asking about Zachary Taylor's condition, and asking her to call back. The call back, two hours later, was little better. Flooded with calls from people who thought they knew Zach, thought they might have served with Zach, wanted to know Zach, or were looking to be quoted in her next article, Amanda's patience with the public had worn thinner than Prudy's smile each time she walked by the administrator's door on her way to sit at Zach's bedside . She had been sitting with Zach every day since he'd taken a turn for the worse with double pneumonia. Amada wasn't feeling very charitable at the moment.

"I see you're calling from the Phoenix hospital, Mr. Pingree. Just what is your relationship to Mr. Taylor?" she asked trying hard to copy Prudy's officious manner.

"We're friends. I'm just calling to find out how he's doing," said Corey.

"Oh really! And how long have you two known each other?" Amanda said coolly.

"We met two or three years ago," Corey replied. "Can you please tell me how he's doing? Is he out of the coma yet?"

"I suppose the two of you met in a Phoenix bar?" Amanda said in a mocking voice that sounded like she was getting ready to hang up.

"Huh? I wasn't aware that Zach had been to Phoenix. No, actually, we met in the Ponca Wilderness Area, just south of you. Look, perhaps if you could just give me the number of the hospital?"

Amanda's phone was half way to its cradle on her desk, when she heard Ponca Wilderness. She snapped it back to her ear so fast, her head was ringing. "Would you repeat that please?" she said.

"Look, Zach and I only met once, but I think he'd tell you, if he could, that we have a very special kind of relationship. Now, please, tell me, is he going to make it?"

"No!" said Amanda, "I don't think he's going to make it. Not unless you believe in miracles," she said with an audible catch in her throat.

"I'll be there the day after tomorrow, " said Corey. "Oh, by the way, Ms. Cousins, I really do believe in miracles. In fact, I just saw one yesterday!"

Amanda Cousins sat staring at her phone for a very long time. She'd been working on a follow-up story about Zach when she heard the message from Corey Pingree. It was his voice, not his message that had finally convinced her to call back. And it was the voice that wouldn't allow her to get back to her story. She'd gleaned gobs of information over the phone during the past two days. Some of it was clearly legitimate, like the little girl from Wichita, and much of it was just as obviously bogus. All of it, however, made for a good story. But, from Corey Pingree's few words, she somehow suspected that he held the key to the real story about Zachary Taylor.

27

DEATH OF AN UNKNOWN

Amanda was asleep in the chair beside Zach's bed when Corey slipped quietly into the darkened room. The gaunt figure on the bed, waxy yellowish skin, cleanly shaven, breathing loudly through an oxygen mask, looked nothing like the Zach he remembered. Not sure if he was in the right room, he turned to open the door and check the room number when he noticed the corkboard covered with cards, all reading: "Dear Zach." There were get well cards from all over the country — there must have been close to a hundred. His eye caught two, side by side. One was addressed "Dear Mr. President, please get better, so you can come back to Kansas, We miss you! Love Becky." The one beside it was a picture of a couple standing in front of a rustic cabin, with a dog that looked like Pup's twin. The writing around the margin was in a feminine hand, reading: "We love you Zach, Miro, Mirin, and Cody."

Corey went to the bedside and studied Zach's face. He'd only known Zach with a beard and long hair. Still, he was shocked. His gaze shifted to the woman beside the bed. She looked as though she had been crying, her hair hadn't been combed recently, her face was devoid of make-up, and yet she was beautiful. He sat down across the bed and began to study the face. It was the face of someone who was not young, and not old, strong but sensitive, and clearly very tired. Corey liked what he saw. But, he felt embarrassed at having spied on her while she slept. He coughed and she opened one eye, then quickly the other. They were great blue eyes!

What Amanda saw through those eyes was the carefully trimmed beard and eyes of a man she thought she knew. It was a face she'd seen before, one of the doctors perhaps? No, it was strikingly like the face on the cover of a book she'd been reading about the last Czar, it was the face of Nicholas Romanov — the same sad, penetrating eyes.

"I'm so sorry to have been caught staring," the eyes seemed to say, while the voice simply said: "Hi! I'm Corey Pingree, you must be Amanda." It was not a question. Royalty does not ask questions.

"Did you bring your miracle, Mr. Pingree?" Amanda asked. And, then, as he rose, she noticed his left arm was in a sling. "What happened to your arm?" she inquired solicitously.

"The miracle comes later. The arm is a long story. Let me tell you over dinner. I'm famished and you look like you could use a change of scene. Is there a cafeteria in this place?" he asked.

Amanda was ready to say no thanks, when she realized that she too was famished. She hadn't had a decent meal in days. And, somehow she couldn't see herself saying "No" to Nicholas Romanov! In fact, the Czar had somehow moved around the bed and extended his hand to her. In her still sleepy state she wasn't quite sure what she was supposed to do with that imperial hand.

"The cafeteria is closed. Do you like Korean?" she asked, grasping his hand. His grip was firm, lingering perhaps a full second longer than was necessary.

"Your choice," Corey said simply. "I'm afraid you're driving. I took a taxi from the airport."

Ah, the commoner's touch, Amanda mused, the chauffer and limousine would be bound to bring out the Springfield paparazzi.

"It's just down the street," she said. "I'd like not to be gone long," she added. The way she said it had an ominous ring, like she knew that Zach didn't have long to live. That coincided with Corey's prognosis on his first look at Zach.

Over dinner, Amanda explained that Zach had back been in intensive care until yesterday. At first, she'd thought that the move back to his room signaled the miracle she'd hoped for. But then, her friend,

Ruth Ann, explained that the hospital had no way to justify keeping him on the equivalent of life support. There were no next of kin to request it, and it was probably just making him more uncomfortable anyway. Zach had never regained consciousness, since coming in two months ago. He'd been in and out of the ICU twice since then.

"Does anybody know what happened?" Cored asked.

"No. He was found alongside a county road, unconscious and bleeding. They're sure that the blow to the back of his head didn't come from a fall. He was struck by someone or something."

"Has anyone come to see him besides you?" Corey asked.

"Just you," said Amanda. "Do you think that there is anything you could say to him that might register somehow? You said you met him in the Ponca Wilderness. Surely there's something. Please try to think!" she implored.

"I'll try when we get back. He had a coyote that lived with him that he called Pup. Maybe mentioning Pup would get through."

"Well, that's a whole lot more than we've had to work with so far," Amanda said with a note of resignation in her voice.

"There's a woman down in Ponca that he'd talked with. Perhaps her voice might register with his subconscious," Corey mentioned, as he was trying to think of other possibilities.

"If you mean Miss Lucy Duckworth, I'm afraid were out of luck there. She recently suffered a stroke. I missed seeing her by a matter of minutes when I went down to Ponca. I've since checked with her nursing home and found that she's too frail to travel. They say her speech is so slurred she refuses to talk to anyone."

"Oh, I'm sorry, I was planning on going down to see her," said Corey.

"I suppose you'd take a taxi?" Amanda said looking at his sling.

"No, I was thinking you might like the drive," Corey shot back. "Tell me, how did you make the Ponca connection?"

"Like your arm, that too is a long story. I flew out to the Portland VA hospital and talked to a doctor who knew him many years ago. The good doctor seemed to have this crazy idea that the reason the bureaucracy keeps records is to use them for the benefit of the rest of us!"

"What a quaint notion!" said Corey. "I think I might like him! I don't suppose his records told you anything about Zach's family?"

"He doesn't seem to have a family. Dr. Norton believes that Zach is, at least partly, Nez Perce, based on where he was inducted into the Marines. But, please, tell me how you happened to meet Zach."

"I didn't. That is, I didn't happen to meet him. I'd gone looking for him." Over the next hour, Corey related the story of his sister, Sarah, and her death on the Buffalo, and how Zach witnessed it. He described, with caring detail, their encounter on the bluff, Zach's openness in showing the cave, his affection for Pup, and his admiration of Miss Lucy.

"You probably aren't aware of what's happened to his cave," Amanda cut in, "but it's no longer like you remember it. Apparently, Zach left it over a year ago, and it has since been vandalized and had to be sealed by the Park Service."

"How, can that be? It doesn't make sense," said Corey. "That cave was almost impossible to find! And where has Zach been all those months?"

"I've got some local press clippings about the cave that you might want to see. But, where Zach's been is a mystery that I've been piecing together since my article started to get widely distributed. I've only been able to follow up on a few of the cards that have come to the hospital, but I'd say that for some reason, Zach headed out on a trip across the country. I've pinned him down at a number of spots on the map with approximate dates. He spent last Thanksgiving with a trucker's family near Wichita. After that he apparently spent some time on a prison work gang out of Phoenix. Say, that's right! You called me from Phoenix! Any connection?"

"Sorry! I wish there had been," replied Corey. "But, at that time, I was living in a cliff dwelling in New Mexico and wondering about Zach. I can't imagine how anyone could have put that gentle soul in prison!"

Amanda studied her plate, bemused by the incongruity of a Russian Czar living in a cliff dwelling in New Mexico. Deciding that she couldn't deal with any more mysteries at the moment, she looked up and said, "I think we need to get back to the hospital. Maybe you'd like to tell me about your arm on the way?"

Corey's greatly abridged version of getting accidentally shot, left Amanda with more questions than answers. But, since none had anything to do with Zach, they weren't questions she had any interest in pursuing. Tomorrow, when she got back to her desk at the paper, she'd do a little internet research on Mr. Corey Pingree!

Back at St. Jude's they both tried to rouse some reaction from Zach, mentioning Pup and Miss Lucy without response. Amanda thought she saw a slight eyelid flutter when she told Zach that Corey was here, but she couldn't be sure.

For some reason not worth thinking about, Amanda wanted to keep Corey around until Ruth Ann came on duty at 9:00 PM.

"Why don't you just try talking to him," she suggested. Maybe the sound of your voice could be the miracle," she said hopefully. "I've tried reading all of those cards to him, but he doesn't know my voice. You could try reading them to him—please?"

Instead, Corey sat down by the bed, took Zach's hand in his own, and started telling him the story of how they met, repeating the few words they spoke, and describing in detail his wonder at all he saw inside the cave. Amanda sat entranced, listening not just to the story and the description of the cave, but the tenderness in the voice of the man telling the story. How could this be the same man who, just four days ago, have been shot during a sting operation a thousand miles away?

They looked up together to see Ruth Ann pausing in the bright light of the opening door.

"Okay, kids, time to go home," Ruth Ann said. Then looking Corey right in the eye, she added, "Do I know you?"

Corey introduced himself as a friend of Zach's, and asked to be called at the Airporter anytime day or night, if there should be any change in Zach's condition. Ruth Ann pulled Amanda aside after Corey left the room.

"Honey, there's lots of room at my place. He doesn't need to stay way out there at that drafty old airport inn!"

"That would be *your* dream!" said Amanda.

Amanda dropped Corey at the Airport Inn and went reluctantly back to her apartment, exhausted, head swimming with questions she was too tired to even try putting into words.

During dinner with Amanda, Corey had become painfully aware that he hadn't taken one of the pills they'd given him since leaving Phoenix. As much as he would have liked to visit longer with Amanda, she seemed ready to leave, and with the pain pills in his hotel room, it sounded like a good idea. But, she was a puzzle. Did she get this involved with all of her stories? Aside from the Amanda question, which kept pushing all the others back, he tried to prioritize the growing list of questions about Zach: Why did Zach leave? Why come back? How did he get so badly injured?

Corey could understand why he might have been on the prison work gang. As a drifter, himself, he knew how easy it was to be treated as a social problem needing to be swept out of sight. And, he could easily understand how Zach might have made so many friends during his travels. Zach was likable, if a little off-putting at first. The most important question he wanted to tackle was what happened that put him in the hospital? Why would anyone hurt harmless Zach? He decided that a visit to the deputy who'd called for the ambulance was his first assignment.

Then, he'd go visit the site where Zach was found. Drifting off to sleep, Corey realized the most interesting puzzle he needed to solve was the puzzle of Amanda Cousins.

Luck! Pure fool's luck, Corey concluded over breakfast the morning after arriving in Springfield; that's what had saved him. There wasn't the slightest doubt in his mind that Wes Turner would have pulled the trigger. In fact, he did, but fortunately Ben had distracted him. No doubt there was some adrenalin along with the luck. Wes had triggered the adrenalin, but where does the luck come from? Why did he seem to have it all, when people like Zach never had any? Even his sister, Sarah, seemed to be plagued by a string of bad luck.

When he looked in the bathroom mirror earlier, he was planning to shave off the beard and mustache. They just weren't him, even though it was a distinct improvement over the past two years as a bearded drifter. That's when he started thinking about luck. Maybe the beard was lucky? Without the beard, Wes might have identified him. After all that was part of the plan, and maybe he'd be in the morgue now, alongside Wes. The beard, or the sling, or maybe both, got him the upgrade to first class. Maybe he was imagining it, but Amanda, and her friend Ruth Ann, seemed intrigued by the beard. He decided to keep the beard, for a while, at least. And, he decided to call Amanda and ask her to join him for breakfast. Don't mess with Lady Luck, when she's smiling your way!

Fifteen minutes later, Corey looked up, from studying his reconstituted hash browns, artificial scrambled eggs, and extruded sausage links, to see Amanda coming toward his table. There was certainly nothing artificial about that smile and that walk.

"So, Mr. Corey Pingree, do you have a plan for the day?" she asked extending her hand.

It was the first time Corey had seen her smile. He got up from his seat and helped her to hers. Along with Ben's smile when he came into the hospital room, Amanda's was only the second smile he could remember seeing in a very long time. Maybe he was feeling smile deprived? But, surely that smile was more than anyone deserved to see at breakfast!

"As a matter of fact, I do, Ms. Cousins. And, it involves you, I hope you don't mind?"

"Me or my car?"

"As another matter of fact, I **am** in need of a driver," said Corey, holding up his left arm. "I'd pay extra for someone who knows her way around these Ozark roads!"

The waiter came by the table with a steaming coffee pot and a menu. "Good Morning, Ms. Cousins," he said, clearly enchanted by that same smile.

"Nothing for me, Andy," she said waving off the menu with a sympathetic smile in Corey's direction noting his barely touched plate.

"It's not really that bad," said Corey, "compared to airplane pretzels and cliff house food! Say, you seem to be pretty well known around here," he added.

"I do occasional special features on public television, Amanda explained. "You've got my curiosity up on cliff dwellings; maybe there's a story there? But, first, let's hear your plan?"

"I thought I'd like to see the spot where they found Zach, and talk with the deputy who called for the ambulance," Corey explained. "After that, maybe talk with the head ranger on the Buffalo about the vandalism. If he's still the same one as a few years ago, his name is Seth Greer. He's a very nice guy! There's probably no connection between the vandalism and Zach, but it's a possibility I need to set aside."

"I can tell you that we did a story on Seth Greer a while back. He's the new superintendent of the Buffalo. I'll dig up a copy for you," Amanda offered. "As for the first two items on your list, I talked with the deputy — name's Frank Erbe. He's pretty upset about his role in this. He saw an old white Ford van earlier that night, down the road, and he blames himself for not turning around and going after it. It had only one head light, but he was in a hurry to get home.

It was the only other car on the road, and he thinks they might have had something to do with Zach, or at least they may have seen something, like Zach walking. I told him that he'd done the right thing. Otherwise, Zach might not have been found until morning, and by then, it would have been too late.

Frank went back the next day and picked up a few things in addition to the backpack. They're down at the sheriff's office, but there isn't much: a few battered road maps, a poncho, a couple pair of socks, no money, a couple of water bottles, a bag of oatmeal and another of raisins. There'd been a hard rain, so it was a pretty soggy mess. Something was written in pen on the front of the maps but it was illegible."

Corey was a good listener. He waited to see if Amanda's review might get her to recall anything else. She finally gave him a puzzled look. He was deep in thought.

"What is it?" she asked.

"Did anyone put out an APB on the white van?" he wondered half aloud, "Old white Ford van, one headlight. How about an appeal to the public for help?"

"Yes, the sheriff did, but nothing turned up. It may not have even been registered for years. That's a real possibility in the hills!" she added. "I thought about putting something on the air asking if anyone might remember seeing a vehicle that fits that description. Do you think it's too late?" she asked.

"No, but it's a police matter," replied Corey. "What about the admitting physician's report, do you think your friend, Ruth Ann, could get us a look at it?"

"Sure, but I don't see how it could help?"

"Probably can't. I'm just a curious sort,"

"Well, now you've got me curious. I'd call Ruth Ann, but she's probably just getting to sleep and would bite my head off."

What Amanda knew, was that Ruth Ann would quiz her unrelentingly about Corey, and she wasn't in the mood for her horny friend's innuendos.

"So, you think like a cop." Are you a federal agent of some kind? Is that how you got in the middle of a shoot out in Arizona?"

Corey explained how, for the last two and half years, he'd been working as an undercover agent with the US Fish and Wildlife Service in the Southwest. But, over the course of next two hours and several cups of coffee, he mostly talked about the wonder of the high desert and the red bluff country he'd come to love so much that he would never have left except for Amanda's piece in *USA Today*.

So, you'll be going back soon?" she asked.

"Just as soon as I can," he answered directly, feeling decidedly homesick from his own descriptions of the land.

"That good, huh?" Amanda commented just as directly, coloring, and immediately wishing she'd said nothing.

Corey stopped daydreaming about Amanda and the rain check he'd got from Ben on the line shack, and looked at her face just in time to see the smile drain away and be replaced by her down-to-business look as she stood up saying, "Well, times a-wasting. Let's get going on your plan for the day. But, first let's go check on Zach, okay?"

As they walked by the administrator's open door, Prudy called out, "Amanda, can I see you a minute, please?"

The look on Prudy's face was even more unsettling than her use of the word "please."

"Ruth Ann has been trying to reach you for hours. She wanted to tell you that Zachary Taylor died during the night," Prudy said matter-of-factly, adding almost as an afterthought, "I'm sorry!"

"Goddamnsonofabitch!" Amanda sobbed and turned to Corey, burying her face in his chest. She felt his chest heave with her own silent sobs as she implored him: "Please, get me out of here!"

Ruth Ann was perplexed. Amanda's phone answering message was not the usual cheery set of helpful instructions. It had been replaced by a terse, almost rude, "Call me back in a couple of days, I'm out of town!" The voice was Amanda's, but it was definitely not her best!

She'd been calling off and on since 7:00 AM, always getting the usual message, and leaving a short note for Amanda to call back as soon as possible. There had been no call back, and now the message had been changed. She called the hospital, and talked to the day nurse in Zach's ward. No, no one had seen Amanda today. It was now 7:00 PM. Where could she have gone? Ruth Ann thought about calling the Airport Inn but couldn't remember Corey's last name.

Amanda had driven Corey back to her apartment.

"Please, she said, don't leave me alone right now!"

The two of them sat and talked for hours. Corey reminisced about Zach and Pup and the cave. Amanda cried some more as she told him what she'd learned from Doctor Norton — the story of a young man seemingly without family or friends, all alone in a world he didn't understand.

They argued, at times heatedly. Corey had lost all interest in focusing on Zach's death. His plan for the day was discarded. Zach was dead. How he died now seemed almost immaterial. In fact, when did Zach really die? Did he die on a county road in Missouri? Didn't he really die all those years ago in Vietnam?

"I think I'd like to go see your Dr. Norton," he said, adding, "I'm more interested in Zach's life story than his death story!"

"Well, I'm sorry!" Amanda flared back, grieving over Zach's death, and his having been left to die all alone. "I can't just walk away from what happened here. What if that white van killed him? Don't you want to see them pay?"

"Of course I do, Amanda. But, that's your story, and you need to finish it. And, now you can do it. The public wants to know what happened. You can see that from all the messages he's received. Zach belongs to them now! Your story needs to include the mystery of his death. Maybe someone will come forward. Do it! Please do it!" Corey implored.

"I intend to," said Amanda. "But right now, let's drop it for a while, okay? Let me fix you something. I can top that breakfast you never finished. How about some Thai stir fry with a salad and beer?"

Corey busied himself examining Amanda's bookshelves, while she filled the apartment with the tantalizing aroma of a stir fry that awakened hunger pangs he hadn't heard from in years.

"Why don't you pop open a couple of beers, and call your friend at the Buffalo while I finish this? she suggested.

"Good idea! The beers, that is," he said heading for the refrigerator. "But, I need to think about that call. It'll just open a lot of sad memories, and I don't want to get talked into coming down for a visit.

"I guess I'd prefer to remember things the way they were. I'm sure that's what Lucy would prefer as well. You know, I doubt that Greer ever knew that I'd visited Zach at his cave, unless Lucy told him, which I doubt."

Over a lunch that didn't disappoint either Corey's taste buds or his hunger pangs, he told Amanda about canoeing the Buffalo with Lucy, and what a remarkable asset she was to the Park and to the children of the area. Corey's bittersweet memories of his brief time at the Buffalo, the loss of Sarah, his discoveries of Zach and Lucy, the winey aroma of the Buffalo River Valley in fall, combined with the magic of this moment, had him talking nonstop. He realized that the long months of silence at the line shack had made him hunger for someone to talk to. But, he also knew that Amanda was not just "someone!"

In the middle of relating how Lucy had struggled over whether to tell him about Zach, Corey looked up into Amanda's blue eyes that smiled even when her mouth didn't, and he said, "You have no idea how much I wish things were different. I would have loved for you to meet her, and to see Zach's cave, and to have really known Zach. But, none of that is possible now! I just hope your story will include the description of the cave that I gave you. That way, Lucy might read it, and know that you and I talked. I think she'd be pleased."

Amanda caught the sadness in Corey's voice, and reached across the table to hold his hand. She squeezed hard. It felt good. She smiled and he squeezed back. It was a smile as inviting as a desert sunset! Amanda and Corey spent the next two hours making love, falling in love, knowing love, and finding love in ways that neither had ever known, or imagined! It was love in search of new life where the old had been severely jolted by death. Through passion, Amanda could momentarily forget her heartache for Zach. Corey found all that and more, the renewal of a spirit devastated by too many months of living close to meanness and cruelty.

They had known each other less than a day, yet in that brief interlude, they had glimpsed eternity, accepting the inevitability that life goes on and the hope that all is not in vain. Each rediscovered the promise of sharing. Their grief, though still present, found its home in the larger perspective of the magic of living, the necessity for moving on, and even a touch of the humor in life. At one point, gasping for breath, Amanda laughed, wondering out loud, "And what might you be able to do without one arm in a sling?"

Ruth Ann and Amanda finally connected the following morning.

"Where in Hell have you been, girl?" Ruth Ann demanded. "I gather you know about Zach?"

"Please tell me he wasn't alone." Amanda implored.

"No. He wasn't alone, at least no more so than he's been for the past nine weeks. He never came out of the coma."

"What will happen now?" Amanda asked.

"Cold room." Ruth Ann said. "At least until the police decide if there is going to be any further investigation. After that, I don't know.

Now, tell me what's happening with that beautiful man you were with?"

"Oh, he left this morning. Portland, I think," Amanda said casually.

But, Amanda was feeling anything but casual. For the last hour, she'd been mentally replaying their parting. "I hope you'll think only good thoughts of me?" she'd said, blushing, as they hugged their good byes.

"He laughed. "How could I think otherwise of the woman I plan to spend the rest of my life with?"

28

LETTING GO

The story was a gem! Maybe even a prize winner. It had been rerun by just about every major newspaper in the country. The Stone County sheriff's office had been flooded with over a hundred tips on old white Ford vans. Amanda Cousins was, likewise, flooded with not just requests for follow-up stories about Zach, but with a dozen offers of jobs from newspapers and television stations all the way from both coasts and north to Alaska! She had read a draft over the phone to Corey's acclaim. He only asked that she refer to him simply as a friend of Zach's, not by name, which added a further note of mystery to the enigma of Zach Taylor that, almost overnight, captured the hearts of veterans and anyone who loved a real-life mystery.

During the last two weeks, Corey and Amanda had several long talks about Zach, about the white van and the sheriff's investigation, and about what was to happen with Zach's body. Several veterans groups, along with their elected representatives, were adamant that Zach must be buried with honors at the Missouri State Veteran's Cemetery. Privately, both Amanda and Corey felt that returning Zach's ashes to the Buffalo would be more appropriate, but they knew there wasn't a chance. That was where Zach had been heading when he was killed. He was going home! Amanda left little doubt about that in her reporting of Zach's lengthy visit with Miro and Mirin in Oregon. For their own reasons, like Corey, they, too, had asked that their names be omitted from her story. The fact that he was headed home to certain disappointment, with the cave now sealed by the Park Service, wasn't lost on the readers!

Zach's final year of travels across the country, seemed to arouse an intensity of human interest, exceeding even that of his life in the wild, or his artistry with a whittling knife, or his mysterious death, and the blank pages of his earlier years. Amanda had captured the paradox of this gentle soul from the wild having been treated as a vagrant in a way that would bring a tear to the eye of the most hardened reader. Zach was not just a soul lacking memory, but one deprived of everything that goes along with having a memory: beautiful moments of nostalgia, the comfort of having roots, of belonging to a special place; the mellow familiarity of knowing your beliefs; the joys of having loved and been loved. Amanda's readers were subtly left to decide whether they could live easier as Hale's "Man Without A Country," or as a man with no memory of his country or of ever having fought for that country.

The little vignette, provided by Joe Figuroa, whose name and telephone number Amanda had been able to retrieve from the sodden maps found near Zach's backpack, had been the hardest for her to write. Joe, in return for anonymity, had provided her with details that only another sensitive insider could have known; of a man whose only possession, his identity, was his freedom. To lose his freedom, after having already lost his memory, would have broken most men. In Zach, Joe saw the raw material of greatness, the one thing that no one could ever take from him, his dignity. Joe expected to be forever haunted by what Zach might have been, by what his country had most certainly lost.

As her story developed, Amanda came to realize what Corey had sensed at the outset. The mystery that was Zach would only be diminished by drawing attention to the few individuals who had barely touched his life. The absence of names, except for Miss Lucy's and Becky Capp's, could only accentuate the starkness of Zach's aloneness while surrounded by millions!

The portrait of Corporal Zachary Taylor as drawn by Amanda Cousins was not just bigger than life. Amanda's Zach had somehow exposed the pain of a generation of Americans who needed real human closure to match the scale of The Wall—something bigger than death, some uncluttered symbol of the thousands more who survived, though damaged, each in their own way. For every letter she received following her first article, the second piece on Zach's death generated a hundred more! The *News-Leader* hired extra staff to cope with the flood. Amanda was pressured daily to write a book focusing on the heartbreak in the letters. She found herself on the verge of celebrity status, and she hated it. She would not use Zach for her own gain. She would not become the spokesperson for a man she never spoke with. She knew she had to get away or risk becoming someone other than the person she was comfortable with!

Every phone visit brought Corey and Amanda closer in their appreciation of each other's lives. It was as though each had vowed to avoid any discussion of their only day together. The more she learned of his devotion to his sister, Sarah, and of his love of nature, the more she felt assured that his parting comment was sincere, at least at the moment. The more he learned of her self-confidence in the face of a difficult childhood with alcoholic parents, and her single-minded drive to become a writer, the more he realized that blustering his intentions that day may have been honest but not exactly as honest as admitting that he was rushing away for no good reason other than to give them both time to recover from the tornado that had swept up their lives. Without saying so, neither of them chose to regret that day, but both were trying to see if the romance of a lifetime could be built from the passion of the moment.

Corey's visit to the Northwest had been disappointingly unproductive. His visit with Hugh Norton at the VA Hospital, and then at dinner with his wife, Constance, was well worth the six days he'd spent travelling back and forth across northern Oregon. Without his knowledge, Amanda had set things up for him by telephoning the good doctor to alert him to a visit by one of her colleagues who was working with her in pursuing the Zach Taylor story. Corey's request to see Zach's file was treated as a legitimate press inquiry. The patient, regrettably, was dead, and there was precious little nonmedical information to share anyway. In a matter of days, the file would be archived. So, in Hugh Norton's philosophy, anything anyone could do to shed a little light on Zach's story was all to the good. Hugh had taken an immediate liking to Corey, and he obviously wanted to talk outside the confines of the office. Corey remembered Amanda's description of Hugh as a man with little patience for the bureaucracy's rules, so he arrived prepared to like the man. Over a simple dinner, almost totally produced from Constance's garden, Corey began to look at the devoted couple with guarded envy. Their life together seemed to be storybook idyllic. If he closed his eyes, he could almost see himself and Amanda in the way they looked at each other. Outrageous as he knew it was, he was audacious enough to ask how long they'd known each other. "Forever" they replied in unison. "Well, honestly," Constance said, "it's only been fifteen years. Life before then, seems to belong to someone else. Perhaps, you find that hard to understand?" she asked.

"No, not in the least," Corey replied. "I'm beginning to feel the very same way!"

"Might I presume to wonder if that has anything to do with a young lady named Amanda Cousins?" Hugh smiled, perceptively.

Over brandy in Hugh's den, Corey learned of Hugh's suspicions about the blow to the back of Zach's head. He'd already retrieved the designation of Zach's unit in Vietnam, and the induction information from Joseph, Oregon. Corey didn't really want to open old wounds and spend months researching military records, but he did think he ought to pass it along to Amanda in case she wanted to mention his service connection in her story. There are times when just a passing mention in the press can start information flowing from sources that have been dammed up for years.

He did want to visit Joseph, despite Hugh's previous experience there. But, he doubted that any car rental agency would rent to someone with one arm in a sling.

"Why not take mine?' insisted Constance. "We hardly ever use it, and I'd like to see it get some mileage that's a little better for the engine than just running around town."

The day he arrived in Joseph, Amanda's story had aired and was already getting lots of local attention. Now, contrary to Hugh's experience two decades earlier, Corey found that everybody remembered Zach. Everybody had a story to tell about Zach. And, everybody wanted to be sure that their name got spelled right. Before deciding to chuck the whole thing as a waste of time, and head back to Portland, Amanda encouraged him go over the mountains and see if he could locate Miro and Mirin Kiraly.

The Kiralys, even Cody, were delighted to meet Corey and share memories. Zach's presence was profoundly still there, kept alive by far more than his beautiful carving of the three of them in its candle-lit place of honor on their kitchen table. Corey slept where Zach had slept, in the moss shed. Then, in another day, he was on his way to return Constance's car.

"Where the Holy Hell have you been!" Ben sounded more relieved than aggrieved at hearing Corey's voice over the phone.

"Is your offer of the line shack still open?" Corey asked, sounding appropriately chastised.

"Never mind Silver City! The doctors at Phoenix want to see that wrist!"

"I had a doctor here in Portland look at it," Corey replied, stretching the truth a little.

"What are you doing in Portland? Listen you're still on the Department payroll, you know? There's another job waiting for you if you're interested."

"No way! I'm a civilian and loving every minute of it!"

"Okay, but you are being kept on extended medical leave status until we're sure that the wrist isn't going to need further surgery. The Department is taking full responsibility, and I have a personal stake in this as you may recall, so don't just up and quit. You are coming back here aren't you?"

"Yes, I am. I can't imagine living anywhere else. But, first I need to get back to the Northeast Kingdom to clean up some loose ends."

"Good! Just stay in touch, okay? This job is nothing like the last one, I promise. In fact, it's not even with the same agency. No risk, and the Secretary really wants you on this one!"

"Ben, did you ever sell used cars? Okay, you've got my interest. We'll talk soon, I've got to run and catch a plane to New York. And, by the way, forget the wrist. My new personal physician says that I'm already doing amazing things with it!"

Corey's new personal physician was at her desk on the second floor of the *News Leader* building, glaring at her overflowing in-box, and even more menacingly at the ever-ringing phone. She was not one bit interested in feigning politeness to one more person claiming to have fought with Zach, or one more job offer that she had no intention of considering. She glanced at the caller-ID screen as she reached to shut off the phone. It was a New York area code. She knew no one in New York. On impulse, she answered the call.

"Still answering your own phone! I'm impressed." It was Corey's voice.

"Something in my subconscious remembered you saying that you were going to New York! You were one breath away from getting cut off!" Amanda confessed.

"I'd have just called back, again and again," Corey admitted. "It occurred to me that you probably have never seen northern Vermont in October. Can you take a few days off?"

"Oh, Corey, I'd love to, but . . . . ."

"I thought you might like to see the old homestead before I put it on the market."

"So, you really are serious about the southwest!" Amanda mused aloud. "Okay, I think I've about worn out my welcome with the sheriff, and I'd really like to see the land that did such a good job on you!"

"Tell you what," Corey offered, "just get a one-way ticket to Albany. It's time you got rid of that clunker you're driving. You can have Sarah's Honda Civic if you want to drive it back. I'm going to be driving my pickup back to New Mexico, so I'd just have to let the Honda go with the farm if you don't take it."

III
GRAVE ROBBERS AND GHOSTS

29

THE SKY PEOPLE

The mother and daughter lay in the shadow of the overhanging bluff. Beyond their line of shade, the dessert sun was quietly going about its eternal task of baking the red sandstone to a fine dust. In the distance, tall stone pillars could be seen to have crumbled and collapsed in the unrelenting heat. The two were nearing the end. They had prepared themselves for it. The fact was, they had been close to death all of their short lives. Preparation for death began at birth for the cliff people. It was the price they paid for living in a place of relative security and indescribable beauty.

They lived on the brink, four-hundred feet above the canyon floor. A few years earlier, the girl's younger brother fell to his death while chasing a wooden ball she had rolled to him. Just yesterday, her father had died while going in desperation for water along the narrow crack in the face of the cliff, two water jugs fastened around his waist. Perhaps his toes slipped from the crack greased by a broken egg from a cliff swallow nest above, or, perhaps he succumbed to the heat. He died silently. It was not the Anasazi custom to draw attention to themselves. But, the girl and her mother knew he had died, and with him died all hope for their own survival, barring the miracle of rain to refill the reservoirs of their empty village. Even if the torrents should come, it would be too late! Death had won its prize.

They did not expect rain. It had not rained in recent memory. For many moons, their few neighbors had been trickling away from the village of their forefathers. With each departure, the girl's mother had argued that they should leave too. Her father insisted that the rain god would reward them for having faith. Now, they were the last ones. They had grown thinner with nothing but bat flesh to eat. For months, their only water had come from licking the little bits of morning dew from the cool rocks at the back of the shelter. Even after the always-reliable stream dried up in the valley below, and the giant cottonwoods shading the stream had died, they had been able to get water from the hot spring in the stream bed. Now, it too barely flowed, and the pool was covered with green slime. The water was foul-tasting, but it was wet.

When the father did not come back, the girl's mother began gathering their meager possessions, and moving them to the back wall of the dwelling. She lined up her pots along the wall, in progression from the oldest to the newest. The grain pots were long empty. They hadn't bothered with the rope ladder to the grain fields and the kiva, sixty feet above, since the fields burned up and disappeared in the heat two years ago. Her prize cooking pot, the one she made when their daughter was born, she placed in the middle of the line. It was delicately incised with connected lightning, thereby increasing the heating surface. It had a single v-shaped chip on the rim where, in later years, her daughter had nicked it with her stone knife while cutting dried deer meat. The bottom and sides were smoke stained, but it was treasured for the wonderful aromas it had filled their home with during the good years.

One pot contained the father's arrows. In another she placed all of their beads, and there were many, some strung, some not yet drilled. She spat a turquoise bead from her mouth into the pot. It was the final admission of the loss of all hope.

She gathered up their baskets and nested them neatly in one corner. Then she rolled up the grass mats from the floor, all except one, and leaned them against the back wall, out of habit, to keep them dry. There were no pouches or leather goods of any kind. There was not even much clothing. The leather had been eaten, the clothing burned for a bit of warmth, but mainly to remind the gods they were still alive. The sun went down early beyond their south-facing cliff. She walked stiffly to where her daughter lay on the remaining mat. Lifting the emaciated, barely breathing girl tenderly in the mat, she carried her to the back of the cave where she sat heavily on the bare stone ledge. Once covered with layers of hides and furs, the ledge had been the family bed. Her feather-light charge was lovingly cradled in arms of skin and bone that were once brown and beautiful, and claws that had once been strong sensuous hands for embracing her man, and for making the finest pottery in the village. There was not enough moisture left in the mother's dehydrated body to fill the tear that formed in her barely functioning mind.

The mother crooned a low sweet song, more of a hum rising and falling with her shallow breath. Her lungs had started to shut down weeks ago, but she needed the air, she needed to sing, despite the wracking pain in her chest. She needed to give her child music to die with, music to carry her spirit to a better place. She hummed the songs of her people, the Sky People, and their love of the land. She was singing the songs that the three of them had sung together since the days when the child first spoke. Then, sensing that something had changed, she looked down at her daughter and she began to wail. It was a long, piercing, mournful wail that reverberated off the lonely stone walls becoming a living part of the canyon — and the source of its enigmatic name, Place of the Mournful Wind. When the last of the air was gone from her lungs, she gently kissed her daughter, and without a struggle for breath, began her centuries-long sleep.

Six-hundred years is but a catnap, a flicker of the eyelid, in the geologic time clock of the Southwest. When the orange nylon rope appeared, dangling from the overhanging cliff above, the interior of the dwelling had changed very little. The whitened back wall with its colorful paintings had almost returned to its natural gray. Centuries of dust lay upon everything. But, nothing had been disturbed. And when the intruder inevitably arrived, descending the colorful rope, what he would see was a place where time had, with little exaggeration, stood still awaiting his hopefully reverent disbelief. And then, when his first words desecrated the spirit of the place, change could only follow obscenely fast:

"Gordy, get your fat ass down here! You won't believe your goddamn eyes!"

By the time Gordy arrived, Tim was already at work pulling apart the dried out baskets, and dumping the contents of the clay pots on the floor of the dwelling. Gordy was left to his own devices to swing himself into the cavernous entrance. And, when he did, his reaction was equally erudite. "Christ a' mighty, Tim, we've hit the fuckin' jackpot!"

Gordy's glance fell to the opposite corner from where Tim was methodically tearing things apart in his search for obvious wealth, gold and jewels.

"Whoa, what's this?" he yelled to Tim. "Looks like mummies, don'tcha think?"

Six-hundred years of dry dessert air had, indeed, mummified the remains of mother and daughter. The few remaining patches of leathery skin and ephemeral hair fell from the skulls as Gordy tossed them, one by one, to Tim. Over time, the two skeletons had slumped, bonding together in death as they had in life. Now, they collapsed into a single pile of bones, those of the daughter indistinguishable from those of the mother, as the looters searched among the bones unsuccessfully for jewelry. Tim walked away, disgusted. "Just take the goddamn skulls, them bones ain't worth a fuckin' thing," he hollered as he went back to searching the rest of the dwelling. In practically no time at all, working silently and swiftly with the hands of practiced looters, the two had roped together all of the unbroken pots, with as much plunder stuffed into them as possible, beads, skulls, arrows, scrapers, baskets, and an assortment of stone and bone ornaments and tools that they didn't understand, but looked like they might bring some decent money.

"The line of suckers for this stuff is fuckin' endless," observed Tim cheerfully.

"Come on," yelled Gordy, already halfway up the orange rope.

Only one pot got smashed, hitting the rock outcrop, as they hauled in the rope. It was the one containing thousands of beads which poured out laughingly to the valley below. Freed from their centuries of dark captivity, the beads produced a momentary rainbow the likes of which the valley had never seen, and would never see again! Gordy let out a stream of curses, while Tim reassured him that there was plenty more where those came from. And, he was right, they had only visited one of the five dwellings in the remote ancient village. Gordy and Tim would be coming back, and soon. The MD-500 was a marvelous helicopter for getting in and out of the dessert wilderness rapidly and without arousing suspicions. And, Gordy Stubbs knew how to use the rules to his own advantage. He was just a struggling businessman shuttling tourists in and out of the wilderness. After all, that's what he'd been doing ever since the Gulf War, and mostly on the other side of the inconvenient line that was the law. That's where the money was!

Ever since his close call with the Turner brothers, Gordy was being much more careful. Jesus! A shootout with the feds! Those jerks were crazy! After that close call, he vowed to work only for himself, no more risks with assholes like those guys! If he'd failed to convince the judge that the brothers had only hired him as a driver one week earlier, he could have lost everything, the Bronco, the chopper, everything! The Turners couldn't have testified that he'd worked on and off for them for years without incriminating themselves. But still, it was too close for comfort! Of course, Gordy knew he was a small fish compared to the Turners, hardly worth wasting time prosecuting. But he also knew there was a part of him that yearned to be a big fish. Just once in his life! It was a side of him that led to risks, seldom very far below the surface, and infinitely more thrilling than anything he'd ever known, including sex! The Gulf

War had given him a bit of that feeling, but it was too short-lived. What a joke! It shouldn't even have been called a war! He needed to get that high back! He needed to be able to see it in the eyes of his wife Erica, and his daughter Angela! He wanted it for them!

Gordy dropped Tim and their loot off at The Pair O' Dice, Tim's and his dad's failed dude ranch twenty miles outside of the tiny village of Coyote and went on to Espanola in time for dinner with Erica and Angela. At dinner, the three of them ceremonially held hands and closed their eyes as Gordy offered a blessing for their food, their health, and for living in the land of opportunity. After dinner he retired to his magnificent den, adorned with Navajo rugs, rustic pine furniture, and his collection of books and maps of the public lands. The public lands! That's where his future lay! It was the world of his childhood where the only rule that mattered was the rule of Finders Keepers. Only a damn fool would leave something valuable for the next person to take! The tall Anasazi pot beside his desk, filled with rolls of public land maps, stood in silent testimony to Gordy's philosophy.

One more trip to the remote cliff top in the bright red chopper, and the partners had completed their work. The loot from the last four of the five dwellings was considerably less than from the first. There were no more skeletons and far fewer personal possessions to be found.

There were a few earthenware jars and jugs, but none in as good condition as their initial finds. They did find one jar full to the brim with colorful beads of all sizes. An archeologist might have been able to conclude something about the nature of the exodus from the evidence left behind, but the partners destroyed all chances of a scientific investigation. The two adventurers went away with their few relics, feeling cheated out of what should rightfully have been theirs.

Three weeks after the first cliff dwelling had been desecrated Kathleen and Colin Devine were pulled over by the Arizona State Police. Colin was in a hurry to get back to LA, to turn in their rented SUV, and catch their flight back to Dublin. Their extended vacation in the Southwest, with fourteen-month old Duncan, had been exhausting. With Kathleen asleep, and the teething Duncan finally quiet in the back seat, Colin had been carelessly speeding. The trooper, only the second generation out of Ireland himself, was about to let them go with a warning when, glancing into the back seat to be sure that the boy was safely strapped in, he noticed that Duncan was teething on what looked like a child's skull. "And what have you got there, lad," he asked, peering into the darkened back seat, and obviously not making small talk. Kathleen twisted around with difficulty, and let out a gasp.

"Duncan, how did you get that out of its box?" she scolded.

"Is that what I think it is?" asked the incredulous patrolman.

By this time, Colin was unstrapped and had turned in his seat to retrieve the skull from a most unhappy Duncan, and pass it to the officer.

"We were told, by the woman who sold it, that it was authentic Anasazi. It had better be; we paid $250 for it!"

The officer looked at the yellowish-brown skull in disbelief, then, without changing expression, glared at the couple, saying, "I'm going to have to ask you folks to follow me to the police barracks, if you don't mind!" It was not a question.

The wailing Duncan had pretty well shattered the peace of the barracks by the time that separate statements had been taken from his parents, and their SUV thoroughly searched. The only other item of interest was an obviously ancient clay pot, beautifully shaped and meticulously incised all around with a continuous lightning pattern. It had a small v-shaped crack in the rim. But, the crack appeared to be ancient as well. The pot was purchased from the same roadside vendor as was the small skull.

The three tourists were released without charges, and without their two souvenirs, after a forensics expert and an archeologist from nearby Walnut Canyon had been called in. The Park Service archeologist had decided that she also wanted to talk with the couple, once she had read their statements. "Hello, Mr. and Mrs. Devine." She spoke softly so as not to waken the now sleeping banshee in his mother's arms. My name is Renee Marquis. I'm an archeologist with the National Park Service. I'm no expert on Anasazi earthenware prices, but I'd say that you got quite a bargain on the cooking pot. However, I'm afraid that the police aren't going to allow you to keep either of the items you bought from that roadside peddler. At least, not until they have determined that they weren't stolen."

"And how long might that take?" barked the obviously stressed Colin.

"It could take months. I don't really want to predict the outcome," Renee replied. "But from the price you said you paid, $575 for the pot, I'd have to guess that these are stolen items. I am sorry."

"What do you think the pot is worth?" asked Kathleen.

"Anywhere from a few thousand on up," replied Renee. "Personally, I'd call it priceless!"

"So, are we free to go?" grumbled Colin, obviously further stressed by his financial misfortune.

"I gather that you are, said Renee cheerfully. "However, would you mind taking just another moment to look at a road map and see if you can pin down the location of the old peddler and her beat-up pickup truck. You said she was somewhere between Taos and Espanola?"

"I'll try," replied Kathleen, pointing to a spot on the map. "It was on the right side of the road just about halfway. There were half-a-dozen along that stretch, all selling stuff under canvas awnings, and out of the backs of their pickups. I finally got Colin to stop at the last one."

At that point, Duncan awoke with a scream of pain. Undoubtedly, Colin would have liked to do the same!

"Let's get going," he grumbled at his wife. Then, addressing the slender, dark-eyed, young archeologist, and anyone else within earshot:

"That stuff wasn't stolen. You'll be hearing from my barrister!"

30

ON A VERMONT HILLSIDE

Corey regretted saying it as soon as the words were out of his mouth. It was like that stupid parting comment he'd made at the Springfield airport. What was it about Amada that made him act like such a jerk?

She's thinking that I am trying to control her life, make her obligated to me, he thought miserably as he waited for her answer. Damn it, he just wanted to see her. It had been nearly three weeks!

"Sorry, Corey, my editor was trying to get my attention. Now, what were you saying? Oh, Sara's car! Yes, of course. That is so sweet of you! How about the day after tomorrow? I was thinking of going to Albany anyway, I got a really interesting offer from WNYT. I don't suppose you'd know anybody there?"

"No, afraid not. Actually until rather recently, I've been able to keep a healthy distance from you reporter types."

The five-hour drive from the Albany airport to the Northeast Kingdom of Vermont, kept Amanda exclaiming over the brilliant fall colors, the pastoral rolling countryside, the quaint villages, and even Corey's adeptness at driving one-handed.

"I've done it more times than I can remember," he admitted. "Not one-handed, of course. And, no tickets so far! I'm actually using the left hand already. Have to, with the stick shift. Ever drive one?"

Corey explained how his former secretary, Jen Gilmore and her husband Clark, had been using the pickup for the past two years in exchange for keeping it registered and insured. On their return trip to Albany they'd get the Honda registered and checked over for the trip to Missouri. Hopefully, the porcupines hadn't eaten the tires while it was stored in the barn at Island Pond.

They stopped for dinner at the Trapp Family Lodge. Corey was not going to rush this trip! He wanted Amanda to experience Vermont while she was here. And, he particularly wanted her to see the Vermont that had meant something to him as a young man. But Amanda noticed that he seemed different somehow, more reticent than when they first met in Springfield. While they sat waiting for their dinners to be served, she reached across the table and took his hand in hers. "Okay, what's on your mind?" she asked. "Why so quiet?"

"Not quiet," he said, "cautious. I'm trying to avoid saying something stupid, like I tend to do whenever I'm around you."

"Honestly, Corey, I've never heard you say anything stupid!" The smile on her lips told him that she was being totally honest too.

"Okay, then, how about this? I'm nervous about tonight. The farm is pretty Spartan. No, it's pretty rough. I haven't been there in years, it could be falling down for all I know."

"Sounds interesting!" Amanda said. "Is that all, or are you afraid of me?"

True to form, their waitress arrived just in time to hear Corey reply, "I'm more afraid of you than I was of getting shot by that smuggler!"

They both laughed as the waitress pretended not to hear, almost spilling their grilled salmon in the process.

"If it's good enough for you, it'll be just fine for me! You should know that I've slept in some pretty rough places chasing down stories," Amanda reassured him.

"Oh, tell me," Corey raised his eyebrows. "I bet I can top yours. Just last week I slept in a moss shed in Oregon, and over the past two years, I've slept in everything from line shacks and cliff dwellings to park benches and bus stations."

"Ok, you win, but I did sleep in a few sorry shelters when I did the story on the homeless last year."

"Well, there are three bedrooms, so the chances of a leaky roof in all three are pretty slim. However, if a window got broken and the bats got in, it could be pretty bad. Also, we aren't going to get there until well after dark and the electricity is disconnected. So, really, wouldn't you rather stay here tonight and see the old place in all its charm tomorrow?"

"You must have known! Bats are the one thing I'm petrified off, you sly devil!"

If their wild fling in Springfield had been the stuff of romance novels, Corey and Amanda's night at the lodge was a litany of biographical catch-up. Their hunger for really knowing each other revealed a shared yearning for a foundation that was fully as lusty as their physical desire. Both had known lives of powerful family obligations and sorrow, only to be followed by a driving ambition that left little time for romantic interludes that could only be diversions. Family had acquired a connotation of pain, not just for the losses of loved ones, but for the loss of freedom it implied. For Amanda, at least, family had become the "F" word! Corey had been engaged, twice! But both times, it had turned into controlling situations that he couldn't, or wouldn't, deal with. Amanda had lived with a lover for two years, finally breaking the news to him that she didn't see herself as ever marrying, when he took to introducing her as his wife. Amanda fell asleep in his arms, as they both wondered whether there was any truth at all to the old saying about opposites attracting.

"So, do you think that you might like to work in Albany?" Corey asked over breakfast in the inn's coffee shop the next morning.

"No, I really don't think so. But for some strange reason, this is the only offer that I decided to check out," Amanda smiled.

"Do you have an appointment?" Corey asked.

"No, I thought I'd just drop in. You learn a lot more that way! You see, there is this remote chance that I would move to Albany, if I had any friends in the neighborhood."

"I think you'd find that we're all friendly people. The northeast has gotten a bad rap for coldness. Now, the winters! Well, they can be cold!

When I was growing up we expected to have to break the ice of the top of the water pails every morning in the kitchen. That was always my job!"

"Poor little Corey!" laughed Amanda. "I can see him now, with his little red mittens stuck to the frozen pail. Oh my gosh! He just got his tongue stuck too!"

"You think that's funny? It actually did happen, and I've been tongue tied ever since!" Corey shot back in mock irritation.

"Well, your parents only had the two of you, so how cold could it have been?" Amanda said, deciding it was time to change the subject. "So, what did you think of Hugh Norton?"

"He reminds me of our old family doctor. I hope that you get to meet his wife, Constance, some day! I found myself envying their life together. Oops, there I go again. Sorry! Honest!"

"Corey, do you think it might help if I confessed that I'm not ready to make any commitments right now either? But, when I am, you will be the very first to know!"

This time, when Amanda squeezed his hand and smiled, Corey didn't feel the expected sense of panic. Instead, he felt a sense of contentment that he'd never known before.

When they pulled off the paved road, onto the long gravel drive, overgrown with weeds, winding up through a hayfield to the old house and barn, Amanda's breath rushed out in shock:

"Oh no, Corey, do you really have to sell it? It's an authentic living Wyeth!"

"No, I don't. I don't even particularly want to sell it. But, I can't just leave it empty, and let it decay. Come on! Want to see it up close? I'll give you the professional real estate agent tour."

Amanda took the tour in silence. The Cape Cod style farmhouse was, indeed, Spartan. But, it was fully furnished with old, if not necessarily antique, furniture. Alongside the slate kitchen sink, with its single nickel faucet, was a long-handled pump for filling an upstairs tank with icy-cold water from the ancient hand-dug well. The table and chairs were pressed oak and creaky. Everything was neatly in place, even the beds were made in Corey's and Sarah's rooms. Every door was open, except the father's bedroom, which was locked, with the key conveniently resting in the keyhole. Corey unlocked the door and everything was the same, almost unnaturally neat. The only bathroom was on the first floor. The claw foot tub and heavy porcelain sink were badly rust stained, otherwise, everything had the look of having been cleaned and walked away from. Amanda knew there was a story here. What she didn't know was whether or not she wanted to pursue it.

Corey, reached for her hand, and she jumped, so deep in thought had she been about this strange house. His touch jolted her back from the puzzle of its exterior charm and its interior mystery.

"Let's go out to the barn and check on your new car," he said cheerfully. "I noticed the barn door was blown open as we drove up."

"Corey, is your father buried here?" Amanda asked.

"Up on the hill, there's an old family cemetery where my mother, and my father's parents, are buried too. Would you like to see it?"

After they'd checked out the Honda, which had miraculously started on the third try, Corey left it running in front of the barn, and took Amanda's hand to guide her to the cemetery with its rusted gate and headstones tilted askew by the winter's freezing and thawing.

As Corey stood looking at his parent's headstones, Amanda noted the dates: Thomas Pingree, 4/12/31 – 7/17/76; Marie Lafleur Pingree, 7/19/32 – 12/19/60.

Your mother was French?" she asked.

"Uh huh, French Canadian. The border is only thirty miles from here, Corey affirmed. "She was beautiful. I remember her picking flowers and bringing them here every week in the summertime."

"And, who are the Pettigrews?" Amanda wondered, looking at the older, lichen-encrusted marble slabs.

"They're the folks that my grandfather bought the land from. Old Sam Pettigrew built the house and barn back in the mid-1800's. The family is all gone now.

"So, why isn't Sarah buried here?" Amanda asked.

"Well, it was really up to me, and I knew that she was never happy here. She was happiest at Olana, Frederick Church's estate. So, that's where I brought her ashes. I'll take you there when we return to Albany."

Amanda was beginning to think that she was letting her imagination take her to places that were ridiculous. It was just an old New England farmhouse, neglected and slowly dying like so many Ozark farms that she'd seen die around Springfield. And then, Corey added, "She was never happy here, and yet, she was adamant that I should never sell it."

"So, why sell it now?" insisted Amanda.

"I think she always thought of it as a place to come back to and paint someday, if her marriage with Theo didn't work out," Corey said. "That's probably the best thing you can do with an old Vermont farm that's this far north of good skiing!"

"Couldn't you rent it?" asked Amanda.

"There's always a market for buying land in the Northeast Kingdom, but no market to rent. Farming died out years ago, and there's no place to commute to from here! Well, shall we head for the garage in Lyndonville and get your car checked over?" suggested Corey.

"Let's go!" said Amanda. Inexplicably she felt an urgent need to get away from the place that had enchanted her less than an hour earlier.

Following Corey, in Sarah's Civic, Amanda kept going over and over her feelings of near-panic while at the farmhouse. She'd barely been inside the stark old dwelling long enough to recall its layout, yet it was long enough to have planted questions—questions that she couldn't put into words, let alone expect answers from Corey. It was as though the walls were trying to talk to her. But, that was silly. She began to wish that she hadn't been in such a hurry to leave. She felt an enormous mismatch between her warm and lively image of Corey, and his having grown up in a setting so cold and lifeless. Something was missing! The enigma of the place was spreading to her feelings about Corey, reminding her of how little she really knew about him!

Over a late lunch, while the Honda was getting checked over to be sure the field mice hadn't eaten holes in the gas line or the fan belt, she abruptly shared her unease with Corey:

"I had the strangest feeling, Corey, when we were upstairs in your folk's bedroom. Maybe my imagination was running on high, but I had the distinct impression there was a ghost in your father's room."

"No kidding!" Corey smiled. "Could you make out if it was male or female?"

"Now, you're laughing at me, and I don't blame you. But it gave the shivers."

"No, I'm not laughing. In fact, I felt you jump when I took your hand, but I just assumed you were daydreaming," Corey reassured her. "The fact is, the place is haunted, or at least it's reputed to be. And, according to local lore, it's cursed as well. Frankly, I've never seen the ghost, but I've tried to keep an open mind. Sarah claimed to not only have seen her, but to have talked with her many times. Dad said that my mother was obsessed with the ghost. Apparently she only makes contact with females in the house."

"She? Cursed?" Amanda was beginning to feel rather proud of her ability to sense a story worth pursuing, as well as hugely relieved to be rid of the dark thoughts that were beginning to crowd in on her.

"Well, the ghost is supposed to be that of Abigail Pettigrew, old Sam's wife. As the story goes, she shot herself in the bedroom grieving over the loss of her son in the Civil War. No one knows where the curse comes from, but it supposedly damns everyone who lives there to an early death. It does make you wonder when you look at the gravestones. My grandparents, my folks, even Sarah, all died way before their time.

For a long while after Dad died, I thought that, if I ever had children of my own, I'd name them after my folks, Thomas and Marie; sort of give the names a second chance for a full life."

"Oh, Corey, how could you even think of selling a real haunted house? Let's go back, I'm dying, no pun intended, to see if Abigail will talk to me. I want to sleep in your folk's room! Shall we?"

Back at the garage in the center of town, they found the head mechanic, who also doubled as the assistant mechanic and tripled as the owner, just closing the hood on the Honda and scratching his head. "Wouldn't go too far without changing them hoses and belts," he offered in his best Yankee imitation of English.

"How long would that take?" asked Corey.

"Well, guess I'd have to order the parts from St. Johnsbury."

"And how long would that take?" said a smiling Corey.

""Not long at all. Got a telephone right inside!"

"You're Silas Peabody, aren't you?" asked Corey as they followed the owner/mechanic into the cluttered office.

"That's my name. See it? Right there over the door. Do I know you?"

"Probably not, I grew up north of here. Name's Pingree, Corey Pingree."

"You must be Tom Pingree's son," said Silas as he dialed the grease-encrusted phone. "You folks ever want to sell that place up in Island Pond, let me know. Make a damn fine huntin' camp. I been huntin' them fields for years. Sorta keepin' an eye on the place for you," said Silas in between placing an order for the Honda's parts. "Your hoses and belts will be here in the morning. Leave 'er here and I'll have 'er ready for you by noon," he announced hanging up a black telephone that looked like it belonged in the Smithsonian. Corey and Silas shook hands, with Corey promising not to sell the farm without giving Silas first shot, so to speak.

"So, is this something that you and Abigail arranged?" Corey asked as they headed back to Island Pond, with a full tank of gas in the truck.

"Silas wouldn't take any money for the gas; call it my huntin' fee," he said.

About ten miles up the road, Amanda said simply, "Yes."

By then, Corey had forgotten the question.

"Yes, what?" he asked

"Yes, I will marry you. I take it that was your idea of a romantic proposal at the Springfield airport?"

"You will?" replied a stunned Corey.

"Uh huh, someday. But first, we've got a lot off thinking to do about where the twain shall meet."

"How's that?" Corey asked, still sorting out the first yes.

"Well, it seems that, for the foreseeable future at least, you're going to be living in the Southwest, and I'm going to be in the Northeast!

If Abigail Pettigrew had been waiting for years for another woman to talk to, she must have been disappointed that night, and no doubt shocked at the silhouettes dancing across the faded wallpaper in the flickering candlelight of her old bedroom.

31

HERDING ELEPHANTS

The first meeting of the Inter-Agency Task Force on Heritage Protection was brief. Its mandate from the Secretary was even more so:

> "To work together to put an end to the theft of ancient artifacts from the public lands of the Southwest."

Ben Tanner Richardson, as the Secretary's personal assistant, was nominally in charge, even though every one of the task force members outranked him. The Secretary wanted there to be no doubt about the importance of their mission, so he had appointed the regional heads of the agencies under his control as the formal members of the task force, the National Park Service, the Bureau of Land Management, the Bureau of Indian Affairs and the Fish and Wildlife Service. Invited to participate, the Forest Service and the Corps of Engineers could hardly do otherwise. Of course, everyone knew, the actual work of the task force would be carried out by whomever these folks designated. Probably not more than one or two of those present knew that, in addition to having the Secretary's confidence, Ben's Navajo heritage gave him a powerful motivation to make this task force succeed.

Ben stood at the head of the highly polished walnut conference table, at the Inter-Agency Information Center, smiling faintly as he looked at the regional chiefs and their assistants engaged in their private conversations over their second or third cup of coffee. He'd prepared well. Herding elephants was indeed possible. You simply had to change the playing field to one that was unfamiliar to the elephants.

When the secretary asked him to coordinate the task force, Ben stared blankly at him. They both laughed. Coordination is a kiss-of-death assignment in the feudal world of federal agencies. Ben had left Washington with that word struck out of the letter that went to the regional chiefs. He also left with a strong personal mandate to run the task force as he thought best, along with emergency hiring authority, substantial budgetary discretion, and a promise of noninterference. With Ben driven by his cultural heritage, and the Secretary driven by ambition, the elephants never really stood a chance!

This morning he'd avoided coming to the coffee hour, knowing that at least some of the chiefs would try to put forth their own agendas for the task force privately. Ben had seen his share of power plays over his years in the department, and he knew where the pitfalls lay. Starting the meeting ten minutes late was part of the scenario. Now, he was going to shift the field even more by ignoring protocol and the printed agendas that he had carefully positioned at each place around the table. He tapped his pen lightly, almost contritely, against the water pitcher.

"My apologies, everyone, for the late start. However I've been on the phone with the Secretary to see what last minute instructions he might have. Now, in the interest of conserving time, and being not unmindful of your own busy schedules, I'd ask your indulgence in shifting the printed agenda just a little. We'll return to the introductions and round-robin of your concerns in just a few minutes."

Ben then usurped the chiefs' prerogatives by asking each to designate their top law enforcement officer and their chief of cultural resources as working members of the task force. Ben caught the anxious looks on the faces of several of the chief's assistants. They, no doubt, had been promised the assignment. He ignored the shuffling of papers and continued. This time, he dropped an even bigger bombshell:

"Our original mandate to provide legislative and executive recommendations by next August still stands. However," Ben paused to let the however sink in, "however we are also encouraged to crank up existing law enforcement efforts so as to produce high profile results as soon as possible. I interpret that to mean arrests!" Ben smiled at the looks of consternation around the table. He'd stretched the Secretary's mandate to the limit, not only usurping the regional chief's discretion in appointments, but now toppling their administrative priorities, as well!

Ben asked that he be provided with the best facts and figures they had on the extent of the problem in their agencies, their arrest and prosecution records for the last three years, their latest artifact inventory records, and where the greatest threats of future losses were most likely to occur. He would appreciate receiving the requested information within the next two weeks. He concluded his opening remarks by telling them that he had secured the services of the best available undercover agent to work with the task force. For obvious reasons, he couldn't share the agent's name. It was another bit of imaginative agenda-setting, but Ben felt sure that he could cajole Corey into signing on. Given Corey's interest in cliff dwellings it should be a shoo-in. In fact, he'd already started his persuasion by using the Silver City line shack as bait. He'd even arrange for a long-term lease on the shack and its faux cliff dwelling if he had to!

Ben then returned to the printed agenda, opening the discussions by turning the meeting over to his deputy, a young Park Service archeologist, Dr. Renee Marquis, generously on loan to the task force. It was actually a last minute precondition Ben had thought to get from of the Secretary before leaving Washington. Ben asked Renee to begin with a brief recounting of a recent incident of theft that had come to light purely by chance, courtesy of the Arizona state police.

Over the next two hours, the elephants grew increasingly restless, excusing themselves to take urgent phone calls, visit the restrooms, and recharge their caffeine level. A few were clearly getting ready to excuse themselves from the closing luncheon, prominently printed at the end of the agenda. Ben decided it was time for his closing gambit:

"Since we seem to be approaching the end of what has been a very productive first meeting, let me thank you all for your strong commitment to this effort. Now, I know that I've already encroached on your crowded schedules, but lunch is being served, as we speak, in the next room." Fastidiously avoiding eye contact with one of the elephants trying to get his attention, Ben continued. "And, the Secretary will be joining us, via closed circuit television, to thank each of you personally, and hear your thoughts. So, let's eat! Oh, Mr. Director, I'm sorry, did you want to say something?" Ben said to the regional director who had been trying to get his attention.

"I simply wanted to compliment you Ben on running a very efficient meeting! And, I am sure my colleagues all join me in wishing you every success," mumbled the regional director of the Bureau of Land Management, initiating a perfunctory round of applause for Ben.

In the span of less than three hours, and at the cost of a luncheon, Ben had acquired a top notch staff at almost no cost to his budget, and it was a staff of his own choosing. Better yet, it was a staff that had access to an army! He'd also demonstrated his own willingness to share the leadership with, not just a woman, but a PhD specialist in a field he knew nothing about. He'd even prepared a draft news release for each agency to use, mundanely explaining the work of yet another government task force. It might be boring to the press, but, in fact, Ben had just declared war on poachers and thieves. And, he was the general! Herding elephants was not just possible, it was a helluva lot of fun!

Ben felt that the most significant outcome of the preliminary task force meeting was the fact that nobody really seemed to have a good idea of the magnitude of the problem, or even where the public's resources might be at greatest risk. He set a meeting for his new task force staff in three weeks, and reminded the chiefs that he wanted all of the requested records in the next two weeks.

He had a lot of studying to do before he could work out a strategy for co-opting Corey. His first challenge was to convince Corey to take the assignment. And, since he didn't even know where Corey was at the moment, that might be his toughest challenge!

"Ben! How in Hell did you find me at the New York Motor Vehicle Registry?' asked a dumbfounded Corey.

"Simple, really. I just called your old secretary at Fish and Game. Jen is a real jewel. She had a pretty good idea of what you were up to. So I had them call me the minute you showed up at the Registry.

We enforcers can work together sometimes, without screwing up, as you've always said!"

"And what else did Jen share with you?" asked a miffed Corey.

"How come you didn't tell me that you knew a celebrity? That gal you're with made quite a splash with her Zach Taylor story. Now, I'm beginning to understand your fascination with cave dwellings."

"Well old friend, it's swell to know that you are so worried about me and would go to all this trouble just to make sure I'm not getting shot at," Corey replied with not altogether feigned sarcasm.

"Actually, I was wondering how soon you could get here?" admitted Ben.

"Ben, I told you 'No Way' the last time we talked. Nothing has changed. The answer is still the same."

"Corey, I respect your decision. How about letting me tell you the full story when you get here? I don't think you're going to want to pass this one up. But, if that doesn't motivate you, you might want to turn around. That guy against the wall is an officer of the federal court, That piece of paper he's holding is a federal warrant. Seems the judge on the Turner case has some questions he wants to ask you."

"Okay, okay, you didn't need to use strong arm tactics! Just have the line shack stocked and ready for me in a week!"

"It's a deal, but why a week?" asked Ben.

"That's how long it takes to drive from here to there."

"You're driving? With one arm?"

"Sure! Why not? See you a week from today."

"Okay. And, Corey, don't shave off the Cossack beard!"

"Too late!" said Corey as he hung up. It was a lie, but, if Ben wanted it, it might be time to get rid of it. Somehow, he didn't think Amanda would mind.

Corey thanked the receptionist at the information desk and went looking for Amanda who had wandered away to admire the art work on the Registry walls. He walked past the heavyset gentleman fully intending to tell him what to do with his subpoena when he realized the guy didn't have any papers in his hand, and wasn't even looking at him. "You Son of a Bitch, Ben! he muttered to himself."

"What was that all about?" inquired Amanda.

"Oh, nothing, really. Just a former colleague from New Mexico wondering when I was coming back." Corey replied evasively.

Amanda decided not to pursue how his former colleague happened to find him! This man she'd agreed to marry was obviously still very much of a mystery!

"Okay," she said, "Let's get the paperwork done and get on our way."

Corey had shaken off his anger at Ben, but his curiosity about the assignment Ben was offering wouldn't go away that easily.

"Good idea!" he said, enthusiastically. "We got back to Albany in time for me to take you out for our engagement dinner!"

Over dinner at the Catskills Creek Side, they talked about the last time Corey had been there, with Sarah.

"It's still hard for you to talk about her, isn't it?" Amanda said, as she reached across the table for his hand.

"It's just that I encouraged her to apply for that residency, right here!" Corey explained. "She'd still be here now, if I'd never shown her the announcement."

"Of course, you're right. But, then, we wouldn't be here either, would we?" Amanda replied, adding, "Sarah may not be here, but I feel her presence. I'm glad you wanted to bring me here for our engagement dinner. Seeing where you grew up, and then coming here, I feel like, suddenly, I'm part of your family!"

"You are!" Corey responded with a toast. "Here's to Amanda Cousins, newest member of the Pingree family! Now, tell me what you meant when you said that you thought that you were going to be living in the east?"

"I will, but first you tell me what the call from Arizona was all about!"

"It's a deal." Corey said. "Ben Richardson, the guy who shot me in the wrist, wants me to help him with a case. He wouldn't tell me anything about it, but he was very convincing. Frankly, I doubt that I'll do it, but I should go back to have this wrist looked at, so I said I'd see him in a week."

"Why would you want anything to do with him? I understand he saved your life, but I thought you were through with the undercover stuff?"

"So, did I, but Ben is a very persuasive guy. He seems to be able to get things done. And that's refreshing in any bureaucracy. According to Ben, the Secretary of Interior specifically asked for me. Of course, it's probably just another of his convenient fabrications. Can you believe it, he actually lied to me on the phone and said that if I didn't agree to come, he had a subpoena waiting! Anyway, I'm only going to check it out. No commitments. Now, your turn!"

"Well, I do have to go back to Springfield," Amanda said, " but I thought I'd stay here long enough to check out the NYT offer, and see if it's something I could work with. And, if it isn't, we could drive back, at least half of the way across the country, together."

"What do you mean, work with?" Corey asked.

"Well, I've had an idea for a long time that I need to try some serious writing, a novel maybe. Then, yesterday and today driving all by myself, I got to thinking that if I could work part-time for the television station, and if you'd let me use the Island Pond house, I could get some writing done there. What do you think?"

Corey reached into his pocket and handed Amanda the key.

"It's yours!" he said enthusiastically. "I'd bet you can write your own ticket with NYT, otherwise they wouldn't have written to you. Are you sure you won't be scared off by Abigail?" he quipped.

"Actually, it was Abigail who gave me the idea! I want to write a really different ghost story, something with a whole new twist to it. And, Abigail seems like a good ghost who might just have a great story to tell."

"Well," quipped Corey, "she's just never had a ghost of a chance before," adding, "I like it! I like it a lot! She could be your ghost writer!"

Amanda simply flashed that incredible smile from across the table, wiping away any of Corey's emerging feelings of foolishness.

"Okay. Tomorrow we'll run up to Saratoga and I'll introduce you to Jen and Clark. They will be thrilled to help you get settled here if that's what you decide to do. In fact, you could leave the Honda with them, fly back to Springfield, and it would be here when you're ready."

"I'm dying to meet Jen. She sounds like one in a million!" Amanda replied. "So, will you be heading for Phoenix tomorrow?"

"Funny, Ben said almost the same thing about Jen. I need to talk with her about how to handle people like him!" Corey replied.

"I think you're being hard on Ben. If he saved your life, he can't be all bad! I hope I get to meet him someday!"

"I hope you do too! Actually, I have to admit that I like Ben too! As for heading back, I thought I'd wait and see how things go for you at NYT. But, if they decide to keep you around for a few days, I may have to let you to find your own way back to Springfield. I promised Ben I'd be there in a week."

Realizing that this might very well be their last night together for who knows how long, Amanda brushed aside Corey's suggestion for a moonlight drive along the Hudson in favor of just sitting by the fireside in their room at the Saratoga Inn and talking about the life-changing decision she had somehow arrived at when, barely thirty-six hours earlier, she had sworn that she wasn't ready to make a commitment. It was a decision that she felt enormously comfortable with despite a lifetime of avoiding entanglements that might interfere with her dreams of a writing career.

"I suppose emotional decisions have their own logic, don't you?" Amanda suggested. "Perhaps we humans are at our most human when we stop being logical? All the time I was writing that article I kept wondering why Zach left his cave. Now, I think I know. I think he left because of you! Maybe not exactly you, but something you may have triggered in him. A need; a very human need!"

"How on Earth did you come up with that? What did he need that I could offer?"

"Think about it. You were the only person to ever visit him at his home during all those years. And you came there asking for his help. Am I right?"

"I guess so. Go on."

"At some level, Zach needed to be needed. Perhaps, in a way, Pup filled that need in him. Perhaps, you further awoke the need. And then, when Pup no longer needed him, he went looking."

"So," mused Corey, "what are you suggesting?"

"Just that our lives, yours and mine, haven't been that different from Zachs. Like him, we finally awoke to the need to be needed! The day that Zach died, I think I needed you because I needed Zach not to die. You were my only real connection to him."

"I like it!" said Corey, pulling Amanda close and staring into the fire. "I particularly like the idea that Zach was the catalyst! Maybe, aside from your powerful writing, one reason for your article's instant popularity is that we all need a Zach Taylor to wake us up to the kind of inhuman world we've created for ourselves."

"Maybe. I only know that if Zach could head out into the unknown, leaving the security of his home, going in search of something that he didn't really understand, something that you gave him, I want to continue that search. I needed you, Corey, on more than a physical level! I had to admit that to myself before I could say yes to you. I need you to complete my life!"

Long hours later, Corey still lay awake beside Amanda, watching the flickering shadows from the fireplace dancing on the ceiling and trying to understand why it had taken so long to begin to fit the pieces of his life together. Now, suddenly, it was happening, and happening so fast it seemed as if he'd become a passenger on a lifeboat that was no longer his to control. Strangely, that loss of control was making him deliriously happy, way too happy to sleep, he thought as he fell into the best sleep he'd had in years. Beside him, a peaceful Amanda Cousins slumbered, oblivious to how drastically her own life was about to change.

32

JOINING THE TEAM

"Corey! Good to see you!" Ben Richardson grabbed Corey in his grizzly bear embrace. Let me introduce my deputy, Dr. Renee Marquis. At this moment, the three of us are the full complement of the Secretary's Task Force on Heritage Protection in the Southwest."

"Pleased to meet you, Mr. Pingree. Welcome to our little group!" Renee said, matching the firmness of Corey's grip. "What happened to your arm, or shouldn't I ask?"

"Good to meet you, Dr. Marquis," Corey replied. "You should ask Ben about the arm. Also, you might ask him what makes him think that I am part of his little group?"

"Regrettably, Renee," Ben cut in, "I had to shoot Corey on our last assignment. I'm not usually that poor a shot, either! But, I think he'll be eager to join us, because next time it might be his kneecap!"

Renee had seen Ben in action, herding elephants, as he called it, so she wasn't quite sure what to make of this exchange, other than the two men obviously held each other in high regard.

"I think I'll leave you two alone, and go work on my maps."

"Thanks, Renee. We'll join you in the War Room in a little while." Ben replied with the self assurance all good generals need to have.

"Can you believe that gal's got a PhD as well as looking like a fashion model?" Ben said, as she closed the door on her way out. He didn't wait for an answer.

"Corey, I'd take this as a huge personal favor if you'd just let me brief you before you make up your mind. But, first, let me assure you that, compared to our last little fling, this is going to be a piece of cake. No risk, I promise. If everything goes as planned, your part in this can be wrapped up in no more than three or four months. But, you can stay on if you choose to. And, I hope you will. The Secretary really does want you on board. Here's his letter."

Ben waited for Corey to be suitably impressed with the letter's personal appeal, as well as its promise of the assignment of his choice once the Task Force completes its work.

"Very nice!" Corey said, handing the letter back to Ben. "Of course you wrote it for the Secretary's signature!"

"Of course I did, and if you don't like that one, I'll write another! You want out, I'll hire you as a private contractor at five times the money. Here, read his letter to me, giving me absolute hiring and budget authority. And he'll agree to whatever you want. We both thought that the money wouldn't mean that much to you. He wants people with your dedication working **in** the department, not just **for** the department."

"Okay, convince me," said Corey, sinking into the comfortable leather chair across from Ben's desk. Ben briefed Corey on the magnitude of the problem and why the Secretary had made it a top priority. "The loss of irreplaceable artifacts from the public lands has been going on in a steady trickle for decades. But lately, with the prices skyrocketing, the pace has accelerated. The stuff is making its way into private collections not just in this country, but in Europe and South America as well."

Then he acquainted Corey with the Task Force and its first meeting, and the fact that the regional chiefs had been shunted aside into a committee of the whole to develop needed new legislation. On paper, they still ran the task force, but in fact, Ben had their top law enforcers and archeologists working for him and his new deputy.

"We've been overwhelmed with their files. Renee is making a lot of progress in mapping where the reported losses have occurred on each agency's lands, and where the highest risks might be in the future. It's preliminary, but she's already starting to draw some interesting conclusions, as you'll see when we join her in a few minutes."

"And, just how do you see me fitting into the picture?" Corey asked, in a noncommittal tone.

"You are going to be a very well-heeled buyer. I've got you staying at a villa in Santa Fe that belongs to a friend of the Secretary's. And, I've even got your Lincoln Town Car locked in the garage, with a brand new set of California plates on it. We'll go into the details in a bit. But first, I'm going to join Renee while you relax at my desk, and make any calls you need to. I've cut off the phones at your villa. Sorry, but I had to. You'll see why later! Oh, by the way, there's a letter on the desk to you from Amanda. That's quite a gal you've got there, my friend. She and I had a nice visit on the phone a few days ago!"

"I don't even want to know how that happened!" cracked Corey.

"It does seem to be a small world, doesn't it?" said Ben. "And, in the small world category, you'll be interested to know that we're keeping an eye on an old friend of yours, by the name of Gordy Stubbs. Seems he owns a small helicopter. And, according to Renee, the only way you can get into some of these sites is with a helicopter."

33

BUYERS AND SELLERS

Island Pond, VT
September 11, 2007

Dear Corey,

It's a good thing that you didn't try to sell the Island
Pond house. You might not own it! Abby (she said it was all
right for me to call her that) has got me doing some research
at the local library and county courthouse. It seems that your
grandfather got a real good deal on the property ($650!)
because he agreed that it would revert to the Pettigrews if
he, or his heirs, ever stopped living here for a period of five
years. So, how long has it been? I suppose you'd only have to
have slept here once in every four years and eleven months?
Do you think that Sarah knew about this, and that's why she
said to never sell it? Don't worry, there are no Pettigrews in
the phone book.

Corey, call me if you can. I need to hear your voice.
I had a long talk with Ben after you left, courtesy of Jen. I
guess your talk with her didn't stick very well! Anyway,
he's letting me use his address to write to you. He thinks
the world of you, as do I! He told me several times that he
doesn't think you will be in any danger if you decide to
work with him.

I'll tell you more about Abby's and my ideas for the book
in my next letter. For now, just know that she has agreed to be

my coauthor! The NYT job is great! They're letting me do just one show a week, so I only have to be in Albany Wednesday through Friday. The Honda is running beautifully! I plan to have Silas check it over and winterize it for me next week. I hope you won't mind if I let him use the farmhouse for a few days when I'm not here? Bird season starts in a couple of weeks, and I thought I'd exchange the Honda checkup for rent? Had to get a new pump for the well. Otherwise, everything is working fine. Of course, cold weather isn't really here yet!

Until I can find an apartment in Albany, Jen and Clark insisted on letting me stay with them in Saratoga. They tell me that you stayed there a couple of times too. So, I get to sleep in your bed when I'm there as well as when I'm at the farm! Maybe that's where all my inspiration is coming from? I am getting a lot of writing done.

Take care of yourself!

Love, Amanda

PS: My boss in Springfield has been very understanding. He's given me a three-month leave, just in case NYT doesn't work out. But, I do need to get back there. I'm running out of clothes! An exaggeration! This job comes with a clothing allowance! Can you believe it?

Corey decided he needed to call Amanda. He'd only talked to her once on the trip down. Two other times he had to leave a message. And, frankly, he didn't give a damn if he tied up Ben's office for the next two hours doing it!

An hour later, when Corey walked into the War Room, next door, he found Renee and Ben huddled over a collection of aerial photographs spread out on the conference table. He looked around the room at walls totally covered with maps that were highlighted with numerous colored markings.

"What the Hell are we planning here, an invasion of Mexico?" Corey wondered aloud.

"I'm going to let Renee brief you. Right now, I've got to run across town and smooth some ruffled feathers," said Ben, as he headed for the door. "Renee, take Ben to lunch for me, I may not be back for a few hours. Corey, you and Renee need to spend some time getting to know each other. For the next week, she's going to be taking you to museums and giving you the Anasazi Archeology 101 Course, so you'll know exactly what to be looking for. See you guys later this afternoon."

"I'm famished," said Renee. "How about lunch first and a briefing later? Do you like Mexican, Mr. Pingree?"

"My favorite, and it's Corey. May I call you Renee? Also, I need to fit in a visit to the hospital, sometime today, since it appears I'll be relocating to Santa Fe soon."

"Good!" agreed Renee. "There's a great place just across the street. And, it's my job to get you to the hospital and back. That way we can visit along the way. Did Ben really shoot you?"

"It's a long story, but yes he really shot me, though it was an accident—I think!" They both laughed.

Over the course of lunch and arranging the therapy for Corey's wrist and hand, then dropping in on a couple of downtown antique shops that Renee frequented, Corey was rapidly brought up to speed on the task force. Renee's primary job had been to plot all the information they got from the land managing agencies on the wall maps in the War Room. She explained the color coding: red dots meant a verified theft location on public lands; yellow was a theft from a museum, visitor center, antique shop, or private collection; green signified an unverified theft location based on police reports, and orange dots were where the highest risk of future thefts might occur on public lands, based on agency guesses.

Obviously, the War Room was considered top secret. No one, not even the agency chiefs, got to go in without Ben's approval! To date, less than half of the mountain of files had been plotted, but already Renee was seeing potentially useful patterns emerging. She hypothesized that they were dealing with two distinct types of theft. Sites within twenty miles of populated areas were getting hit in what appeared to be a random, unorganized manner, probably the work of locals living nearby. Sites deep in the Indian lands, and sites not protected by the agencies, were hit much less frequently, but the losses were greater. The latter locations, were not easily accessible by four-wheel drive vehicles and, because of their remoteness and the absence of possible witnesses, they were highly vulnerable to raids by helicopters. Two types of theft, led to a two-pronged strategy. Ben was encouraging the agency folks to concentrate on the more readily accessible sites, while the three of them would go after a major bust on one or more of the remote locations. Hopefully, Corey's undercover work as a rich buyer might encourage someone to drop their guard and provide some clues. They might even be able to pull off a sting, at some point if Corey could arrange it.

"The situation today is nothing like it was a hundred years ago, when major new sites were being discovered almost monthly," Renee told him. "Those sites were almost always looted, and then poorly investigated. Back then we just didn't have the tools and the procedures in place that we have today. I personally doubt that there are any major undiscovered sites left to find. But, and this is a huge but, there may be as many as a dozen or more sites where we can still learn a great deal because they have been largely undisturbed over the centuries. I believe one of those sites was found recently by looters. That pot you saw sitting in the War Room may have been stolen from that site. And, we have no clues as to where it may be!"

"And, the reason it sits there is because it is both our goad and our goal!" mused Corey. "Sounds like one-hundred percent Ben Richardson thinking to me!"

"You've got it!" said Renee. "Along with the fact that this has to be a helicopter operation. We do seem to have to fight fire with fire. I gather you know that he owns his own helicopter and that he has Indian blood. So, this whole operation fits him like a glove! And, he is a superb organizer! I have to tell you, my opinion of the Secretary has shot way up for giving Ben this assignment!"

"So, how did you get pulled into this?" Ben wondered aloud.

"Some reporter on the state police beat picked up on the recovery of that cooking pot and an ancient child's skull, and the fact that I'd been called in to examine them. There was a small item in the Flagstaff paper and, the next thing I knew I was being given a short-term reassignment and was to contact somebody named Ben Richardson in Phoenix. Supposedly it was on orders from the Secretary's office. A case of being in the right place at the right time, I guess."

"You mean, no interview, no choice, and you'd never even met Ben before?" asked Corey trying not to sound too incredulous.

"I think we're dealing with people who know how to make the bureaucracy work for them." suggested Renee.

"Yeh, I get that impression too." replied Corey, as Renee pulled back into her reserved parking space at the Interagency Center. "Speaking of the devil, looks like he's back from smoothing feathers."

They found Ben's door closed with a Do Not Disturb hanger on the knob, obviously borrowed from a Travelodge Motel. Renee unlocked the War Room door and led Corey to a closer examination of the ancient cooking pot.

"The skull is still being examined by specialists at the Anasazi Heritage Center Museum at Mesa Verde," she said. "You'll get to see it on our tour. I'd be just as glad to see it stay in the basement of the museum. Though I gather Ben would like to have it here. So far, they seem to have pinned it down to a thirteen-year-old who died of starvation some six hundred years ago."

Corey finished his examination of the pot, wandered casually around the walls studying the maps, finally sitting across the conference table from Renee with a puzzled look on his face.

"So, any questions?" asked Renee.

"Uh huh, lots," replied Corey. "Let's begin with the Santa Fe connection. I only see orange dots around Santa Fe. There aren't any red dots within fifty miles, so why am I being lodged there?"

"I should probably answer that one," said Ben, who'd come in behind Corey. "We want you to look rich and authentic. A Santa Fe address gives you that. You can give out the phone number, but all it will do is record messages. Again, authenticity. You can only respond to messages with your cell phone, and that number is blocked from showing up on anyone's screen. You can even give out the address, in fact, we want you to. The Lincoln will be partially obscured by the landscaping, but still visible through the electronic gate. Your job is to flash your big bills in the places you think will be the most effective."

Ben paused, then continued, "And be looking for specific kinds of artifacts. That's Renee's job. You are going to be an expert on Anasazzi culture before this is over, my friend. I only wish you hadn't shaved off the beard! It was authentically rich, and it fit with your new name! You are a rich South African collector by the name of Hermann "Sonny" Van Derbur."

"I'll have to work on my Boer dialect. You still haven't explained the lack of red dots in the area," Corey observed.

"Your job, for now at least, is to be prominent in the marketplace, and it's huge, extending above Taos in the north and below Albuquerque in the south. That's the only way we're ever going to entice any of the helicopters that we're watching to move. However, the hot spots in the marketplace are actually not that far from Santa Fe. In fact, that pot you're looking at was purchased by tourists from Ireland about forty miles north of Santa Fe. We've been keeping an eye on the roadside spot for a couple of weeks hoping the seller will show up again. Also, if it seems appropriate, you might drop a hint from time to time that you'd love to visit a really remote Anasazi site, if there are any, before you head home to South Africa."

Ben paused again and this time Corey jumped in:

"Which brings me to question number two," said Corey. "You suspect Gordy Stubbs of being involved. What if he recognizes me?"

"Not likely, the big guys in an operation like this almost never deal directly with customers. They're strictly suppliers. But, even if he did, all it would do is alert him, and he'd start to cover his tracks, maybe buying stuff back and alerting anyone he is working with to lay low, for example. And, we'd know the minute he started acting out of the ordinary. What we need now is leads. Any way we can get them!"

"So now for question number three," said Corey, staring directly into Ben's unflinching eyes. "You weren't being entirely candid back at the line shack, when you said that it was the director's idea for me to walk in on the Turners, were you?"

"You mean did I lie to you? Yes I did, Corey. And, I'd do it again in just the same way. Look, I'm sorry as Hell that you got shot. That wasn't part of the plan. How could I have guessed that you were going to jump at Wes at the very moment he turned?" As for the director, Hell, the fewer people involved in these operations, the safer we all are."

"I accept that, and thank you, Ben. But, I really have to ask one more question, before I agree to any of this."

"Sure, fire away!"

"What about the Secretary's role in this operation. Is that on the level? Because, if the offer of any job I want when this is over is for real, I want to be your boss!"

"Everything is one-hundred percent on the level. And, frankly, I'd like having you on my team permanently!"

All three laughed. Each had their own reasons for not wanting a commitment out of Ben for no lies in the future. He needed a free hand,

and they knew he could never have made such a promise without compromising their safety and the project.

"So, what's the medical report on the hand?" asked Ben.

"Ten weeks of physical therapy. Any residual disability will have to come out of your retirement" panned Corey.

34

A FALLING OUT

"You stupid sonofabitch!" yelled Gordy, causing Tim to almost drop the phone. "I coulda got four times that much for that pot!"

"Maybe," agreed Tim. "But I needed the money now. Besides, you ain't payin' me nothin' for storage."

"Of course I'm not, Goddamnit! I'm providing the fuckin' helicopter. I thought you were bright enough to understand that's how a partnership works!" fumed the irate Gordie.

"Okay, Gordy, if you want to find another partner, go ahead. This is a pretty risky business, maybe too damn risky for me."

"All right, all right, just calm down! And don't sell any more of that last batch without clearing the prices with me. Understand? You haven't, have you?" Gordy asked with obvious anxiousness.

"No, I haven't, not yet anyway. But we gotta start movin' some of this stuff. I'm hurtin' real bad right now. I was getting ready to head to town before you called. Dad's outa medicine."

"How 'bout I advance you a thousand?" asked Gordy.

"That'd be great, partner! I'll be by later today. But, you know we gottta start movin' some of this stuff outa here, okay?"

"Okay, but for Christ's sake don't be selling to Elena or any of those roadside dealers. We can do a lot better by sticking with the established shops, like Maria's. And, nothing leaves the ranch without my approval! Agreed?"

"Screw you, partner!" Tim cursed as he headed for the stables. If he was going all the way into Espanola anyway, he was damn sure going to bring along a few trinkets to sell. Gordy didn't know half the stuff they had stored away under the hay in the old stables anyway. Gordy might have the damn helicopter, but by Gawd, he wasn't the only one who knew the location of every one of those dwellings they'd visited over the last year and a half. If necessary, he could sell that knowledge! He didn't need Gordy as much as Gordy needed him. But, maybe Gordy was right about the established shops. He might just go the extra thirty miles and see what Maria would give him for a couple of small pieces, nothing too large, or anything that Gordy might miss or recognize if he happened to see it.

Tim was feeling better already, just knowing that good old Gordy might be advancing him the thousand. But the payback would be coming out of Gordy's own pocket, for damn sure. Honor was neither affordable or relevant in some partnerships.

Tim Dice and Gordy Stubbs had been off and on friends since high school. Tim had put up with Gordy's lording it over him, with his money, his looks, his war record, and now his helicopter, simply because nobody else ever bothered to give him the time of day. They'd joined the Army together. Tim gave his enlistment money to his dad, Tim Senior, to start the dude ranch. It might have made it too, if his dad hadn't gotten sick. Over the years, Tim found little to pride himself on, certainly not his rotted teeth or his pock marked face, or his dishonorable discharge for stealing from his buddies' footlockers while they slept. But he knew he was a good son! He would do whatever he had to do to get pain medication for his dad. Tim, Senior, was dying of cancer, almost completely immobile, pretty much confined these days to one end of the old ranch house. The house stunk like Hell most days, but neither one of them would consider hiring a helper.

Tim struggled with the creaky old barn door, grabbed the pitchfork, and looked wistfully at all the empty horse stalls. It had been hard selling off all the horses. Another admission of failure. Piss on it, he said, meaning the lost dream, and piss on it he did, as if to rid himself of a bladder full of life's rejections! He poked around under the hay with the pitchfork, being cautious of rattlesnakes, and came up with a couple of interesting items, a tiny basket that the pitchfork had pierced, and a small obsidian hand chopper that the pitchfork had scratched. He stuck both behind the seat of his beat-up old jeep, checked in on the sleeping Tim Senior, and headed for town.

Gordy Stubbs maintained a tiny office down at the hangar that he visited daily to listen to his phone messages. There weren't any, as usual, although today he found himself wishing that someone might have seen his one-line ad in the yellow pages and called. Gordy didn't believe in advertising. He'd had three clients in the last year. The business was just an excuse for owning the chopper. Flying gave him a feeling of power. Whenever he had to fly a client, it was like giving some of that power over to the client. He hated every moment in the air with a client. It was like pimping his chopper. He owned a speedboat on Lake Powell and had a couple of ATV's in his garage. Machines were power, particularly machines that could get him to places where others couldn't go. Taking paying customers defeated the whole purpose! It really galled him to realize that, thanks to his wife's money, he was probably better off than most of his clients.

Even if he'd received a call, he would have had to turn it down. The chopper was being serviced. That machine got more attention than did his wife. But then, Erica was a low-maintenance wife. One of the top real estate salespersons in the area, she was pretty self-sufficient. Once in a while she'd go trail riding with him, but ATV's weren't her kind of power. Besides it was more fun to go with someone like Tim. Tim's dad might own hundreds of acres, but there was no question who was in charge when the two of them went for a day of ATV riding in the hills behind The Pair O' Dice.

After Gordy hung up on his conversation with Tim, he started pacing the small office. When he'd seen those pictures of the pot and the skull in the newspaper, along with the story of the Irish tourists, he felt like he could have killed Tim with his bare hands. Tim had him over a barrel and he knew it. He sure as Hell couldn't be seen unloading the chopper anywhere around here. The ranch was the perfect remote location. Even Tim's housebound dad wouldn't suspect anything other than another friendly visit from Junior's buddy.

Gordy knew that Tim had been stealing from him. But until now, it had been small stuff. This last lot had been museum quality, worth thousands, and Tim had stupidly sold a couple of items for hundreds.

Gordy had to protect the rest. He knew that his loan wasn't going to keep Tim from dipping into the bank again and again. The loan, at best, was simply to buy some time. If only he hadn't arranged to have the chopper serviced he'd fly out to the ranch right now and retrieve as much as he could load on board. But, then what? If Erica ever found out it would be all over. He might never see her or Angela again! What he should do was leave Tim behind in the desert. He wouldn't last two days! But, then he'd have to explain it somehow to Tim Senior. There was just no way to avoid a full-scale search, which would mean a search of the ranch as well. Slowly, a plan began to form in Gordy's mind.

When Tim arrived at the hanger later that morning Gordy had worked out most of the details.

"Look, partner," Tim said as he burst in on a glowering, red-faced, Gordy. "I know I should have cleared it with you but, like I said, I needed some cash in a hurry for Dad's medications," he began, defensively. "So, just add it to the thou, and I'll pay you back. I promise, okay?"

"No, Goddamn it! It's not okay," Gordy shot back, knowing that he would have to browbeat Tim to get him to go along. "What's not okay is the way you're treating your old man. He needs to be in a nursing home, where he can get real care! And, you damn well know it!"

"Shit! You know he'll never leave the ranch! Besides where would I get the money" Tim replied, morosely. "Like you always said, the Dice's are land rich and cash poor!"

"You've been promising the old man a helicopter ride for ages. We could give him a ride and, instead of taking him back to the ranch, we could deliver him to the nursing home" Gordy offered. "You know, damn well he's dying! Don't you think he deserves a ride before he joins the gang at the ghost ranch?"

"Course I'd like to give him that! But he'd be madder than Hell at me. Might never talk to me again! Besides, it's crazy, we don't have that kinda money!" Tim lamented.

"Suppose we just forget about you paying me back? Suppose I was to buy the ranch from you? Right now? I could see my way clear to giving you a hundred, no, a hundred and fifty of these thousand dollar bills for it. Whadda you think?"

"I dunno," said Tim, his eyes lighting up at the thought of a stack of hundred and fifty one-thousand dollar bills. "Dad would never go along with selling the ranch, you know that!"

"Oh, for Christ sakes, your dad doesn't even have to get involved. All you're doing is selling me your interest in the Pair O' Dice. If you ever wanted to buy it back you'd always have the right to do it. Now, I've got the papers all drawn up down at the bank. All you've got to do is sign and go home with a hundred and fifty thou in your pocket. That'll sure buy a lot of medicine for your dad! Then you and I'll go make the arrangements for the nursing home, and we'll fly him back here this weekend. He'll love it! Hells bells! I don't know why I didn't think of this months ago."

"Thanks, partner," said Tim, trying to control the excitement that was bringing tears to his eyes. "You are the best friend I've ever had! But, you've got to promise me that you won't ever tell Dad anything about this, okay?"

"Forget it, partner." Gordy said, wrapping an arm around Tim escorting him to the door. "You'd do the same for me, if you could, and we both know it. I won't even register the deed. I'll just keep our agreement here in the office. Hell, I'd just give you the money if I could get away with it. But, you know I've gotta have some kind of collateral in case Erica finds out. You understand, don'tcha?"

Tim nodded sagely, as if he could divine the intricacies of collateral. Whatever it was, all he knew was that he didn't give a shit about it.

"Tell you what, old Buddy," Gordy said, "let's seal the deal over lunch. Now that you're a rich man, I'll let you buy me a nice thick steak down at Ruby's."

After visiting the bank, and a three-beer lunch, Tim felt a little edgy about going on to Maria's to see what she'd give for the old basket and the stone chopping knife. But, the more he thought about it, the more he concluded that Gordy had really screwed him out of the lunch. "That cheap bastard should've bought the steaks!" With luck, whatever Maria might give for the treasures would offset the cost of lunch! Each passing mile added to Tim's guilt about selling out on his dad, while firming his resolve to sell every bit of their loot. "Fuck you Gordie!"

Tim Dice, Senior, awoke from a fitful sleep knowing that death was overtaking him at a full gallop. He'd been a cowboy all his life. All he knew for sure, at this very moment, was that he didn't want to die indoors, in that stinking little room, and in that stinking uncomfortable bed. Slowly, painfully, he struggled to his feet and lurched into the walker that Junior had given him last Christmas. Junior was a good boy, even if he was a lazy little shit! Just like his mother. Hard to believe the kid was almost fifty. He needed to get outdoors, needed to get down to the stables. Maybe that's where Junior was, he thought in his confusion, taking care of the stock.

As he came alongside the corral, he pushed away the filth-encrusted walker, and leaned against a weathered post, peering in between the poles to watch the horses. They saw him, and came running. There were scores of horses all running to see him, every horse he'd ever owned in his seventy-seven years. He tried to remember all their names as he reached between the poles to stroke their noses. His cracked lips parted, in what might pass for a smile, as he thought: How good Junior had been to round up all the horses for him to see!

The last thing that Tim, Senior, felt was the blazing New Mexico sun burning through the long thin hair of his scalp as he slid to the ground against the weathered fence post. The flies buzzed through his straggly beard and into his eyes and ears and nose and gaping mouth, but Tim Dice, Senior, was where he wanted to be. It was where Tim, Junior, found him five hours later. Junior brushed away the flies, closed the blankly staring eyes, picked up the still limp body, amazed at how light it was. This once two-hundred-pound bull of a man didn't weigh more than a bale of hay thought Junior as he carried his dad back to the house, tears dripping onto his father's face. In the passing of a moment, in the fading of a dream, Gordy Stubbs had, without knowing it, become the sole owner of six-hundred-and-forty-acres of rock and mesquite along with its rattlesnakes and the decaying buildings of a failed dude ranch.

The wraith that was once Tim Dice, Senior, sat propped in one of the two rickety, paint-chipped, kitchen chairs while Tim, Junior, got a beer out of the refrigerator, and sat across the chipped enamel table just as they used to do in the old days. He'd no sooner sat down than he jumped up with a mumbled apology, got a second beer, which he placed in front of his dad, and for the next hour they reminisced about horses, about Junior's short tour in the Army, about their dreams for the Pair O' Dice. The conversation was a bit one-sided, but that was okay, because it was a talk that was long overdue.

Death was not a subject that either of them had ever been comfortable with, so Junior steered the discussion toward the long-awaited rain. He was clearly at a loss about what to do next. He knew he was supposed to do something, but he was damned if he knew what. Digging a hole was a lot of work, so he quickly dismissed that idea.

With the last of the cold beers gone, he asked his dad if he wasn't going to drink his. No answer. Maybe he ain't dead at all, wondered Junior reaching for the Coors and brushing the fly off the open top. Later, staggering to reach the wall phone behind his dad's chair, to call Gordy, he lurched against the chair toppling the corpse against the dingy kitchen window. "Oops, sorry, Dad!"

"Jesus, I'm sorry as Hell to hear that, Old Buddy! But we both knew he wasn't long for this world way back when. It's just a damn shame he never got to go on that helicopter ride!" said Gordy, doing his best to sound appropriately consoling, while realizing that he was now the sole owner of the Pair O" Dice ranch.

"Gordy, I don't what I'm supposed to do next. I know he wouldn't want a funeral of any kind, but I just don't know what I'm supposed to be doing. Hell, I'm not even sure if he's dead!" Tim sounded like a man who'd lost his only real friend in the world. Which is exactly what he was, except for the half-empty whiskey bottle in his other hand!

"Don't you worry 'bout a thing, Old Buddy!" Let me take care of everything. I'll call the nursing home and see if we can get your deposit back. Then, I'll call the coroner's office and get 'em out there pronto. But first, there's some things I need to know, like did the old man have a will? Is there anybody else that should be notified? Did he have any other kinfolk? Where do think he'd want to be buried? I should imagine right there on the ranch, right?

"Hey, slow down, you're confusing me! No, there's no will. Dad had a brother and a sister up near Four Corners, but I think they're all dead now. Listen, thanks for taking care of these things. I ain't thinking straight right now."

"'Course you ain't!" This is what buddies do for each other! Hey,

I got an idea. What about cremation? We could spread your Dad's ashes over the ranch from the chopper, give him that ride after all. Then we could head back out to the canyon and have a look around. We ain't been out there for weeks! You need a change of scene! How about it?"

"Yeh, that sounds like just what I need!" Tim slurred. Gordy smiled as he heard the sound of the bottle and the whiskey gurgling down Tim's throat. "Look, I'm probably going to have to get your signature on a few things, like the cremation go-ahead. I'll get everything together and fly on out after I call the coroner. In the meantime, save some whiskey for me! You got enough, or shall I bring a few more bottles when I come up with the papers?"

"Yeh, bring a few more. I'm gettin' low. Bring some Coors too."

"Will do, Buddy. See ya soon."

Gordy decided he'd bring along a case. Maybe Tim might just stay drunk until it was time to drop the ashes. Be a Goddamn shame if he were to fall out of the chopper along with the ashes!

35

FITTING THE PIECES

When Corey got back to the villa, it was after eight in the evening. It was his third long day of visiting antique shops and cruising the byways in the big silver Lincoln. Pressing the remote control to open the gates, he decided he'd come a long way in the undercover business in less than two months, from being hustled out of town by the marshal of Silver City to living in a Santa Fe mansion! He fixed himself a tall gin and tonic, flipped on the answering machine, and opened the sliding glass doors to better appreciate the lights of Santa Fe as they were just starting to wink on below the terrace.

> *Hello! You have reached the answering service of Herman "Sonny" Van Derbur, please leave a brief message with your name and phone number. I will try to get back to you before I leave the country next month. Thank you!*

Got to figure out those damn buttons, he mused for the fourth or fifth time, while critiquing the clipped Boer accent he'd affected.

> *BEEP! You have four new messages. Message number one. Received today at 2:59 pm: "Hello. This is a message for Mr. Van Derbur, from Maria Vega-Rivera. You stopped by my shop looking for Anasazi items yesterday. A couple of items came in right after you left, that might interest you. If you care to drop by, my hours are ten to four most days, except Monday."*

> *BEEP! MESSAGE NUMBER TWO. RECEIVED TODAY AT 4:10 PM: "Corey, they buried Zach today at the Missouri Veterans Cemetery.*

Please call me. I need to talk. My boss in Springfield called the other day and asked if I could come back to cover it for the News. I declined. My closure with Zach happened several weeks ago, and I'm not going to keep this alive for anyone else! The sheriff found the white van and they've made arrests, but I don't want to know any more about it! Please call soon. I hate this phone system they've got you tied into. I need to hear the comfort of your real voice right now. By the way, Abby has told me some great stories about you. You were her favorite. I bet you didn't know that! Did you really fall out of the hayloft when you were nine?"

Corey scratched his head in disbelief.

BEEP! MESSAGE NUMBER THREE. RECEIVED TODAY AT 5:47 PM: "Corey? Renee. Got some further information for you from Ireland. Meet me in the parking lot of the Santa Fe Opera at noon tomorrow."

BEEP! MESSAGE NUMBER FOUR, RECEIVED TODAY 7:12 PM: "Mr. Van Derbur, you indicated to a colleague of mine that you'd like to see some Anasazi ruins that public doesn't get to visit. I may be able to put you in contact with a helicopter service if you're still interested. You can call me back at this number anytime.

That's strange, thought Corey. The voice sounded vaguely familiar. Gordie? Maybe? The tech crew could probably figure it out. He didn't leave a number. I must be able to retrieve it somehow he thought, promising himself once again to reread the instructions. It could wait. First, he had to call Amanda. He got her on the first try.

"You must have been sitting on the phone," he cracked. "Thanks for telling me about Zach. You absolutely did the right thing, not going to the funeral."

"Corey, it's so good to hear your voice! And, thanks for saying that, even if you don't really believe it. I've been torn apart by not being there."

"Amanda, I believe it, or I wouldn't have said it," Corey assured her.

"We both need to move on. At least, I do. If I'd found any connection at all when I was Oregon, some living person, anyone, who gave a damn about Zach other than Hugh Norton, I'd probably feel different, but somehow, I just feel it's best for Zach, and for us, to let it end. Had you gone to his funeral, it would have breathed new life into all those side issues, like the white van, and why wasn't he buried at the Zachary Taylor National Cemetery in Kentucky, and how can someone find his cave on the Buffalo? It's the end of a chapter, and I want to let it go. It seems more respectful to the man, rather than continuing to feed the endlessly curious."

"I agree completely. Well, almost completely, I'd really like to reconnect with Hugh Norton some day! I'm just glad that you came along and gave me a chance to know the real Zach. Zach sort of woke up for me when you walked into my life. I hope you don't mind?"

"Not at all! Now, tell me the truth, have you really been talking with Abigail? And, just how did you find out about my fall from the loft?"

"Well, I did find an old diary of your Mother's out in the barn in a box of books that had been well chewed around the edges by mice. But, I do believe that Abby called me out there to look. Honestly, Corey, it's really weird, I don't try to listen for her to say something, I don't ask questions, or go into a trance, I just go about my writing, or washing dishes after a meal, and sometimes I get the strangest feeling that someone's helping me. I wish I could have a talk with her!"

"Sounds like your healthy doubt is eroding," observed Corey.

"Corey, I lost my skepticism the very first day! Anyway, I feel so close to your Mother after reading her diary. I know that you will cherish it even more. I think that she must have died that same year. The diary just stops. Her last entry is September 29th. It's almost seems as though your Dad just packed up a bunch of her books and got them out of the house, probably with a lot of her other stuff, to ease his pain. I realize how different things might have been for you, had she lived. At first, I thought your dad must have been a very harsh man, but the more I read, the more I realized how much they loved each other, and how much he must have suffered. I started at the end of her life and read from back to front"

"You're right, I think Mom died in early October. I'm eager to see what you write about her. My memories of her are very sketchy."

"You're also right about their love. It's something that I clearly remember from those years. I can't remember specific examples, I just know that there was a lot of love in our home, particularly after Sarah was born and Mom started being sick all the time. Eventually, Dad had to give up his job and stay home to take care of her. Mom kept a goat in the barn and taught me how to milk it. When she couldn't get out of bed any more, I used to bring her fresh goat's milk and flowers from her garden. When I brought her new flowers, she always had me take the old ones up to the graveyard."

"Was the flower garden on the path between the house and the barn?" Amanda asked.

"Uh huh, why do you ask?"

"No particular reason," Sarah said. "I just noticed a few straggly flowers there almost lost in the tall grass. In the diary, your Mom refers to it as Abigail's garden."

"So, let's see? Abby calls you to find the diary in the barn. Mom refers to the garden as having been Abby's. Why do I think that you are about to tell me something weird?"

"Not weird, Corey, wonderful! You are so perceptive! Okay, here it is. I picked those few straggly faded flowers, and brought them up the hill and placed them on Abby's grave. When I headed back down the hill, a wind came up and blew the flowers right back at me. One of the blossoms landed in my hair. I've pressed it in your Mom's diary. But first, I looked it up. I bet you can't guess what it was?"

"Nope, not even going to try."

"It's a coreopsis! I'm thinking it may have been your Mom's favorite flower. Now, tell me truth. Do you know where your name came from?"

"No, I don't have the foggiest idea." Corey replied. "But, I like your suspicion. Does it look like me?

"Well, the book says it's a sunny perennial. That sounds like you!"

"Listen, speaking of sunny, is there any chance you could come down here for a few days. I'd really like you to see this place."

"Oh, Corey, I'd love to, but I don't see how I could leave right now. NYT has given me a really great opportunity, and they'd think I wasn't very serious if I took time off so soon. Maybe later? How long do you think you'll be there?"

"I don't know. It was just a wild thought. Tell me more about Abigail. I like listening to your voice as I sit here on the terrace looking at the lights of Santa Fe. There's no telling how long this will take. Ben thinks that we might be able to make a really big bust within the first three or four months. What happens after that is pretty much up to me I think."

"Okay, Good! We've got some time. Next month, at the latest, I promise. Now, you promise me that there's no risk of you getting shot again."

"No risk at all of that. But, I can't promise anything about these roads and drivers."

"No, I suppose not. But, I hope you can promise me something about that archeologist you told me about?"

"Yeh, I can, Renee and I have a date tomorrow at the Santa Fe Opera."

"Very funny. Maybe I'll just drop in on you next weekend, after all. Oh, before I forget again, something has been bothering me ever since that day you first brought me here."

"Only one thing? You're lucky."

"Just one, for now. How come your father's bedroom door was locked?"

"Oh, that! We always kept it locked. The latch doesn't work."

"Now that's really interesting. Abby asked me if I'd fixed that latch yet."

"You're kidding, right?"

"Wrong! See you soon, my love! Be careful."

The next day, Corey arrived early to an empty parking lot. Renee had picked the ideal time and place for a rendezvous, except that there was no shade anywhere. Fortunately, he'd brought along a couple of museum books to study, and fortunately, the Lincoln had good air conditioning because Renee was forty minutes late. When she arrived, she jumped into the seat beside him, "Sorry, I'm late. I'm afraid I'm not very good at this cloak and dagger stuff yet! I headed out of the parking lot in my usual gray GSA Ford, and called Ben to let him know I was on my way. He asked me what I was driving and laughed when I told him. So, I had to go back and get an unmarked car. Hence, I'm late, sorry."

"Not a problem, though I am glad you changed cars. The chances of your being recognized are remote, but, nevertheless, a good idea. I guess that's why Ben gets the big bucks! So, what have you found out?"

"Let's go for a ride. I'll show you. Head north on 84 when you get to the bottom of the hill, about five miles on. If it's still there, there's an old pickup that belongs to a woman named Elena Sanchez. It seems that on the flight back to Ireland, Mrs. Devine remembered having introduced herself and her son to the vendor, who responded with her own name, Elena. Elena had been very taken with Duncan, and was making him laugh while Kathleen and her husband were looking over the merchandise in the back of the truck. Ben had his agents in this area start asking around for an Elena who sold Native American curios on the roadside out of the bed of an old pickup truck. In no time, he had an answer. There was only one Elena, and she owns a 1971 Chevy Fleetside."

"Okay, so what do we do when we find her?" asked Corey.

"Well, it's only an idea. And, I've not cleared it with Ben, but I thought if we stopped and chatted with her as husband and wife, we might learn a lot more than if you tried to do it all by yourself. But, it's your call."

"What makes you think so?" wondered Corey.

"Nothing in particular. Just a gut feeling from Kathleen's wording."

"I like gut feelings!" Corey said. "However, you are going to have to play the dummy. You know nothing about this stuff, agreed?"

"Agreed!" said Renee, enthusiastically.

The beat up old Chevy Fleetside was parked under the shade of a huge cottonwood. Elena Sanchez was sitting in an aluminum lawn chair beside a playpen containing a toddler surrounded with plush animals and toys. Elena was clearly a babysitting grandmother who made what little money she could selling whatever she could. The sign on the truck indicated Navajo blankets, beads, and fruits and vegetables in season.

Renee dutifully made a beeline for the grandmother and baby, engaging Elena in what was obviously her real interest, while Corey looked through the items in the back of the Chevy, and then ambled over to join his "wife."

"Let's go, darling," he said. "We've got to get to Santa Fe by three o' clock."

"Couldn't find nothin' in the truck?" asked Elena.

"No, but Thank You," said Corey taking Renee by the hand and turning away.

"What you looking for?" asked Elena.

"Antique Indian pots and baskets," Corey said over his shoulder continuing to walk. "Do you ever have any?"

"Sometimes," Elena said.

Corey stopped and turned part way around. Renee continued to hold his hand. "Well, can you tell me where I mind find some? Where do you find them?" he asked.

"I don't find them. Not any more. Too old! Now, they come to me. Different people bring them to me."

"Can you give me any names," asked Corey. "I, we that is, are only going to be here a few more days, and I'd hoped to find something really nice for a friend in California."

"No, no names. Very expensive," intoned Elena. "Come back, if you can, maybe Tim stop by."

"Tim?" asked Corey. "You don't know his last name?"

"No, haven't seen Tim for a while. Maybe he come by soon," Elena added, hopefully.

"I don't suppose you know what Tim drives, just in case we happen to see him along the road somewhere?" Corey asked.

"Jeep, old Jeep," Said Elena, trying to be helpful. "Come back tomorrow."

As they headed back to the opera parking lot, Renee was clearly impressed. "Wow. You're really smooth. Tim and an old Jeep?"

"Yeh, better than I could have hoped for. I'm betting that Tim is Elena's source for the Devine's pot and skull! Can you pass that along to Ben, and see if he can come up with another computer match? Meanwhile, I'm going to drop in on a dealer in town by the name of Maria. Know her?" She left a message yesterday that she's got a couple of items that might interest me."

"Okay, let's meet later and compare notes. There's a Georgia O'Keeffe gallery just off the square. How about five 0' clock?"

Corey pulled up in front of Maria's just as she was locking up.

"Maria, Sonny Van Derbur. You called."

"Oh, okay," Maria said, as she unlocked the door. "You can park there for a few minutes you won't get a ticket."

Corey left his flashing lights on, just to be on the safe side, and followed Maria into the dark jumble of Southwestern curios and antiques. It was total chaos, reminding him of pictures he'd seen ages ago of the inside of King Tut's tomb. It was dark and depressing with hardly room to move around. One aisle was completely blocked, stuff hung everywhere from the ceiling, even the display area behind the fly-specked show window was packed to the ceiling. When he'd stopped by two days ago, Maria had been just leaving. She'd stopped him at the door and wrote down his name and telephone number. Looking around now, he got the idea that Maria spent most her time collecting, hating to part with stuff so much that she spent little time in the shop. It was her warehouse more than her shop. He'd known people like that. It was a sickness. He felt like he might be her worst nightmare, a paying customer! Or worse, one who wanted to haggle over prices. He decided not to haggle.

Maria disappeared behind a curtain and reemerged carrying a couple of small items that he couldn't make out.

"You want old? These are old! Oldest I've seen in a long time." Maria said holding out, for his inspection, a small, delicate basket with a hole in the side, and an obsidian knife. He recognized them immediately as authentic from the crash course that Renee had given him.

"How much?" Corey asked.

"They're damaged," said Maria in a display of candor. "But, I need a thousand each. You don't find quality like this every day!"

Maria was surprised to see Sonny reach for his wallet, and peel out two one-thousand dollar bills, as if they were tens! It was the fastest nine-hundred percent profit she'd ever made! She was regretting not asking for more, when Sonny Van Derbur said, "These are very nice, Maria, but they're not what I was hoping for. Do you suppose that whoever brought these in might have some pots?"

Maria's fascination for Sonny's bulging wallet put her off guard, and she too quickly replied, "Maybe. I'll check with Tim tomorrow, and give you a call. Okay?"

"Thanks, Maria." Sonny said as he headed for the door. Then, he turned around, dug out his wallet and pulled out another thousand.

"Here, this is for your trouble." The bell on the door jangled loudly, as he went out, louder than Maria ever remembered hearing it.

36

ABBY'S GHOST

    Amanda had gone to bed early. Tomorrow she had to get started back to Albany before daybreak. Besides, she liked falling asleep in the old brass bed with its feather mattresses, flannel sheets, and old patchwork quilts. She liked lying in bed and staring at the kerosene smoke stains in the intricate patterns of the tin ceiling. She liked remembering how she and Corey had made the feathers fly. Each night, she hoped that Abby would come to her in her dreams.

    Abigail Phelps Pettigrew awoke with a start. The clock had wound down but she knew it was well past midnight. Her still-sleepy mind registered the passage of one more lonely day since Thomas had left for The War! It was May 6th, 1864. She looked out the bedroom window, across Samuel's sleeping form, at a beautiful starry sky. But, like every moment for the last ten months, the beauty escaped her. She had kept faithful track of the days from the moment Thomas had left to join Colonel Lewis' Fifth Vermont Volunteers. John Randolph Lewis was a distant relative of Abigail's. If her nineteen- year-old son insisted on going to war, she had to believe that he'd be safer with John.

    The last letter she'd received from Thomas was a month old. But, he sounded cheerful and was filled with pride for having been named a sharpshooter. Thomas took pains to assure his mother that being a sharpshooter meant that he would be much safer than the men in the front lines. The sharpshooters were too valuable to be wasted on the battlefront. They were held back from the battle where it was their job to harass the enemy's artillery and their field commanders. Thomas tried to reassure his mother that the war would be over soon. The rebels couldn't survive the

North's superior forces much longer. He inquired about his father, about his favorite cow and calf, and he noted that it would soon be planting time. Abigail had found cheer in the letter. She'd reread it every day. But, now, holding the letter in her hand, under her pillow, she felt anything but cheer. A cold panic had overcome her in her sleep. The horrible dream was coming back to her. She couldn't waken Samuel, she couldn't go back to sleep, and, the dream was replaying in her mind in all its frightening details.

Abigail got up and went downstairs to the kitchen, fixed herself a cup of hot tea, and sat at the kitchen table. Her head was splitting, but she couldn't stop the dream. It had to play itself out. It was so real, she almost thought she could walk into it and be there beside Thomas as he lay in the mud with acrid smoke swirling all about him. She wanted to clear his eyes for him, to wipe his forehead with a cool wet cloth. She got up and dampened a cloth from the pitcher beside the slate sink, and pressed it to her own forehead. She stood looking out the kitchen window into the dark. She saw Thomas struggling to see through the smoke across to the enemy's line of cannon. He had had a bead on one of their cannon crew when smoke from his own cannon enveloped him once again. Then, for a moment, the smoke cleared. He rubbed his stinging eyes. He was looking directly at one of the rebel sharpshooters, when he realized his target was no older than himself. He stared at the youth, transfixed by the incongruity of the situation, as they carefully aimed at each other. Abigail screamed at her son: "Shoot, shoot, Thomas, please shoot." Abigail's dream ended. Wide awake, she feared sleep more than anything she'd ever feared in her life. She knew that there would be no sleep for her until Thomas came home! Samuel heard his wife scream, and had come downstairs. Tenderly, he took her in his arms and brought her back to bed, where she lay, eyes fixed on the ceiling and its smoke stains from the oil lamps.

Amanda awoke in a cold sweat. The bedroom window was open,

yet she was sweating. It was a dream, but what was it? Only the date stuck in her consciousness, May 6th 1864. What could it mean? She went downstairs, she didn't know why, except that she needed to get out of that room for a while. She fixed herself a cup of cocoa, and wrote down the date, May 6, 1864, on her shopping list. She tried to bring back the dream. But, it was gone! What wasn't gone, however, was the nagging realization that she'd seen that date before. And, there was only one place where she could have seen it!

After her second cup of cocoa and her third piece of toast, Amanda went outside. A bright full moon over the western sky gave an eerie light to the wrought iron fence around the cemetery at the top of the rise. She kidded herself into believing that the cemetery would be the ideal place to greet the first light of day. Slowly, almost reluctantly, she started up the moonlit path, her white slippers and robe adding to the ghostly setting. The full moon shone so brightly that she could almost read the ancient words without a flashlight. It was a small stone, for there was no grave. It seemed pitifully lost in the tall grass. She brushed aside the tangle of grass and weeds to fully reveal the inscription:

TO THE MEMORY OF OUR SON
Thomas Phelps Pettigrew
May 11, 1844 - May 6, 1864
Pvt., 5th Vermont Volunteers
Lost in The Wilderness
"For God and Country"

"Oh Abby, how could you bear it?" Amanda sank to the ground, and traced her index finger over the letters in the stone, slowly, over and over again, until the finger started to bleed. Still she couldn't stop, her blood stained the groove of each letter. She reached across to Abby's stone, where the blood lightly stained the top of the "M" on the word

"Mother." Then she sank onto Abby's grave and wept. Amanda wept for all the ones she'd never known, for Zach, for Abby, for Thomas, for Marie, and Sarah, and for the hopelessness of it all!

Slowly she got to her feet and headed back down the path. She felt embarrassed. She longed for just a little bit of Corey's strength. She felt a hand on her shoulder, and turned with a start. There was no one there!

Later that day, Amanda drove with a throbbing, bandaged, finger back to Albany. She would call Corey, and let him know she was coming for the weekend. She needed to bring him his mother's diary from the year she died. But she was bringing him something more. Something he needed to know. Marie's diary revealed, with no room for doubt, that she had talked with Abigail, as had Corey's grandmother. According to Marie, Corey's father had been named for Thomas Pettigrew, supposedly at the spectral request of Abigail. Amanda had a foreboding sense that Marie's diary was a warning to get out of that house. Determined not spend another night at the farm house, Amanda had hurriedly packed up her few belongings, turned off the electricity, locked the doors, and left the key with Silas Peabody in Lyndonville. She told Silas that she felt sure Corey would entertain an offer, if he cared to make one.

Amanda had never thought of herself as being particularly susceptible to the supernatural, but this was different. And, it was nothing she could talk about over the telephone. Whether she and Cory ever married, or if they went their separate ways, he needed to know that she was wrong in trying to talk him out of selling. If, at some future time, he decided to settle at the farm, it was only fair that he understand the risks, particularly the risk of giving his son the name Thomas, and living in that house.

Whatever the cost might be to her own career, Amanda was leaving for Santa Fe! She was undecided about calling Corey. She hated leaving a message for somebody called "Sonny." She had Ben's number, but she didn't really want anyone else to know what she was doing, or why. She felt foolish enough just telling Corey! The one thing she knew that she wasn't going to share with him, at least not yet, was her suspicion that she was pregnant.

Georgia O'Keefe's paintings proved to have greater power than either Renee's or Corey's curiosity. Finally, as they completed the circuit of the gallery, Renee was first to succumb: "Any luck?" she asked in a low voice, as they admired O'Keefe's Cibola Church.

"You first," said Corey.

"Nothing yet. Ben wants me to call back in an hour or two. He asked if you were doing your therapy exercises?"

"Yes, I am. And, as for Maria, another jackpot! She mentioned a Tim and that she might call to see if he had any pots. She obviously has his number. I bought a couple of trinkets, They're out in the car. Maybe you can tell me if I spent the public's money well?"

"Wow! What did you pay for them?"

"Probably too much," said Corey on the way to the Lincoln. "But I was trying to let her know that I was really interested in Anasazi pots, and that there wouldn't be any haggling."

Once in the Lincoln, Renee studied the basket and the knife carefully, handling them with great care.

"Well, they are authentic Anasazi, and prices aren't my specialty, but if you got them for under five-hundred each you probably did well."

"Let's just say I spent quite a bit more than that to impress her. We can hope it pays off."

"I don't think that you need to worry about the auditors," cracked Renee. "I'd guess Ben's only concern is for results. I sure wish we had his budget back at Walnut Canyon!"

"Maybe he'll let you exhibit these two pieces," suggested Corey. "What do you make of the damage?"

"The scratch is definitely recent. The scientists at the museum can probably tell us how recent. I can't say about the hole in the basket, but it looks recent, as well. Again, forensics can probably tell us, not just when it was made, but how, as well as what those seeds are that are stuck between the fibers. A scientific analysis might very well prove that you got a bargain!"

Renee pulled out a couple of large zip-lock bags from her purse and carefully inserted each of Corey's purchase into its own bag. "I'll take these off your hands," she said without sounding the least bit bossy. "Now, how about some dinner, if you haven't already OD'd on Mexican food, there's a great spot a few blocks from here. Another Maria's."

Corey was lost in thought. "Do you think that these came from the same place as the cooking pot and the child's skull?" he asked.

"Maybe Tim can tell us if we ever find him," replied Renee. "The trouble with grave robbers is that they tend not to keep very good records."

"No, I suppose not!" muttered Corey. I'm sure looking forward to meeting Tim, and don't worry, we will find him. This is what the old trackers would call a 'hot trail.' And, he added confidently, "there'll be a reckoning waiting at the end of it!"

Dinner with Renee had been a bad idea. It was his fault. He'd been in a hurry to get back to the villa and see what messages were waiting, while she had been the perfect national park interpreter. He'd learned the history of Santa Fe all the way back to the 1500s, but practically nothing about her, except that she apparently knew his hosts and had been to the villa once for a fund raising event.

When Corey got back to the villa that night, the message light was blinking authoritatively at him. He pressed the button.

"YOU HAVE THREE NEW MESSAGES. MESSAGE NUMBER ONE, RECEIVED TODAY AT 5:39 PM: In case Renee hasn't caught up with you yet, we got a match. Your subject is a Tim Dice, living at the Pair O' Dice

ranch somewhere west of Coyote. That's the good news. The curious news, is that a death certificate was filed by the county coroner on a 77-year-old Tim Dice, same address, late yesterday. Just for the Hell of it, I had them do a cross-check on Tim Dice and helicopter licenses. Nothing! But, hold onto your hat. The younger Tim Dice, age forty-nine, has a criminal record for car theft. He was bailed out by none other than our old friend and helicopter pilot, Gordy Stubbs of Espanola! We don't show any red dots in the area of Coyote, but, I just happen to know that the fuel range of the MD-500 is better than two hundred miles. Call me!*

"MESSAGE NUMBER TWO, RECEIVED TODAY AT 5:51 PM: I hope you don't mind, Love, but I made a last minute decision to fly down for a couple of days. I get into Albuquerque tomorrow at 12:30, on an American flight out of Chicago. If this is a bad idea, please call me right away. I miss you!

"MESSAGE NUMBER THREE, RECEIVED TODAY AT 6:19 PM: Hi Sonny! Thanks for the great dinner! Just a reminder that you can reach me at the Park Sevice training center in town. I'll be there for two more days for a conference, but they will let me know if I get any calls. If you want to take another drive up by Elena's, let me know, I'd like to come along. I'm guessing you got Ben's good news by now. You were right about this being a hot trail!"

Corey went out to the Lincoln to get a highway map. Ben's news about the death of what must be their chief suspect's father suggested that a drive up to Coyote and a little nosing around might be in order. But, Amanda would be getting into Albuquerque in the middle of the day, and he was damned if he wanted to call and head her off. One look at the map confirmed his suspicion that he couldn't do both. It could wait until the following day. He and Amanda would just be a couple of California tourists. But, that would mean no stopping at Elena's. It wouldn't do to show up there with a different woman. And, once anybody saw Amanda's flaming red hair and Nicole Kidman eyes they never forgot her! He needed to call Ben.

"Corey! You got my message." Ben said at the sound of Corey's voice. "Look, I've got an idea that I need to bounce off you. Just as soon as I can find out if there are any funeral plans for the elder Tim Dice, I'm thinking that you might be able to slip into the ranch and have a look around during the funeral. If Junior and Gordy are partners, that's probably where they're hiding their loot. You'd need to rent a Jeep and make yourself look like a prospector, just in case you get caught. That big Lincoln might be bad news, particularly if Gordy were to show up. What do you think?"

"I like it! I like a lot better than my own idea. I was going to go up there in the Lincoln with Amanda and play the lost tourist role."

"Too risky! So, Amanda is with you?"

"No, but she's flying in to Albuquerque on American tomorrow noon."

"Okay, I'll meet you both at the American baggage lobby at 1:00. Things are starting to unfold too fast for me to stay in Phoenix. I'm going to bring my own chopper up and set up a temporary command post out at Los Alamos."

37

DEAD RECKONING

It had only been three weeks, but when Amanda appeared at the head of the escalator coming from Security, Corey felt his heart skip a beat. Her flight had been delayed leaving O'Hare, and he'd been pacing back and forth between the security gate and the arrival screen. She smiled when she saw him, and he realized he was probably grinning like a damn fool! He tried not to grin, and felt even more foolish! She stepped off the escalator and into his arms. Her fellow passengers smiled as they walked by.

"Come," he said. "There's somebody I want you to meet."

"The last thing I want tonight is company, so I hope you haven't invited your undercover friends? I've been thinking about my own undercover operations all the way from Chicago!"

Corey continued to smile, saying nothing. Ben arrived at the baggage claim area just as Corey and Amanda did, quickly ushering them out of earshot of the other passengers.

Corey made the quick introductions. Ben, ever the gentleman, forced himself to take his eyes off Amanda long enough to wink at Corey, saying, "Look I'm sorry to break in on a private moment. But, I can't stay long, so don't even think of forcing me to."

"I've heard that you are a master at dropping in at just the right moment!" Amanda flashed her irresistible smile at Ben. "And, I'm indebted to you for doing it a couple of months ago! It's great to finally get to meet you!" she said as she wrapped her arms around the big teddy bear, jumping when she felt his shoulder holster against her right breast.

Ben recovered from the pleasant shock of Amanda's embrace, asking, "What about your bags?"

Amanda pointed to her overnight carry-on, saying: "This is it. I travel light!"

"Good, you guys can drop me off at the Park Service training center, I'll show you the way, and we'll visit more in the morning. Renee can run me back out here to pick up my chopper."

On the drive to Santa Fe, Ben briefed Corey on the latest of the fast-breaking developments. First, they'd found out that, as of this morning, all arrangements for Tim Dice Senior's remains were in the hands of Gordy Stubbs, and a cremation had been approved by the coroner. It all fit the profile they'd been able to put together of Tim, as being incapable of tackling anything that might be remotely social or complex. Second, the routine servicing of Gordy's helicopter was finished, and Gordy had already made a quick flight out to the ranch and back. Third, they'd managed to get an agent, posing as a temporary mechanic, to get close to the MD-500, and scrape some dust off the skids. The dust was being analyzed by soil scientists now and would, hopefully, reveal where the machine had been recently. The phony mechanic had also managed to hide a small tracking transmitter on the chopper. And, fourth, any casual visit to the ranch by Corey was shelved, since there was to be no funeral. Ben was in the process of getting a number of units on stand-by, and they were monitoring activity at the ranch.

As they dropped Ben off at the Training Center, Amanda couldn't help attempting to shake the unflappable Ben. "You do know that I'm a reporter, I hope?"

Ben smiled as he closed the door of the Lincoln. "I hope you took good notes, I may have to ask you what I said. Goodbye you two!"

"I like him!" Amanda said as they drove off.

"Not too much, I hope. Remember, Ben doesn't have a villa. But, I do!"

"No, my teddy bear days are long over." Amanda said as she snuggled closer to Corey on the front seat.

From the moment Corey pressed the button to open the tall iron gates, Amanda was in complete awe of the villa. Imposing adobe walls, blending into the natural rock of the hillside, landscaped with giant cactus plants, hinted at owners who possessed something more than just monetary wealth. Inside was like a museum, polished marble floors, incredibly large paintings of desert, canyon, and wild creatures adorned the walls of every room. The whole structure was designed to draw the eye onto the decks overlooking the lights of Santa Fe. The drop off, beyond the iron railing was unnerving. Corey watched as Amanda took it all in. Here was a woman to match this house!

"I am so glad you got to see this," he said, simply and quietly.

"Who owns this cliff dwelling?" Amanda whispered, as though afraid to break the spell or wake the owners.

"I don't really know. Some friends of the Secretary of the Interior, I gather. They're off on an extended trip to China. So, we are the beneficiaries of their concern for preserving Southwestern heritage! Don't you just love rich people?" he said as he guided her toward one of the three master bedroom suites.

Hours later, they sat on the deck outside the kitchen, sharing Corey's singular culinary achievement: huevos rancheros, with cheese enchiladas, tortillas with homemade guacamole, and a pitcher of frosty margaritas.

"Tomorrow night, I'll take you to Maria's," Corey said apologetically.

"So, what made you change your mind, so suddenly, about coming down?"

Back in the king size bed, Amanda told him, in detail, of her dream, Abigail's dream really, and how it seemed to be a message of some kind from the past, a warning that was emphasized by the dates on Thomas Pettigrew's memorial stone. She dug out his mother's diary from her overnight bag and gave it to him, telling him to read it and see what he might make of it. She had half expected Corey to laugh the whole thing off as nothing more than a string of silly coincidences. Instead, he reached across the glass-topped table and took her hand in his own, and squeezed it gently. She squeezed his hand, and neither said anything for a very long time. The lights of the city were winking at them, shutting down for the night.

In the dark, Corey lay on his side, and placed his hand on her bare stomach. "There's something else, isn't there?" he said, matter-of-factly.

For a long time, Amanda said nothing, struggling within herself, finally saying "Yes."

Corey's finger tip moved, tracing the sensuous line of her stomach up between her breasts, stopping to feel the beat of her heart, finally reaching the silhouette of her face in the darkness, where his forefinger touched her parted lips. "Don't tell me," he said. "Not unless you're sure!"

Amanda's return flight alternated between amazement at the landscape spreading out beneath her, sadness for those like Zach, and Sarah, whose lives were so much a part of that landscape, and an almost unspeakable joy in the knowledge that the tiny life within her was destined to share all the wonder and all the amazement. Somewhere over Kansas, Amanda knew that she had to make one last very brief visit to a tiny hillside graveyard in Vermont.

38

THE WAGES OF GREED

Three days after Amanda left for Albany, Corey was sitting with Ben and the Forest Service's southwestern chief of law enforcement in Ben's temporary command post at the Los Alamos airport. They were in radio contact with spotters at Espanola and in the hills above the Pair O' Dice ranch. The GPS monitor in Gordy Stubbs chopper turned automatically when the engine started. Gordy's position was constantly shown on a small screen in Ben's chopper. But the MD-500 hadn't budged for fifteen minutes. "What the Holy Hell is he doing?" demanded Ben of the Espanola monitor.

"Can't really tell, Boss. He's moving around in there. Looks like he's working on the passenger side door. He's opened it and closed it several times. He lugged in a backpack, and a couple of heavy boxes. One looks like a liquor box. The other is probably the old man's ashes he picked up this morning. Okay, he's taking off now, you got him?"

"Yeh, we're tracking now. Just stand by there in case he comes back."

Had he only known, Gordy Stubbs might have been oddly proud of all the attention he was getting. The movements of the President of the Unites States probably didn't get monitored this closely. Gordy didn't know it, but he had achieved his dream. He was finally a Big Fish!

Less than half an hour later, the Forest Service monitor above Coyote confirmed that the chopper had landed at the ranch. One person staggered out from the ranch house, fallen twice, and got on board. They'd circled the ranch for a minute or two, did a couple of crazy banks, dropped something small, and then took off heading southwest.

"Okay, Corey, let's go. If he keeps heading southwest, he's up to something!" Ben had his own, blue and silver, MD-500, ready to fly. "I'm going to stay a good half-hour behind him, but as long as he's headed southwest, we're just going to sit here and wait and watch. No sense in wasting gas. Just watch his position on that screen above your head and try to follow him on the map. If he keeps going in a straight line, extend that line out about a hundred miles and tell me what's on the ground."

"Goddamn it! Gordy, what'd you do that for?" Tim slurred. "You damn near made me fall out. I dropped the whole jar of Dad's ashes, trying to catch my balance."

"Sorry, Buddy, I was distracted for a moment by a Jeep parked up on the hill. Good thing I caught you! Now, let's get outa here!"

Tim almost immediately fell asleep to the steady beat of the rotors. Good! thought Gordy. He proceeded to bounce the chopper a couple of times, to see if he could wake him, without raising a response. He stayed on course, heading for an area of deep canyons that he'd explored a year ago, right after getting the new chopper. There was nothing there, which was exactly what he wanted now. It wouldn't do to have searchers scrambling around in areas where he hadn't finished scavenging for artifacts. He was flying low, looking for a box canyon he'd seen back then. He was about ten miles from the continental divide, when he spotted it, and quickly set down on the table rock that jutted into the canyon. It was an ideal landing spot, except that there was no place to go. Three sides dropped off abruptly and the fourth led gradually, through rocks and mesquite, upward toward the divide. Tim kept snoring heavily all the while Gordy was busy unloading the backpack, the whiskey, and the box containing the camp stove, sleeping bag, and provisions, mostly salted meat. There was one large canteen of water, which Gordy uncorked and left laying on its side. "C'mon old Buddy, here's your camping spot, Gordy said as he struggled to help

Tim out of the chopper. "Let's have a little drink before lunch!"

Gordy helped Tim to a rock seat on the mini mesa, and popped open a bottle of bourbon for him. Returning to the chopper, he got out the backpack, the rest of the bourbon, and a bucket of fried chicken.

"Picnic time, old Buddy," yelled Gordy, sitting down on another of the many rocks strewn across their landing site. Gordy helped himself to a piece of chicken, while the half-conscious Tim downed an unhealthy slug of bourbon, and slithered to the ground. Gordy watched his partner of over thirty years, lapse into unconsciousness.

"Well, Hell, if you ain't going to drink with me, I guess I'll be heading on home." He got up, walked back to the chopper, kicking over the bucket of fried chicken on his way, and prepared to take off.

"Looks like he's landed, about ten miles straight ahead." Said Corey. "And, his GPS has shut off."

Ben veered abruptly, ninety degrees, and began looking for a place to land. "I don't want to get too close. Let's give 'em time to do whatever it is they're up to. Let me know if he starts up again."

Ben found a place to land in the bottom of a draw, and they sat in the chopper waiting. Less than five minutes passed, and Corey announced that the GPS had come back on and was flashing. "Okay, let's sit and see which way they head," Ben said. After another five minute wait, Corey announced that they were apparently returning home.

"What the Hell?' said Ben. "They can't be running low on gas, and they didn't have time to do anything. "Mark that spot on your map. I'm going to call our spotters and have 'em keep an eye on these guys, while you and I try to figure out where they went and why."

Corey's navigation proved to be a whole lot better than either of them expected. "Well, would ya look at that!' Ben exclaimed, setting down on the spot vacated by Gordy not twenty minutes earlier. "This gets weirder by the minute. Looks like the boys had a falling out." The two got out of the chopper and walked toward an unconscious Tim Dice, surrounded by whiskey bottles, and an extra large bucket of fried chicken spread around him. Ben looked up, responding to something in his Indian heritage, and saw a buzzard circling high above them. He got up from kneeling over Tim, and sprinted for the chopper. Radioing to the Forest Service monitor in Coyote, he yelled, "Andy, get your Jeep outa sight, but hang around and get ready to move in fast."

Ben sat in the chopper watching the GPS display, checking the coordinates, while Corey tried, ineffectually, to rouse the snoring Tim Dice. The last readings, before the display went blank, indicated that Gordy was back at the Pair O' Dice.

"Okay, Andy, can you see what he's doing?" asked Ben.

"Yeh, he landed right near the stables, and he's gone inside. Want me to move in?"

"Negative! Just watch and keep me posted," replied Ben. "Can you rouse Tim?" he yelled to Corey.

"No way, we probably need to get him to a doctor," Corey yelled back.

"Okay, see if you can drag him over here and get him into the back seat. I need to stay with the radio for a while," said Ben.

Ben's radio crackled. "Okay, Chief, he's coming out of the stables lugging a couple of big pots toward the helicopter. Now, he's loading them in the back, and heading back to the stables."

"Good! Move in and 'cuff him. The charge is theft of government property, for now. There'll probably be more charges before we're done here. You probably ought to read him his rights. Whatever you do, do not let him get back in that chopper, okay? Book him at Los Alamos. I want to talk to him!"

"Renee, have you been monitoring this?" Ben asked.

"Yes, I have, Renee answered.

"Well, you probably need to get out of Los Alamos and head for the

Pair O' Dice. Bring some help if you can find any. It looks like you may have an inventory job ahead of you."

"Roger, will do. Where are you going to be?"

"We'll be in touch. Corey and I are headed for the Los Alamos hospital."

"Everything all right." inquired Renee.

"Couldn't be better!"

The inventory of the stables at the Pair O' Dice actually took a team of specialists two weeks to complete. Of the eighteen horse stalls, fifteen had stuff buried under dried and dusty hay, some with as many as four dozen precious artifacts just dumped on the floor, and hastily covered over. Tim Dice, within his limits, tried to be helpful in connecting each stall to the dwellings where he thought the stuff came from, scattered over nearly 12,000 square miles in three States. Ben offered him immunity from prosecution, in return for his full cooperation. However, after learning how his long-time buddy had left him to die, the immunity may not have been necessary.

The State charge of attempted murder probably wouldn't have gone very far. Gordy was adamant that Tim had asked to be taken to a place where his Dad had taken him forty years ago, and to be left there for a week, "to be with his dad," thereby explaining the backpack and "supplies." Gordy had planned well, just not well enough! One thief's word against another's wouldn't have been very convincing in any court, particularly once Gordy had wisely destroyed the bill of sale Tim signed for the ranch. If Tim could stay sober, and pick his friends more carefully, he might be able to do something with the ranch now that he had a little working capital!

Christmas Eve found Gordy in federal prison unhappily looking forward to tomorrow's visit from Erica. Their daughter wouldn't be coming. Angela's embarrassment, and anger at her father, wouldn't allow it. He feared tomorrow like a bad dream out of Dickens, but with no happy ending. Tim Dice got his Christmas presents early. Tomorrow was just another day at the Pair O' Dice.

Ben and Renee, along with Amanda and Corey, were having dinner at Maria's in Santa Fe. Amanda had moved to Santa Fe in time for a Thanksgiving wedding. The newly-weds were headed off to a honeymoon with a stop-over at the line shack and its adjacent cliff house outside of Silver City. Ben raised his margarita grande in a toast to "The Cliff Dwellers," jokingly suggesting that they might consider naming their first-born "Ben." Amanda and Corey replied, in unison, "Sorry, the poor guy is going to be stuck with 'Zach,' Zachary Taylor Pingree!"

"What if it's a girl?" asked Renee.

"It's not!" replied a beaming Amanda.

EPILOGUE

PLACE OF THE MOURNFUL WIND

The Interagency Task Force for Heritage Protection of Public Lands submitted its recommendations to the Secretary of the Interior on schedule the following August. Sweeping recommendations for tough new laws, along with the continuation of the task force approach to law enforcement, created hardly a ripple of public notice compared to the turning over of two ancient skulls, those of an Anasazi woman and her daughter, to tribal officials for a ceremonial re-uniting with their skeletons in The Place of The Mournful Wind. There are few better protected archeological sites today than this tiny remote cliff dwelling which continues to greet the dessert sun as it goes about its eternal task of baking the red sandstone to a fine dust, a dust that rises and falls with xeric winds as oblivious to human folly as to the insatiable appetites of dinosaurs. The desert winds tell many stories. One story is of their role in Earth's creation, fathered by a passing comet. Another, buried among the sands of the final chapter, written long ago, is the briefest of footnotes describing an astonishing form of life, having almost unbelievable mental powers, yet ultimately destroying itself because of its one fatal flaw: greed.

"We are all cliff dwellers staring into the abyss."

www.ingramcontent.com/pod-product-compliance
Lightning Source LLC
Chambersburg PA
CBHW031055020726
47495CB00007B/1887